THE HAMPSHIRE
PROJECT

To Christine with love, Kitty

A NOVEL

KITTY BEER

"A dystopian sci-fi novel imagines a future New England crippled by pollution and under the control of ruthless corporate patriarchs.

"In 2082, ongoing opportunistic development and runaway pollution have rendered the planet nearly uninhabitable. Lack of resources, coupled with an endless succession of natural disasters, including tornadoes, tsunamis, and wildfires left a crumbling infrastructure and the rise of religious and economic autocrats who battle one another for power over the vulnerable population. Tiny Tully Island is an enclave of independent resistance to both the cult of the Hartford priests and the false benevolence of the Sanmart Corporation based in Albany. Herbal healer Fair and her adopted daughter, Terra, have a happy life there until concern for the safety of Fair's son Orion takes them on a rescue mission, where they discover just how dangerous tyranny and elitism can be. In this dystopian novel, Beer (*Human Scale*, 2010, etc.) confronts a number of topical issues in a gripping, quick-paced tale of greed and self-sacrifice set in the near future. In a few careful phrases, Beer evokes the tenuous position of Tully ("Democracy keeps its head up here, along with a canny system of hiding their resources from the outside world"; the desperate squalor of a refugee camp ("rat stew"); and the frightening sincerity of the authoritarian apologist who says of democracy, "Fair to who? Think about it. Do you want folks who are stupid or ignorant or just plain twisted to be deciding your affairs?" One hardly begrudges a few amazing coincidences, such as Terra's ease in finding her long-lost birth father, on the way to the satisfyingly ambiguous ending.

"A view of the possible results of unbridled corporatism that is both unsettling and empowering."

—*Kirkus Reviews*

THE HAMPSHIRE
PROJECT

A NOVEL
KITTY BEER

Plain View Press, LLC
1101 W 34th Street, STE 404

www.plainviewpress.net
Austin, TX 78705

ISBN: 978-1-63210-028-3
Library of Congress Control Number: 2017933617

Cover photo and design by Anthony Arkin
Map of *New England Coastline 2082* by Chris Howard

for Zoë who will be seventy-one,

and Billie Rose who will be sixty-six,

when this story takes place

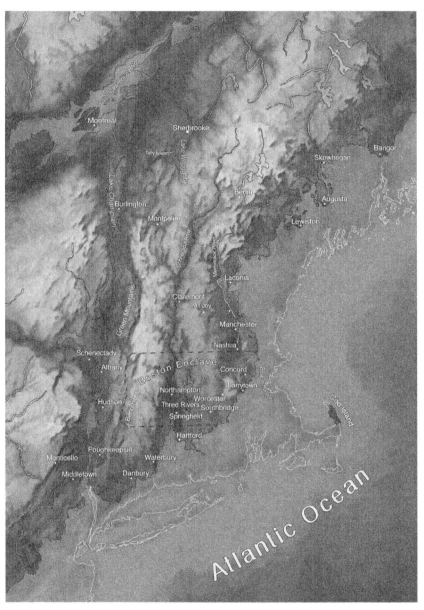

New England Coastline 2082

"…'Tis all in pieces, all coherence gone…"

John Donne
An Anatomy of the World

Part 1

1

A sailboat speeds towards the island. Its hand-stitched spinnaker vaunts a variety of faded colors: aqua, reddish, lilac, gold. It flies in a fast wind from the south straight at Tully's main dock. Already folks are exclaiming and gathering to decipher it. Friend or foe? The militia hastily musters, weapons of any sort ready to hand—bows and arrows, knives, swords, clubs, and the occasional antique gun. Beyond, green water merges into the glaring horizon, tall sheer cliffs sprouting many pine trees still standing.

Fair watches from the upper floor of the main house, where she has summoned the asthmatic children for their morning treat of steaming herbs. The room is filled with pungent peppermint, the kids laughing with the thrill of breathing freely, some even scampering about.

Finally she makes out the flag. Good—it's Boston's blue and white design. But the deck seems to be swarming with people who look ragged and hollow-eyed. If not aggressors, then another hungry horde begging sanctuary? Either one means trouble for Tully Island. They've had to fight off more than one pitiful band of suppliants—Tully has a maximum of two hundred inhabitants, long agreed upon as non-negotiable, a simple matter of survival.

Half a dozen Tully militia are in a boat now, rowing out mightily to head off the intruder, which drops its sail only at the last minute. Those on shore can hear the shouts back and forth. When they see their militia boat turn to head back, every Tully heart rejoices that this means peace. They run to get food and drink ready for their guests.

It's 2082, and Tully Island is thriving. In spite of the crazed storms and ever more unpredictable weather, food shortages, attacks from outside strangers, devastating diseases, and too many dead and deformed babies, the small band survives and lives well enough. Democracy keeps its head up here, along with a canny system of hiding their resources from the outside world. Fair loves her Tully Island. She's been here since that faraway time when she arrived at age seventeen. Thirty-two years ago now.

Tully's stability is all the more impressive in light of the chaos and suffering that's gone on in the rest of what used to be the United States. The northeastern enclaves have had it a lot better than those west of Ohio, or the totally devastated south, but still they've been embroiled in one disaster after another, from tsunamis to wildfires, from plague to war to dictatorship. Boston has been a beacon of hope for some twenty years now, ever since the reigning Zorian priests were defeated. The other major enclaves, Hartford and Albany, are dominated by priests and autocrats. Only Boston can boast elected government and respect for rights. But is Boston too doomed to succumb to autocrats?

Fair prays not, but as soon as she hurries to the shore, the news bears out her foreboding: Boston has fallen to Sanmart.

The newcomers, ten of them it turns out, as soon as they've drunk quantities of water, collapse wearily and tell their story. Boston's governor assassinated, many other elected leaders jailed. It has taken this band weeks to get here, so who knows what's happened since they left. But at that time, the end of August, Boston was rapidly falling into Sanmart's hands. So it's not hard to imagine the present situation. Boston as they knew it is gone.

How did this happen? It was as if Boston's general population was mesmerized by the grandiose, benign claims the Sans were making, until it was too late. There was never even a fight! Trying without success to remain articulate and calm, Fair cross-examines a skeletal young man with a scraggy beard.

"Do you know Orion? You do!! He's my son. How is he? What do you mean you don't know? When did you see him last? Where? How involved is he in this? I know he loved the governor, he must be in trouble."

The poor young man is exhausted, and though he tries to be sympathetic, he eventually retreats into monosyllables. It's her husband Miles who comes to comfort her, tells the man to go get some food and rest, cradles her while she bursts into tears, pounding her fists on his chest.

But of course that evening Miles won't listen to her plans.

"It's too dangerous, he won't want you there!" Gentle Miles is so distraught, he's almost yelling.

12

They're sitting on their porch after community dinner by the shore. The sultry autumn evening has not yet cooled, but darkness and a lake breeze bring some relief. As usual, Terra has joined them. The child is seventeen already, but to Fair as vulnerable, innocent, and impulsive as ever. Terra lives with her grandmother, but "Aunty Fair," though no relation, has been her only mother. Now in a passion, Fair forgets her protective impulse towards Terra to flare up at Miles.

"What you mean is, you don't want me to leave you." She tries to sound understanding, but her anger treads on any tenderness.

"No, no, that's not it. You'll be risking your health, your life, for no reason. You'll only get in the way."

"Get in the way!" Fair splutters, pacing the porch from end to end. "Have you forgotten what I went through, what I'd done by the time I was Terra's age?"

"And how many years ago was that?"

"That's unkind, Miles. Not like you." In a placating gesture she indicates Terra. "Let's stop this argument right now. I am going to Boston to help my son. I'm going. Fact."

And he's not your son, she doesn't add. But the words hang in the charged air. Orion's father, long dead, is still beloved. He's always been a ghostly fourth in their little family. Miles knows it, and Orion knows it. The young man modeled himself as best he could after the father he can't remember.

Terra gets up to stand between them. "You two. Cut it out. I'll tell you what. Fair, I'm going to Boston with you. That will take care of everything."

Fair and Miles start a shocked chorus of "No," making Terra laugh. "Well at least now you two agree," she crows.

2

The boat hits a hurricane just outside Boston, barely makes it into the harbor, straggles past the breakers with one sail intact, drops anchor in a washed-out sunset. To go any closer would risk running into one of the submerged buildings lining Boston's old waterfront. Everyone on board spends an uneasy night, unsure if their battered vessel can withstand the rough hammering that continues until dawn.

Then, suddenly, the water calms. Through shreds of pinkish mist, ramshackle docks take shape, already busy with fishermen. The blurred distance muffles their shouts, bells still tolling fog warnings.

Young Terra is first on deck, even before the sailors, leaning eagerly over the railing peering into her future. She's still lanky like a teenager but with a shapely grace, her serious pointed face warmed by a torrent of auburn hair and arresting amber eyes. They are here to visit Fair's son, but Terra has a secret mission of her own. She hopes to find her father.

"There you are," cries Fair, rushing up, encircling her waist in a hug.

Terra turns to her in the embrace. "I was so worried, you throwing up all night. Okay now?"

"Still a bit shaky. But fine now, sweetie. You?"

"Hungry!"

"Good. Me too."

Fair—small, wiry, carrot-red hair wisping white—usually buzzes with intense energy and bossy bravado, and annoys Terra with her parental protectiveness. But when Fair was helplessly seasick yesterday, Terra found herself caught off guard, feeling vulnerable and alone—it was a revelation to be for a short moment the stronger one. So now she gives her old friend an extra hug.

"We're almost there, Aunty Fair, can you believe it?"

"We'll be seeing him tonight. The captain says the ferry to Barrytown takes less than a day."

"He won't recognize me."

"I guess not! You were only twelve when he left, five years ago now. But you know, Terrie, I sort of wish we'd told him you were coming. He might be furious."

"No, no, I keep telling you. You're his mom. He'll just be thrilled. He would've thought you were bringing a child."

Fair gives Terra's waist another squeeze. "I'm certainly not bringing a child," she smiles wryly. "You're a woman, my sweet. Do you remember those long braids of yours?"

"I know. You kept them, too. Silly."

"Ribbons and all."

They watch as the fog scrolls slowly upwards in strengthening sunlight, revealing a bizarre hulk eventually recognizable as the top floors of a skyscraper. Most of the glass panels are shattered, jagged shards protruding. Glass and steel alike are encrusted with mossy green, the sea claiming them. Terra has heard about these ancient buildings, of course, but she's awestruck to actually witness the remains of that strange world.

Fair says, "That was one of the tallest. An insurance company, or a bank."

Boston's shoreline takes shape as a jumble of lopsided buildings lurching over a seawall thrown together from scraps of anything available, from car tires and wagon wheels to roof gables and rusted girders. People swarm over storm-damaged remnants, clearing and re-building.

Now Thad pushes through the crowd to join them. "Hey there, I was looking all over for you."

Terra laughs at him, as usual. He's not much older than she is, manly but skinny, his big hands and feet out of proportion. He embarked with them at Lewiston and has been entranced with her ever since. Thad ignores her scorn, consoles himself by leaning into her with a mock sad face.

"You break my heart, angel."

Terra doesn't quite pull back. His tall weight and muscle are a comfort. But she shoves at him with her hip, strains forward to watch the new day, trying to discern the ferry that will any moment now take shape detaching from the shore. But instead, an unearthly roar precedes the sudden appearance of a big boat piled with men in black and gold uniforms. Terra holds her ears, and Fair explains tersely, "A motor."

The captain, a wiry leather-faced man, hurries to greet the newcomers. The motorboat is lashed to the side, a few uniforms scramble up a rope ladder to the deck. The captain is beside himself with grimacing smiles.

Fair mutters, "Who the hell are they?"

"Trouble," Thad replies.

A stout woman nearby perks up. "I wouldn't talk like that if I were you."

"I thought Boston's color was blue," Terra comments, but very quietly, unnerved by the display of power and the bestial throb of the motor, quieter now but continuous.

"Was," spits the woman.

"Looks like it's black and gold now." Thad shrugs.

"You better believe it," says the woman, who still wants to fight. Thad's shrug removes him from the field, but Fair willingly takes up the gauntlet.

"These are the new bosses? They're acting like goons."

The woman turns on Fair. "Goons? You dare insult Governor Monty's elite guards? Arrest this traitor!"

Fair fiercely glares at her, but Terra and Thad are pulling her back. A uniform shoves at the three of them, grunting, "Shut up if you know what's good for you."

A few passengers are hurried away, tumbled into the motor boat. Nobody dares protest their arrest, not even Fair. Then the others are interrogated one by one. But the guards are actually quite polite, processing Fair and Terra automatically. There's an eerie disconnect between their official good manners and autocratic behavior.

The journey inland by ferry takes the rest of the day. They travel for hours through increasingly murky water. The ferry is propelled by half a dozen young people paddling bicycle style. Though there's a roof and a lower level, there's nowhere to go to escape the sweltering October heat. Now the water becomes hardly more than a few feet deep as they move down what were once city streets, past shells of roofless, windowless houses, faded stop signs, and upended telephone poles crusted with dusty mud, brittle tendrils of dried

16

moss. Most of the partially submerged trees are dead, but some have survived, waving their leaves in ironic contradiction. Reeds and cattails sprout from porches. The scenes are eerily peaceful, all agony of transition passed, no sign of violence or resistance, everything acquiescing to decay. Life's remnants float gently by, slimy plastic bags, a pink teddy bear half eaten by mold. An oddly colorful chunk of some ancient electronic device, reddened with rust and sporting a little bright-green garden of algae.

Fair is talking about her exodus with her parents from a nearby town in the 40s when she was a little girl. Terra has heard it all before; she's focused instead on the glow of her own limitless future, the wonder and thrill of unknown adventures. While Fair is moaning over the rot and destruction, Terra can't control her breathless anticipation.

"I shouldn't have brought you here," Fair laments. "This is far worse than I imagined. And those thugs who boarded the boat. It's too dangerous."

"Cut it out. You know Orion will take care of us. Besides, you didn't bring me. I brought myself. Grandma was glad to see me go. This is where I'm meant to be."

Fair shakes her head. She's wearing a wide-brimmed straw hat that shadows her small red face. She swipes at the tears joining the sweat on her cheeks.

Terra and Fair have been shown to their room by an old lady with no teeth named Glad. At the ferry dock, they'd transferred to a wagon drawn by two hefty farm horses. What they saw of Barrytown on the way here cheered Fair up considerably.

"It's not half bad, quite pretty in places," Fair comments. "Almost like our Tully, don't you think? I mean, the market place and the flowers and the solar roofs? Look at the darling children waving."

On the contrary, Terra's fascinated by how different it all is from Tully: the houses crammed up against each other, fabricated from every imaginable material, rows of street vendor huts, people dressed elegantly, many women in skirts. Except for Lewiston, this is the largest town she's ever seen.

She says, "It's like the center of the universe."

"I don't see many uniforms. That's a good sign."

The room is large by Tully standards, with two beds, a sturdy oak chest of drawers, table and chairs, a rug, small stove, basin and water pitcher. The women change their clothes hurriedly, expectantly. According to Glad, Orion will be here any minute.

"Now," Fair orders nervously, "you stay out of the way, Terra. Don't say anything at first. Let me prepare him."

"Okay, okay, Aunty Fair. I get the idea. Don't worry."

Terra tears herself away from the window where she's been watching the evening crowds, drags a chair to a corner, sits irritably.

"And here he is," Fair cries.

Her son envelops her in a bear hug. A dark-haired, dark-eyed, solid young man, not the boy Terra recalls. He's looking at her.

He says, "Who's that?" Fair babbles endearments, but he insists. "Mom?"

"Oh, don't you remember her?"

Orion furrows his ruddy brow, his arms still around his mother. "Not exactly."

"You used to call her your little sister."

"Terra? Terra!"

Now she's in his arms too. He holds them both easily, brings their feet off the ground. He pulls back to snap his eyes at Terra.

"Quite grown up," he tells her.

"Quite," she replies archly. She doesn't like his patronizing tone. She feels deprived to have lost her childhood companion to this too-charismatic man.

"I thought we'd have dinner at my place tonight," he says. "I'll introduce you at the dining hall another night. You must be tired, the two of you. How was your trip?"

At Orion's, Terra has trouble maintaining her poise. She's both worn out and on edge. She feels overwhelmed and off balance, as if her world has tilted to one side. Everything is so different from what she's ever known growing up on remote Tully Island. Here in Barrytown, Boston's center, all the buildings are crammed together, so that walking to Orion's felt like navigating an alien labyrinth, with faces of strangers flickering past in the darkening streets, exciting and chilling at once. She had thought he'd make her feel at home, but instead of her old playmate she has found a disconcertingly attractive man who clearly admires her as a female. Further complicating matters, a stunning young woman greets them at Orion's door.

"My partner, Silk," he tells them, proudly and matter of factly. "She's a journalist, works at the News Center."

Fair gives Terra a look, clearly equally surprised. They all sit at a round table laid with a pretty cloth and matching dishes, drinking grape wine and eating tasty lentil casserole.

Silk demurs gently. "Don't forget I have to help with Day Care and pick apples too."

"We all have several roles," Orion explains. "Not so different from Tully. Mom, the Healing Center would've loved your expertise. Too bad you'll only be here for a few days."

Fair coughs, Terra holds her breath.

Fair says, "We thought we'd stay longer than that."

Orion's fond smile falls abruptly. "No."

Fair sips wine, dips her head apologetically. "We can help."

"Excuse me? A fifty year old woman and a teenager? We've got a crisis. It's dangerous. You're both out of here in a week."

During a brittle silence, Silk gets up, puts her hand on Orion's shoulder, serves everyone more wine. Fair, grimacing dissent, is shaking her head.

"Don't you remember what I've been through? I've seen a lot worse. By the time I was Terra's age…"

"I know all about that," snaps Orion. "I've heard it a hundred times. Believe me, you're no match for these types who've just taken over Boston. I wouldn't dream of letting you stay. And you're endangering Terra too."

"I want to help you. I know I can. That's why I came."

Terra well knows Fair's tone, a mix of affection and grit. Clearly so does Orion.

"Listen, Mom. I was hoping we'd just have a calm family reunion this evening. But I'll tell you this—Sanmart's Excell Security Force, Albany puppets pure and simple, took over Boston in a coup on July 20th. Our governor just disappeared. At the time, everyone was in underground bunkers because of the heat. When we came out again, the dirty work was done."

"How could it be so easy?" Fair cries. "Didn't people protest?"

"It was so benign. Life goes on as usual. Life's hard enough. We accepted it."

"The Excells are not so bad," Silk offers. "They mean well."

Orion snorts. "You want to buy their line, be my guest. Silk, honey, don't be a dupe. Changes are happening everywhere already. Libraries curtailed, books burned. A new governor without elections. Our Barrytown militia reduced to the level of babysitting. We're on our way to annexation with the Albany enclave, nobody the wiser."

"The News Center's being left alone."

"Dare to write a risky story," he counters.

Silk sweetly smiles at him, produces a delicious looking dessert of blackberries and yogurt topped with mint. He puts his arm around her waist as she serves him. She's all peaches and gold, everything about her fits into her sleek and glowing blondeness, from her long velvety hair to manicured toenails in silvery sandals. She's wearing a belted bold-patterned tunic over loose pants. She moves deftly in the small space, a flip of the hip here, a curve of the arm there, all with a grace and ease that Terra studies, envies. She assures herself that some day she too will be a smooth and sophisticated woman with a man like Orion.

He accompanies them home with lamp held high. The quiet streets are shadowed, formless, eerie. Walking between Orion and Fair, Terra draws comfort from the sense of his bulk, his hand from time to time taking her elbow, touching her shoulder. She takes a deep breath of him. Maybe it's time to grant favors to Thad, so she won't feel quite so overwhelmed by this unobtainable hero.

3

Because of the drought, Barrytown's rain cisterns are almost empty. Many people are already hauling water from wells, hoping it's purified enough. For newly installed Governor Monty, it's the perfect excuse for privatizing the water supply. On October twenty first, every well in town sprouts a black and gold guard. Accompanying signs read, "In the interest of public safety and equal sharing, the price of water is now twelve dollars per bucket. Water is no longer public property." Long lines of anxious citizens wind away from each well, carrying tin pots, pails, jugs, whatever they can fill with precious water. Those who don't have enough money come away with half-filled containers and stunned eyes.

For a few days Orion harps on their leaving, how worried he is for their safety. Fair responds with stubborn bravado. These scenes usually end with his storming away, Fair grinning in triumph. But towards the end of the week, Orion arrives late for his lunch with them, looking far from confrontational.

"What's wrong?" Fair says at once.

She has dropped from peacock puffed to tender solicitous in a heartbeat. Even Terra can see he's dejected. He sits slowly at the little table, shoulders slumped, shaking his head.

"I lost my job."

"But you were doing so well managing New Pond," Fair says.

"I was coordinator with the old governor's office. Everybody who worked for him has been transferred out."

"Out?"

"My new job's over in Natick. So I've been told."

"You don't have anything to say about it?"

"Apparently not."

Terra serves them all leek soup. She sips at hers, but they lean oblivious towards each other, intent.

"Natick is so far," Fair says. "You'll have to go and live there."

"That's the idea. Look, Mom, you don't know the half of it."

"How about telling me then?"

So he does.

He starts by lamenting, "Boston had such promise. After we got rid of the Zorians back in '62, we became a real democracy, with real elections. In spite of the epidemics, the cancers, the fertility plunge, we've been thriving, staying at a steady 40,000, because so many folks wanted to come here. Hartford's still run by the Zorian priests and Albany's a Sanmart stronghold, but old Boston's been a beacon of hope for everybody. Well, not anymore."

Terra is shocked to see her swaggering cheerful hero so crushed. He's almost on the verge of tears.

Fair says to him tenderly, "Eat your soup." But neither of them does. So Terra gets him a cup of wine, which he downs.

Orion continues, "When I first came here in the 70s, what an exciting dream it was. Now when I look back, the signs were there way before we noticed. Sanmart built itself up in the public mind as a stalwart rock to lean on: solid, trustworthy, resourceful. By the time my buddies and I discovered their link to Albany, it was already an insidious deep-rooted presence. People were starting to use the word Sans to mean solution. As in, 'Leave it to the Sans, they'll know what to do.' So..."

Orion pauses, looks at Terra. "I'm going to tell you something that needs to be kept secret. You must forget I ever told you, for your own sake. Understand?"

Terra nods.

Fair cries, "Oh for heaven's sake, Orie, what is it?"

"Well, we couldn't very well let that happen."

The atmosphere in the cozy room chills with foreboding. Cloudy afternoon light filters through the blinds making silvery ribbons on the shabby rug.

"Sanmart runs Albany with an iron fist. They started as a business organization and still claim to be one. They play the benign protector, they spout terrific slogans, and give folks plenty of thrilling pomp and ceremony. But they're a dictatorship all the same. Excell is their security force, strong arm tactics hidden otherwise. Most worrisome of all, the Sans are making very successful overtures to Hartford lately. We're afraid of an alliance."

"You and your buddies," Fair prods him, "just what are you planning to do about it?"

"Remember the Credos?"

Fair groans. "Oh no."

Orion bristles, slaps the table. "It was the Credos who got rid of the Zorians."

"At what cost," Fair retorts. Then, soothingly, "Go ahead, Orie. I can understand that an alliance between Hartford and Albany would not be good for Boston."

"So you do see. I knew you would."

He suddenly registers the soup, takes a few gulps. Fair jumps up and paces to the window and back. She's pressing her lips together in a huge effort to shut up. Terra watches them both, rocks she depends on, appalled at their consternation. If they don't feel strong, where does that leave her?

Orion continues. "Our opposition group is small but growing. The problem is, most folks don't see the harm in the Sans and their security force, the Excells, even though they don't buy the story that our governor just up and left. The new regime's power in itself is a kind of reassurance. People are still more afraid of drought and disease than dictatorship. Well, it makes sense if you're trying to protect your kids or your grandparents, right?" He slurps up the last of his soup and adds, "We call ourselves the Stewards. Sanmart calls us traitors."

Fair, standing, asks in a strangled voice, "How much do they know about your involvement? What *is* your involvement?"

"Okay, Mom, I'm stopping here. I've risked you and Terrie enough with this information. You only need to know why I'm taking the job in Natick. I can't protect you, far from it. Being my family is dangerous. If this doesn't convince you to go home to Tully, nothing will I guess."

He's making for the door, turns. "Not a word to anybody, I don't need to tell you that."

Fair has no trouble getting a job at the Medical Center. Apparently her association with Orion hasn't countered Barrytown's need for experienced healers; there are rumors about military casualties soon, and wildfires in the Pennsylvania territories are moving east. They even have her teaching a class of beginners, mostly fresh-checked kids from the Boston enclave's outer limits. Terra can see she's flush with this success, diluting worry about her son. He's packing up for Natick, has found a place to live. Silk is to join him there as soon as she finishes an assignment near Worcester, tracking down a new strain of flu that could turn pandemic, she explains. Terra has persuaded Silk to recommend her for an internship at the News Center. "I've always wanted to be a journalist," she begs, and Silk replies in her silky voice, "You have the guts, Terra, I really think you do."

Fair comments that evening, "She just means you're nosy." With her wry smile.

But Terra can see she's proud, and relieved too, not to have to worry what her young charge is doing with her time. If she only knew. Terra and Thad are now lovers—that's easy to accomplish when Fair's gone all day. Terra has bedded boys since she was fifteen, so it's no big deal, but Fair doesn't have a clue. As for Thad, he has joined the Barrytown militia, which needs recruits since its power became so diluted that many of the members quit to join the Excell Security Force, the ESF. He has been advised to consider volunteering for the grand new project in New Hampshire, where he'll get experience and credentials to advance in the Boston enclave.

Meanwhile another week passes. November comes with oppressive heat but sparse sunlight, dull grey skies with small stringy clouds resembling dribbled foam. Instead of turning red and gold as tradition would have it, the leaves on the scraggly trees turn brown, and shrivel before they even fall to the ground.

The mood in Barrytown is peculiar. Governor Monty proclaims a parade for the 15th, after the soccer game, which is a very popular prospect and has everyone gossiping and getting out their special clothes. At the same time, the water situation worsens; a black market scheme to divert and sell it on the sly ends quickly with the hanging of all concerned, which saves on bullets. A strident mixture of excitement and anxiety tenses the very air, already suffocating.

Glad totters into Fair and Terra's room one morning with the news that the high school is closing for a week so all the teens can help with the harvest.

"The drought is shriveling everything," she proclaims in her wavering treble. "We've got to pick 'em while they're still edible. Get ready for pickled green tomatoes this winter. Ugh."

Glad has no teeth but she smiles readily, showing pink gums. She smells of herbs and old clothes. Her hands are long and bony and expressive, she dances them to every word; they flutter even when she's not talking, which is not often. She loves to show up like this very early in the morning before they're even dressed, because they invariably share their breakfast with her. She particularly loves cream cheese on toast. Glad lives on their floor, so they can't very well pretend they're not home. Besides, Fair's kind of fond of the old lady, still so full of energy and passionate opinions. Terra's mostly bored, and can't fathom how anybody could be that decrepit and still be walking around.

When Fair goes downstairs to the bathroom, Glad starts a long story about her youth in the 30s when seasons were predictable, and crops always ripened in October. It's worse than Fair's interminable reminiscences about her emigration with her parents to Canada and the refugee camp they had to live in. Terra feeds Glad toast to occupy her mouth, and goes to the window to look down at the busy street. At this early hour when the heat is bearable, folks are hurrying about their business. A man selling fish is setting up his stand across the way. A wagon full of hay pulled by two tired-looking horses nearly collides with a bicycle piled with a whole family. The two drivers shout at each other for a few seconds but then rumble off.

"Is this sheep's cheese, then, dear? You know I prefer goat's."

Terra ignores Glad. She chooses a loose tunic she's recently sewn with soft materials she found at the market. She's looking forward to her assignment today interviewing kids about their sports preferences.

"So." Glad sounds like she's summing up, but Terra knows this only means she's transitioning. "So, everything's to be harvested at once, ready or not. The teens will be working hard, poor loves, but they kind of enjoy the break from school. Then, the rest of us have to pitch in for the drying and pickling and smoking, to preserve it all. I hope we have an easy winter. Last year we had a terrible flood in February…"

Terra brushes her hair hard to make it shine. She let it grow during the journey and now it cascades over her shoulders. When Fair returns, she's ready to go.

"Pick up some apples will you, if you get a chance," Fair asks.

"And some goat's cheese," adds Glad, but Terra's already out the door.

4

"If I take that gig in New Hampshire, come with me?" pleads Thad. "Women are welcome too, you know."

She and Thad are lying intertwined on her rumpled bed. It's been a week since they last had the chance, so their lovemaking was quick and intense, and they have almost another hour before Fair is due home from work. Through the narrow window, late afternoon sunlight throws an orange shaft across their glistening skin.

"I can't," sighs Terra, kissing his shoulder. "Anyhow, you said it doesn't pay."

"Yeah but we get our transportation there, and free room and board. And then it pays dividends in experience. I could even go into officer training afterwards, they said."

"What's so great about that? You like those pushy autocrats?"

"I have to make my way in the world," he replies pompously. "You listen to your radical relatives too much."

"I do not. I have my own opinions."

"But you aren't accomplishing anything here..."

"Not yet." She cuddles closer. "But Thad, I have a secret. A secret mission."

She hesitates. But she's decided it's time to tell Thad about her father. She needs to confide in someone, and besides he might be able to help her.

When Terra was ten years old, she saw her mother for the first and last time. She'd been aware ever since she could remember that her mother didn't want her, that she'd been palmed off on her reluctant grandmother. Grandma Vita wasn't mean, but her affection was attenuated, conditional. Fair by contrast always had warm arms and kisses, no matter what.

The day of her mother's arrival, Vita told Terra to sit still in her best dress and not move. Instead, Terra took the first opportunity to slip out and run over to Fair's house. She remembers that flight, up the hill through the apple orchard white with spring blossoms, past the docks, to the lopsided old cottage that had once been a yacht many years before. Fair asked no questions, just let her hold on and cry. Terra's tears made Fair's blouse all wet, but Fair only chuckled about that. And so, arriving home hand in hand with Fair, Terra met her mother. Lorna was beautiful in her child's eyes, with lovely golden hair and chocolate-colored eyes, like a fairy tale. But when Lorna spoke a formal hello, her voice was an icy tremble.

Terra stood in the doorway with Fair, tightly grasping her hand. Her mother was sitting at the kitchen table, did not get up. Vita hovered behind her, holding her by both shoulders as if to protect her. In that searing moment, Terra understood that her grandmother loved her own daughter fiercely and deeply, and that somehow this was the very reason Terra was a burden to her.

She vividly remembers one other crushing scene from that short visit. She was alone outside Vita's cottage on a hot and cloudy afternoon, planting seeds in the garden, when her mother appeared. She looked angelic in her Goldilocks way but her face was stormy. She walked straight up to Terra, took her chin in her hand, and said fiercely, "You have his eyes."

Terra was frightened by her violent stare; her grip was tight to the point of pain.

"What's the matter?" she begged.

"You have his eyes. Your father's eyes."

"But who is my father?"

"Ah," sighed Lorna, loosening her grasp. "They really haven't told you anything, have they?"

"No. Only that you had to go far away to fight for freedom, or something."

"I hated your father. I hated them all. I still do. Is that enough for you?"

"Where is he?"

"Don't ever ask anyone that question. Ever again. Do you hear me?"

The fairytale princess had turned into a witch. Terra's heart froze. She must have stammered acquiescence, but in her mournful yes was born the idea that began to haunt her. When she grew up, she would find her father.

Terra has told no one her plan, not even Fair. But from questions she's asked over the years, she knows her father was a Zorian priest in Boston, and that her mother was somehow coerced into a sexual relationship. Nobody in Tully would ever tell her more than that. But the mystery makes her dream even more tenacious. And now her search has finally begun. Everywhere she goes in Barrytown she darts a glance at men's faces, seeking the large amber eyes she studies every day in the mirror.

Her work at the News Center has been confined to helping with proofreading and interviewing children. She's had no luck in persuading them to let her try a real assignment. But now she's come up with a sure winner. She'll go to Hartford, the Zorian stronghold, and turn up a terrific story, all the while on the trail of her father. Just the idea of meeting a priest, someone who might know him, makes her heart jump.

So she takes a breath, nudges Thad to keep him awake. "You said your buddy has family in Hartford?"

"Yeah, Beller."

"Here's the thing. I want to get sent to Hartford. On assignment. Do you think I could have a chat with him? I could get some tips for an inside story."

"Crazy idea, Terr." He nuzzles her neck, starts his hands on her belly. "They'd never let you do that. Crazy girl…"

"Hey, no, Thad, not yet. Stop. Listen."

Something in her tone makes him raise his head to look at her. His sandy hair tousles down over his skinny face, sleepy eyes. He looks vulnerable and sweet. She plunges on.

"Thad, you know I always lived with my grandmother, right? Well, that's because my mother didn't want me, and that's because she hated my father."

Thad has turned over on his back in resignation. He's always impatient with confessions.

"So what can you do about it?" he asks with infuriating logic.

She holds to the momentum of her telling, ignoring him. "I want to find him. I want to find my father. Don't tell me I'm crazy again. I want to see his face. What if you had never known your father? How would you feel?"

"My dad's a drunk."

"Please help me."

Now she's up on one elbow looking urgently down on him. He gazes back at her, irritated, moved. "I'll bet you one thing. He doesn't want to be found."

"Maybe. We'll see. Anyway, I'm not going to bother him or disrupt his life. I'm just going to introduce myself."

"But what have you got to go on? You're operating totally in the dark."

"I know he's a priest, or was."

"That's it? How old is he?"

"He must be somewhere between thirty-five and sixty-five now. That's what I figure."

"Oh that's real specific. How old was your mother?"

"Fifteen. Possibly, she was forced somehow."

Thad's sleepy eyes fly open. "Rape?"

"I don't know about that." But she sinks back, contemplates this thought for the first time. "No, no. Why would you say such a thing?"

"Anyway, she was really young." Thad smoothes back her hair, murmurs, "Sad for you."

"But I don't know what happened."

"Nobody would tell you?"

"No."

"Why don't you ask Fair?"

"Oh, I tried. There was some kind of conspiracy. Everybody in Tully kept their mouths shut. They didn't want to upset me, traumatize me, they said."

"You're a grownup now, you're a grown woman. Make Fair tell you."

"I may be a woman, but Fair sure doesn't know it. That route's hopeless. But here's what you can do. Introduce me to this Beller guy."

"Hell, no. What for?"

She folds her arms across her breasts, glaring. He pulls back from her with a huge dramatic sigh. "Oh hell." Terra waits, rigid. So finally he says, "Okay, I know where he'll be today at six o'clock."

After he gets rewarded with another avid lovemaking, they wash gaily at the basin, prodigal with her allotment of water, dress quickly, and hurry down the stairs to the street. The brutal

November sun has begun to loosen into lengthening shadows. In a few minutes they reach Barrytown's crowded main street, thread their way along hand in hand.

On each side, little shops occupy the first floor of buildings, above them four or five stories of apartments. In front of most stores squat vendors with makeshift displays, selling everything from food to jewelry, potato cakes to seashell necklaces, in a constant cacophony of enticing calls, the smell of cooking oil mingling with horse manure, sweat, and a pervasive musty, rotting odor. The shops offer clothes, crockery, furniture, goatskin boots, rubber sandals made from ancient tires, wheelbarrows, bicycles, and of course drinking water. Almost every other one is a repair shop—in one window an old computer has been turned into a footstool, wrapped in embroidered cloth. On one corner an old man with two teeth plays a broken accordion and sings about love.

At the entrance to the marketplace, grocers call out the wonders of their wares. "Look at these chestnuts!" "Take a whiff of these apples!" "Sweetest carrots you ever tasted!" Now that the sun has softened and the workday is ending, people are emerging everywhere. Terra marvels that she's almost gotten used to being surrounded by strangers, to the novel ways they dress, the wild variety of types.

"He'll be at the market café," Thad explains. "Beller's a news junkie. Because of where his family is, I guess."

"Did you know they had a television there until recently? Silk told me."

"Yeah, I heard. They can't get parts for it any more. But they have a radio."

"I know that. I help write broadcasting scripts, remember?"

"You're *proofreading* scripts."

"Don't quibble. Now listen, when we arrive, don't tip him off. Just introduce me, I'll take it from there. I don't want to pounce on him."

"Most fortunately, Beller is ugly. Or I might be jealous."

Beller is in truth pretty ugly, brooding and furry-browed with round glasses slipping from a shiny nose. His upper lip is raised over his teeth and his bottom lip juts forward, giving him an air of permanent puzzlement. Terra has no trouble at all charming him.

He receives her attentions with childlike wonderment. Thad brings mugs of tea to the table just as the news begins. Everyone's eyes rivet on the raised platform where the cumbersome radio is cranked by a tired-looking woman from the News Center.

"And here's the latest," blares the announcer's metallic voice. "The drought continues, 550 days and counting. Crops are wilting fast. But harvest still looks adequate. Hopes for hurricane season haven't panned out, all we're getting is dust storms and tornadoes. West of Hartford, wildfires have been burning out of control for days now. Hopes of containing them are high, but Hartford is on emergency watch and cooperating with us on communication. From Williamstown comes the welcome news that our Albany allies are helping to defend our major rain cisterns from evil elements trying to steal our water. And we have the Westfield River well defended. But reinforcements are being sent, just in case. The governor's office has announced that with the new incentives, twenty-five new recruits have signed up for the militia this month.

Thad and Beller prod each other proudly.

But then Beller frowns, grunts, "Fire, that's no joke. My mother and cousins live over that way."

"Do you hear from them?" asks Terra.

"Got a letter two weeks ago. They were fine then. But who knows?"

"Is there any way to call or email?"

"I sent an eview but they never got it. Looks like they don't have access to a computer any more. And phones are only for officials unless you have a ton of money."

The announcer launches into crop yields, temperature predictions, and soccer scores, followed by uplifting comments in Governor Monty's singsong voice.

Monty concludes with exhortations to join the volunteers in the New Hampshire settlements who are working on a wonderful new project for the good of humankind. He praises folks who've joined that effort as heroes.

"Must be hard worrying about your family," Terra says softly. Beller melts, sways in her direction as she adds, "Say, I wonder if you could give me a little advice."

He sighs, "Sure, try me."

"I want to go to Hartford for an assignment. That's where the Zorian priests went when they were thrown out of here, right? It's a story about the priests and how they used to run Boston."

Beller's startled stare is close to fear. "Say, I wouldn't try that. You'll find yourself in jail, or worse."

"You're kidding, right? It's just a matter of historical record."

"Not for the Zorians. Don't mess with their version of what happened. Which is, folks in the Boston enclave were so wicked and depraved that the noble Zorians fled from their diabolical influence."

Terra laughs but the two young men are looking at her askance.

Thad says, "Terrie, wake up. This is a crazy idea. I told you that. Anyway, they'll never let you go there in the first place."

"Who's going to stop me?"

"Fair and Orion, and me too, for starters. And Silk and the entire News Center staff. And who knows, maybe nowadays you'll need permission from the governor."

Terra bridles, then sulks. She wasn't prepared for such resistance.

"Well then," she concedes, "how about if I just do a story on the priests in general?"

"Depends," replies Beller. "But that wouldn't be much of a story would it?"

"How about this for an angle: priests and their childhood influences."

Beller is shifting around uncomfortably. "In Hartford we never talk about that. Priests are chosen by God, not by any human influences."

"Oh, I just want to talk to them for heaven's sake. What's the big deal?"

Thad coaxes, "Give it up, Terra."

But he's looking at her hard, trying to figure out how stubborn she's going to be. He knows her well enough by now to worry.

"Mary, Mary quite contrary," he teases. But alarm weights his tone.

5

The following week in the middle of the night, warnings barely precede the strike of the tornado. Terra wakes to the blaring of horns, Fair shaking her, throwing clothes at her, urging her up. They straggle outside, joining crowds surprisingly calm being shepherded by blue-shirted militia towards a hole in the ground. Wind is already dashing objects back and forth in all directions and obscuring everything with swirling yellow dust. At the narrow entrance they have to bend low, making their way in near darkness along a stretch of round packed-dirt walls like a rabbit's burrow. But soon they emerge into an enormous lighted space. Someone hands them a blanket.

"Over here," orders Fair. "We'll stake out this corner."

They spread their blanket beside a family with small children. Terra sits holding her legs tightly to her chest. She knows storms; Tully has always been racked with them. But she's never seen so many people together at one time, and all of them strangers. The noise of talking and shouting is deafening, and there's a sour sweat smell starting. Water is being passed around, ladled from buckets, but there's no sign of food and she's getting hungry. Fair has had a comforting arm around her shoulder, but now she leans down to scoop up a baby that has crawled next to her.

"Look at you," croons Fair, "what a little darling you are. Does it need to be changed?"

The mother gratefully hands her a fresh diaper, and Fair begins to unwrap the unsavory child, alternately commenting on its rash, giving the mother advice, and singing a sappy song.

"This is a horrible place," Terra comments.

"It's an old underground parking garage," Fair explains. "You know, where people used to put their cars when there wasn't room in the street."

Terra in spite of her discomfort struggles to grasp this information. On one of the chipped concrete pillars, she can make out a smudge of orange color and a faded letter C. If that means a level, are there other floors? Like a bee hive?

"A whole huge building just for private machines? It looks like it goes on for miles."

"Well, everybody owned a car at that time."

"But they burned gasoline…"

"Terra, you knew that." Cradling the baby, Fair turns to her with irritation, but softens seeing her expression. "I guess you hadn't really pictured it before."

Terra returns a rueful smile. Really, she shouldn't be asking for mothering, much as she could use a little right now. She's not sure which is worse, feeling suffocated and squeezed in this smelly cave or imagining it crammed with the metal shapes that ruled the insane old world. She looks around for Thad, but it's Beller she spots, in uniform helping keep pathways open in the sea of people. He's gradually moving this way, and she wonders how she can get Fair out of earshot so they can talk about their plan. Beller has gotten leave to go home for Winter Solstice, and Terra is going with him. Just the idea of actually meeting a priest, someone who might know her father, makes her heart jump.

It turned out Beller didn't need much persuading. She'd arranged to meet him two days ago by the pedicab stand, and they took a brief ride to the outskirts, through orchards, past grazing goats and rows of corn and soy, and in the distance marching over the hills armies of slowly twisting wind turbines. The heat had mercifully abated and the autumn air smelled fresh. First she had to guide Beller through his trance induced by her mere presence, then his warnings about dangers to her of such a trip, but soon he grew enthusiastic.

"Takes about five days," he said, "depending on the weather. We sure don't have to worry about flooding this year. The only problem is bandits, and mostly all they want is your money. So, sew it into your underwear and hope for the best. We probably won't run into them, I know the best route."

"You're not to tell Thad, remember."

"I got that."

As they returned to town, Terra relaxed into the sway of the cab, the rhythm of the driver's leisurely pedaling, the approaching view of Barrytown's center, buildings slipshod with mismatched materials but colorful, welcoming, its solar panels glinting gemlike all along the roofs. Beller dared to put his arm around her. His pudgy hand rested on her shoulder, not grasping, lightly perched, caressing with hope rather than demand. She's handled this kind of situation before, getting something from a love-sick boy without committing to physical concessions she doesn't want. Kissing Beller would be distasteful, though she can't rule it out.

"Beller," she tried sweetly, "I really like you. Yes, I do. But you know, I'm going with Thad. It wouldn't be right to give in to our feelings. I hope you understand that."

He frowned with the effort of nodding agreement. But he was placated for the moment with the idea that she found him attractive.

Terra is truly sorry to be deceiving Fair and Orion and especially Thad; they're only trying to protect her, she knows. But she resents that, too. None of them have enough respect for her as a grownup person who can take care of herself. They're always fussing. Now they'll see: she has a life and a goal and the guts and smarts to go after it. Above all Orion, who torments her with his admiring glances and patronizing attitude. Does he even know how he's contradicting himself?

Now that the multitude in the shelter is more or less settled down, lights are dimmed, the surroundings cast into shadowy blur. Beller materializes, sits down beside her. Fair is busy with the children, but Terra only dares whisper, "We can't really talk now."

"I know." But he's enjoying the conspiracy.

"Where's Thad?"

"He's still out closing up the entrances. It's a nightmare out there."

"Will we be here all night?"

"For sure. But the twister touched down miles away so I don't think there'll be too much damage."

"Beller," Terra whispers, "I know it's still five weeks away, but could we have another meeting soon, just to settle details?"

"Sure, sure," Beller beams. "Name your day. Another ride in the country?"

Terra calculates. The pedicab was a bit too cozy for a repeat. "How about we meet at the market? Pick another time you have leave when Thad doesn't. Then come to, say, the cider stall. About five?"

"That'll be next Thursday. Okay."

Fair has turned back, now holding two children. To keep her grasp on the squirming toddler, she hands the baby to Terra, who takes it reluctantly. Beller gets up with a wink.

"Thursday," he says.

Terra watches his receding stomp with satisfaction only edged with misgiving. Just to think that in a matter of weeks she might meet her father! Beller will be fine. In fact he's perfect, if she can just keep him in line.

The baby is a light warm weight. Its eyelids flutter up at her, on the verge of sleep. It reminds her of a kitten she once had, named Cloud.

Around noon the next day, the all-clear sends everyone out into a chaotic scene, like a crazed child's drawing. The tornado has been bizarrely selective. Roofs have completely disappeared from some buildings; from others all the windows are blown into shards. Lampposts lie upended on overturned and smashed carts, limbs of trees protrude from doorways, a bicycle is perched upside down on a street sign. But many things are untouched, looking equally weird in their serenity. One of them fortunately is Terra's and Fair's building, so wading through ankle-deep debris they hurry home to wash and change. Then they head to the Medical Center, which is roaring with emergencies. Many people from the outskirts of Barrytown couldn't make it to the parking garage and were caught either en route or in shelters that were hit.

The admitting area is a madhouse, and triage is difficult. Fair treats a man for a head wound only to discover afterwards, when he faints, that he has a finger missing. He himself was so dazed he hadn't noticed. Sometimes it's impossible to separate screaming kids from screaming parents to find out who's wounded.

For painkillers they have to ration the garlic and marshmallow root, so they depend mostly on whiskey and wine. They're using soap and water instead of antiseptic, the water trucked in by squads of wheelbarrows and then boiled. Gradually the majority of casualties who can't go home are sent over to the hospice behind the old temple, but the emergency area continues to fill up as people straggle in from farther south, where the storm was even worse. They run out of bandages before dark, so Terra and another girl are sent to scrounge old cloth, to sterilize and rip into strips.

Hurrying back from collecting bandages, Terra spots Orion hammering on a broken stairway. She waves, continues on, headed for the boiling pot set up in the central square where she'll help with the sterilizing. But then she turns around, sees that he's looking after her. One foot on a stair, hammer poised mid-action, in his face a mix of affection, worry, and something like anger. It pulls her up short. What's he thinking? The temptation is great to return and confront him. It will be the first time they've ever been alone without Silk or Fair.

"I'll catch up with you," she says to her friend.

Seeing her approach, Orion turns to deliver a few more whacks of his hammer before acknowledging her.

"Terrie," he says. "Hard at work like the rest of us."

"Don't be so surprised. I am grown up now, you know."

"You sure are. I left a little girl in Tully. It's been kind of hard to get used to." He laughs apologetically, shaking his head. "I'm not easily confused."

Terra wants to taunt him, wants to enjoy his unease. But his shirt is open to his broad neck, sleeves rolled up from hairy arms, his tentative smile close to sweetness. She suddenly feels too warm, recognizes the sensations. She wants to put her mouth on his, press against him. Her feelings shock and fascinate her. She tries to make her face merry, dismisses his confession.

"Oh, I'm sure you're never confused, Orie."

"Can you sit down for a minute?"

She sits down on a step, he sits beside her.

"Am I going to get a lecture?"

"Well, I hope you won't take it that way."

The shirt underneath her overalls is soft blue and she hopes attractive. But his face is severe.

"Truthfully, Terra," he continues, "I wish you hadn't come to Boston. I'm pretty mad at my mother for bringing you."

"A lecture it is," she snaps rudely, too late recognizing how childish that sounds.

It's what he expected, which makes her even more embarrassed. She wants to stop looking at his strong hands, fights for distance, control. If only he'd show some sign of falling prey to her charms, she could ridicule and reject him—not irrevocably, of course— just enough to fire him up completely. But his intensity is pure brotherly affection.

He says, "It made me so happy to think of my mother and you safe in good old Tully." When she shakes her hair back in irritation, he adds quickly. "Of course I knew you were growing up. I know you want a challenging life, I understand that. But there's plenty of time for that later, when you're a little older. You go back to Tully now, you will have already had a huge adventure coming here."

"Orion, I didn't ask you for advice. Stop patronizing me."

He grimaces with a mix of chagrin and amusement, pats her hand which she snatches away.

"Look, Terra, Barrytown is dangerous now. It's probably going to get a lot worse. I may be in trouble, won't be able to protect you. I don't want you…"

"You want. Who asked you?"

Terra hopes she's coming across imperious.

Orion gives a beaten shrug to his shoulders. "Just think it through. Please."

She jumps up, tries a friendly smile. "I've got work to do. I know you mean well."

He stands slowly, looks down at her sadly. "If times were different, I'd love to have you here. Boston used to be a heaven, not so long ago."

"Goodbye, Orion," she says solemnly.

She gives him her hand, for a moment acknowledging his sense of loss and his selfless concern. He really is a fine man, she thinks proudly.

6

Terra and Beller are on the road. It's a thickly overcast December afternoon, the air brittle and taut as if straining towards unobtainable wet, the clouds' promise a lie. They slipped out of Barrytown around nine that morning, after Beller got his vacation pass and before Terra would be missed at the News Center. It was easy. All they had to do was take a pedicab to the edge of town and wait for the bus to Newton. Both are carrying backpacks stuffed with emergency rations as well as minimal clothing, and full flasks of water. Terra is exhilarated with her own daring and the prospect of true adventure. Beller has made this trip half a dozen times so she doesn't worry about obstacles. Her only anxiety at this point is whether she can locate her father at all, and what he will do or say if she does. She tries hard to mitigate her golden girlhood dream of paternal embrace. But she never fully allows the idea that he could spurn her.

Her note to Fair was longer than it needed to be. She should have just written, "Gone to Hartford with Beller. Hoping for scoop on priests. Back in about a week. Will try to be in touch. Love." But she'd gone on to explain. "I know you wouldn't tell me about my father because you wanted to protect me, but I really need to know. I need to find him, or at least try. You can't understand what it's been like not having parents. Anyway this is something I have to do for myself. You had adventures when you were young. Everyone should. Don't worry." Then she thought she'd add, "In any case I'll have some solid news stories to offer at work, so you can be glad about that." This last was to get Fair, who would be in a frantic state at her flight, and Orion—who would be in a fury—thinking positively and admiringly about her mature focus.

The road out of Barrytown had been quite smooth, with very few ruts. The swirling dust churned up by traffic gradually settled as they got farther out into the country. Huts and other makeshift dwellings thinned out, wind farms and winter cornfields dominated. Their solar-powered bus ran soundlessly and it was cozy inside. The other passengers were mostly day travelers, going to markets or visiting friends.

40

In Newton they'd had to change vehicles, switching to a van powered by used cooking oil that smells like stale fried food. It also makes a painful chugging noise and stops every now and then, so the driver has to get out and hit it.

"Want any more of this cheese?" Beller queries, his mouth full.

"No, thanks, I'm fine."

"Watch the water. We have to conserve, I keep telling you."

"I know that. Stop babying me, Beller."

"Sorry. Can I have another apple?"

"Haven't you had enough? You said yourself we may not get dinner."

"Oh, we'll get dinner. The camp in Natick is elegant. I meant tomorrow. The route to Woodville is trickier."

"Well, then save it for tomorrow. We only have four apples left as it is."

"We've got carrots."

But Terra takes the cheese and apple from him and stuffs them back into the bag, puts all the food away. Then she defiantly takes a swig of water. Annoying as Beller can be, she's the boss. Out the window the darkly clouded day seems hardly to have dawned at all, has resembled dusk from the beginning. Terra watches the passing traffic, faintly distressed by the bizarre shapes people have managed to cobble together to travel in: wheelbarrows pulled by bicycles, ancient truck shells propelled by foot, a whole family attached in some way or another to one laboring horse. On the trek from Lake Willoughby to the Maine coast, she and Fair had run into many odd contraptions of course, but at the time she'd dismissed them as unworthy of the surely more sophisticated and civilized place she was headed. Now she has to admit that Barrytown so far looks like the best of all worlds.

She's even more disconcerted when the doddering bus finally breaks down fifteen miles outside Natick. The driver keeps on kicking the tires disconsolately long after everyone has disembarked. It's about five o'clock and the only lights in the gloom come from lamps on the vehicles staggering past at various speeds, ignoring them. Behind and ahead, tunnels of darkness.

"Now what, Beller?" But she quickly abandons her accusatory tone at the sight of his worried face. "Does this happen a lot?"

"No."

He stands there slumped under his pack, a picture of failure and dejection.

Terra asks the driver what his plans are. He doesn't have any, hopes that when the bus doesn't show up, eventually a replacement will be sent out, can't say when that might be. While the two men stew in apathy, she looks around for more promising possibilities.

Some people are shouldering their baggage and taking off on foot; others make their way into the meadow and start setting up pup tents or just spreading blankets on the ground.

The old man who'd been sitting opposite them, cradling a basket of turnips, simply sits down on the side of the road. He seems prepared to wait forever. Whatever Beller claims, it looks to Terra like this probably does happen a lot. Just not always at such an unpleasant time, dark and chill and in the middle of nowhere.

She calculates how long it would take to walk the fifteen miles. They wouldn't arrive until the middle of the night, and exhausted. She peers into passing faces. Now and then a man catches her look, but not for long. His expression invariably reverts to stubborn and intense, focused on the way ahead. Traffic is thinning out fast. Not many want to travel at night, wasting fuel on lamps. She notes a mention of bandits, takes another look at Beller's passive stance, and decides to wait it out.

Terra and Beller create a wildly inadequate shelter in the dead grass with their packs and heaviest clothing. They eat the last of the apples. For a long time, she lies looking up at black sky where the moon struggles to free itself, continuously beaten back by sinewy clouds. Beller curls fetus-like beside her, too abject to think of making a pass. Thoughts of Fair and Orion now have time to intrude on her conscience. How distraught she has made them, the two people she's always loved best in the world.

Orion taught her to fish when she was seven. He was part of Tully's fishing team, an expert, and didn't need to spend his time with a little girl. But he did. And patiently, if humorously. That first afternoon when she squirmed at impaling the bait, kept pulling the line out of the water every five minutes, and panicked when she actually hauled in a fish, he chuckled, teased, and guided until she got quite good at it. For a time she harbored ambitions to become an official fisher too, until a year or so later when she decided she wanted to be a healer like Fair. Then he happily let her bandage his every imagined bruise and solemnly drank the herbal concoctions she presented as cure-alls.

Suddenly there are stars, and Terra realizes she's been asleep. The moon, now farther to the east, is shining unencumbered, casting sharp shadows across the sleeping group. Terra badly needs to go to the toilet, sits up to look around for a likely place. She notes a woman and child returning from a clump of bushes to the right, so that must be the chosen place, but she balks at sharing what will already be a smelly spot. So she veers farther off, towards a stand of tall grasses gilded by moonlight. When she steps in, she's immediately surrounded and shielded, the sheaves are so tall, and so dry they rattle as she passes. She needs only to take a dozen more steps to have privacy assured. But in another second she trips, loses her balance, falls. Keeps falling.

When consciousness returns, sunlight is heating her face. She opens her eyes painfully, head throbbing, and sees peering down at her a shaggy grinning head. For an odd long moment she meets its curious and cunning eyes, human but examining her as if she is not. She's lying in a pit about seven feet deep. She could probably crawl out if she could only move her limbs. Cautiously she tries her arms, legs, sits up, puts a hand to her forehead, finds blood on her fingers. All the while the gloating eyes are watching her. Unnerved but getting annoyed, she finally stops testing her mobility and stares back accusingly.

"Are you going to help me or not?"

The person laughs. She now makes out that it's a man, or rather a boy probably about fourteen, dirty brownish hair spiked out all around his sharp face rimmed with a light moss of beard. Instead of answering, he disappears. She hears him calling out, "Over here! Look what we've caught!"

"What is it, Rudi?"

Now there are three faces staring down at her, the boy and two girls as shaggy and dirty as he. One is tiny, though she must be at least twelve; the other, with big teeth and tan skin, is about Rudi's age.

"A girl. No coyotes or raccoons or rabbits or rats. A girl."

"What good's a girl?"

"Good for some things. Fucking, and especially ransom."

"Henry won't let you fuck her."

"Aw nuts."

"We'd better go tell him."

"Why? We could have some fun with her first."

"Cut it out, Rudi. You know the rules."

Then they're gone.

Terra tells herself she can come to no harm at the hands of children. But who is Henry? It starts to dawn on her that these are some of the feral kids she's heard about. As soon as the thought begins, she's clawing at the sides of the pit trying to find a foothold, screaming. Surely the people in the makeshift camp will hear her, surely she'll soon see Beller's ugly welcome face smiling down reassurances. But nothing happens. She only gets her nails clogged with dirt, and when she stops there's silence except for faint birdsong. She finally reluctantly relieves herself, covers the puddle with dust like a cat, then realizes she's burning with thirst. Her pack along with her canteen and food and everything is back over there beside Beller. Where the hell is he? She screams herself hoarse, and then she's sobbing, realizing what the sun has been telling her all along: it's late morning. The travelers will have left long ago. Of course Beller looked for her, must have enlisted help, but how could they have found her down here? She grasps at the hope that he stuck around, bravely let the others continue their journey, determined to search further. Maybe he'll show up any minute, put an end to this ridiculous nightmare.

A rope ladder flips down to her, topped by Rudi's malicious face. He's merely amused when she makes several failed attempts to climb it. Finally anger trumps weakness and she scrambles up, rolls over the edge, sits glaring at him. Now the other kids return through the surrounding grass. They yank her to her feet, tie her hands behind her, shove her forward.

"My pack," she protests. "Go see if my pack is still there." But she gets another shove. "Please."

"She thinks they left stuff for her," the older girl chortles in a throaty voice. She's wearing a pink straw hat that looks half eaten away on one side, and tattered overalls over a sweater missing a sleeve. "Stupid, too."

"She won't sell for much," concurs Rudi disgustedly.

There's no visible path, but the gang moves briskly forward. Terra is faint with thirst, head pulsing in pain. Shortly they emerge into a clearing, where a clump of belongings declares their camp: a small wagon, a lean-to fashioned with twigs, a circle of stones around a recent fire, and a tent patched in so many places it looks quilted. In front of the overturned roots of what was once a giant tree stands a boy perhaps sixteen, legs apart, arms folded, watching them approach. He doesn't move forward. Sheltered within the cave of roots and dirt behind him are two stumps serving as table and chair, oddly suggesting officialdom. Clearly this is Henry. Terra looks into intelligent storm-gray eyes assessing her and dawning his satisfaction. Surely he'll be reasonable.

"You're a prize," he says. "Who do you belong to?"

7

Orion has barely settled in Natick before he's summoned back to Barrytown by a distraught Fair. When she first found Terra's note she went into a rage, but now she's flagellating herself with guilt.

"Anything can happen out there on the road," she wails at Orion. "And what if she does find her father? Disaster! I should've told her about him. Oh, why didn't I? I'm such an idiot."

"Crazy kid." Orion is much more upset than he pretends. He feigns exasperation but his brotherly alarm is mounting. "She could have asked us to help her, at least."

Orion's walking his mother back from the Medical Center, his lamp casting weaving shadows.

"But we wouldn't have, would we? We'd just have scoffed and dissuaded."

"Stubborn, head-strong, ignorant, crazy kid."

"I should have told her the whole sordid awful story. Vita couldn't talk about anything else when they first brought her the baby. She hated poor little Terra, who was pitiful to look at, a few months old but no baby fat, skinny and pasty looking. To Vita, Terra was always the product of what happened to her own precious daughter. Those priests pretended they were sanctifying the girls, honoring them, but it was obvious to anyone with brains that it was all an excuse for lust and rape. How could she ever know which one fathered her anyway? What kind of a twisted person can he be? If she finds him, what will he do?"

"Take it easy, Mom. You've said all this before. Let's focus on getting her safely back. You're wasting your energy."

But all the way to her door, Fair is in a frenzy of outrage and panic.

"It's been almost a week now," she cries. "If she's not back by Thursday we have to alert the governor."

"You must be joking. First of all this Monty guy has no power. Sanmart's pulling the strings, and they're no friends of mine."

Inside, Fair lights the beeswax candle on her table and sits down dejectedly, face in hands. Orion pats her shoulder, pours her a cup of wine.

He says soothingly, "Give her two weeks at least. A trip like that could run into a lot of obstacles. Anyway, maybe she really will get a good story out of it and become a famous little reporter around here."

But he leaves her soon after. He's tired of her frantic fits. Her rages aren't helping; she really must calm down and focus on solutions.

Silk greets him with her usual sweet and sexy maneuvers, and they decide to cook at home this evening, instead of the dining hall. She shows off a plump pigeon already prepared for frying. They chop carrots together, fall into bed before it's all done. Then they eat at their little table half dressed, groggy with pleasure.

"Oh, I'm sure she'll be fine," Silk assures him. "She's a very clever and resourceful girl."

So Orion forgets his troubles. But not for long. The next afternoon as he's heading for a meeting with fellow rebels, he catches sight of a knot of black and gold uniforms near the entrance. He pulls up short, ducks behind a cart. They're dragging out two of his buddies, tossing them into a machine-driven van. A van with no signage or logo on its side. One of those: people taken away in those vans disappear. He forces himself to move slowly, turns away, and as nonchalantly as possible heads back home.

"Silk, baby, wrap up your report on Worcester, and get yourself to Natick asap. I've got to leave now. They've taken Roddy and Saul. I just missed being there for the roundup. Sorry, my love."

Silk starts to cry, but he stops her tears with kisses, and they make love one last desperate time. He leaves after dark, disguised hastily with a broad brimmed hat and old overcoat. He makes it to Natick, but they're waiting for him. It happens so quickly his brain is not involved, just the pain of twisted arms and bruised head. He's in a van, *the* van no doubt, in total blackness reeking with a smell of mixed vomit and blood, laced with that of the van's fuel, stale cooking oil.

Orion, lying on a hard surface, tries to think. He knows Silk will alert Fair, and comfort her as best she can. He curses that he

47

can't help Terra now, whatever happens to her. He worries about Silk—will they punish her for his delinquency? He consoles himself with her status as news leader. What about his poor mother? Tough as she is, she's no match for authorities who can make life very unpleasant for her. He rocks stiffly to the strange rhythm of the motorized vehicle; he's far more used to the gait of a horse. His brain clears, sleepiness staved off by discomfort and fear. He tries to convert the fear into strategy, but with little success. He speculates on where they're taking him. He's pretty sure it's a detainment camp just north of Barrytown, rumored to be filling up with Sanmart opponents. But he grasps at the hope that they won't keep him long. After, all they're still counting on their benign image as the best conduit to power, for now anyway. Aren't they?

For awhile he beats himself up about being so vulnerable. Wasn't there a lot more he could have done to protect himself from this? He'd thought that in quietly acquiescing to the Natick move, he'd take himself out of the center of action, and seem to agree to stay away from politics. Apparently they knew better. Somebody must've ratted on him. He starts to speculate who, then stops himself with reminders of certain torture methods Sanmart's Excell is known to favor. He himself could not withstand such persuasion, he admits. These guys are just too good, he mopes, and finds tears in his eyes, to his shame.

After about an hour, the van stops, the doors open long enough to admit more captives, who turn out to include Roddy and Saul, just enough time for recognition. Then off they go again, at an amazing speed. In the blackness the comrades exchange depressed greetings and speculations. Nobody is badly hurt, it seems, but everyone admits to hunger and thirst. Orion tries to muster enthusiasm for strategizing, but nobody has the guts to pretend, so he finally succumbs to uneasy sleep.

"Thank you for coming to volunteer for the glorious Hampshire Project, appropriately named All Joy."

The speaker, a squat, bulb-nosed man in uniform with medals sparkling, smiles with his teeth. He's standing in front of a big screen using a pointer to emphasize chosen images. Orion and his pals are seated in a row, clean, shaved, fed, and dressed in identical orange overalls, as are a dozen or so other men in rows around them. They disembarked yesterday, at a large encampment including their bare-bones living quarters that must have once been some sort of garage.

"You will find," continues the instructor, "every consideration for your dedication. We know you all fervently want to serve the grand purpose that brought you here, brave and good citizens that you are. If you hear anyone complaining, be sure to let us know so we can remove that person at once. Now here is an overview of our facility, at one time the largest indoor mall in the east—the famous Merrimack Mega Mall, abandoned over fifty years ago. And here we see the incredibly impressive renovations for our project, now on its way to becoming paradise for the chosen ones. You can just imagine the godly proportions we will achieve. Note that it's well guarded, including dogs. Any questions?"

On the screen Orion makes out an enormous domed structure with scaffolding all around. The egg shape fades into the distance, so it's hard to tell how far it extends. But workers swarming it make its magnitude clear. All the figures are clad in orange, except for guards in gray.

Someone has the audacity to ask, "How long will we be here?"

The instructor fixes him with a stare, states, "My friend, as long as it takes. You all will be amply rewarded when the time comes. You may be sure of that."

Orion speculates that the reward will probably be death. But a remnant of doubt remains. After all, though of course none of them ever intended to volunteer, they're being well treated and just may be slated for brain washing instead. Hope invigorates him, but he has found no opportunity yet to confer with his comrades about any possible mode of escape or resistance. They've been separated at the barracks, the bunks between him and them allotted to strangers. But one thing is clear. Joining in the pretense that they are all here voluntarily to devote themselves to a magnificent Sanmart project is the only way to go. He practices grinning proudly.

8

For the first three days, Terra knows they're traveling due west because the sun sets directly in front of them. But on the fourth morning they all wake up coughing, to an unmistakable smell of fire. Henry, who normally never gets frazzled, barks frantic orders. The kids run around grabbing up their things, packing them any which way, almost forgetting to tie Terra's hands. They set off at a run northward, wagon careening precariously.

All day the smell pursues them, ashes floating the air like gray snow, volcanic clouds pouring from the wildfire looming behind them like a pursuer. The smallest child, called Bird, is coughing so violently she cries from the pain in her ribs. They risk the main roads, where others bent on the same blind goal of escape pay no attention to them. After sunset the sky for a while continues lit with an unnatural orange glow, gradually giving way to night. But darkness doesn't stop them. They struggle on, following the lamp on the vehicle ahead of them, a large wheelbarrow with bicycle wheels. The winter dawn takes its time, reluctant, begrudging light. But now the realization of relief penetrates their mindless exhaustion. The air is only heavy, no longer pricked with ash, and most of the coughing has stopped. Henry orders them off the road behind a clump of bushes. After the kids have dropped asleep in place, he makes Terra study a map with him.

"Where the shit are we?" he asks her, his deep man's voice edged with scared memory of a boy's soprano.

The map is a sorry mess, so creased that many roads and towns are obliterated. Terra makes out the word Worcester under his dirty thumbnail.

"Here's where we camped last night," he says. "Somewhere around here." His thumb angles sharply upward. "We must be near that lake now, if there still is one. What do you know about this territory?"

Terra, sitting beside him on a rock, doesn't want to diminish his awe that she's an educated person and therefore "knows things." Ever since he found out she can read and write, he has treated her with more respect. He himself can barely print his name (he spells it Henree), and make out simple sentences if he reads them slowly and out loud, so he treats her ability almost like magical powers.

She says carefully, "I think it's good farming country. Just look at that field of pumpkins behind us."

He grudges a glance, shrugs. "Yeah that's good news food-wise, but what about the situation? I mean, how about militia and laws and that?"

"I haven't seen any yet."

He's not satisfied with her answer. He looks at her. "You'd better fetch a good price," he warns. "Or you're not worth the water you drink."

Henry has turned out to be a baffling mix of astute and crude. He looked her over, interviewed her, and assessed her worth in cool business-like mode. But, like the others, he eats with his hands and pisses in full sight of everyone. He thinks like an arrow, manipulating his little gang with ruses and insights as much as raw authority, figuring out almost at once what makes Terra tick, what scares or cows her. Yet he will almost beg her to show him how to write the alphabet. He's a sturdy and amazingly healthy looking young man, but he's missing a tooth and reeks of unwashed sweat. None of the kids want to wash, even when fairly safe water is available. They don't even own soap. Terra has already sacrificed her dignity more than once in pleading to be allowed to bathe.

She skirts his threat and replies, "Henry, let's get some rest. Later on I can study the map and get a better sense of what to expect."

He stands up and takes a long look in all directions, importantly brandishing binoculars they recently stole in one of their raids. The bushes shield them from the road, other travelers lie asleep at a distance, and behind them, beside the pumpkin field, twirls a row of small wooden wind turbines. This all apparently satisfies Henry well enough. He ties her to the wagon, throws her a blanket, and tucks himself into a sleeping bag. She tries to stay awake and plot once again some way of escape. But Henry has always been too smart for her, and the kids are as vigilant as animals when it comes to sensing her purpose. So far she has managed only to run a few feet into a ditch, where they all tackled her, gleefully and savagely. Once when they were near a bunch of other people she tried screaming, but the strangers only stared at her, sadly and scornfully, as if she was out of her mind. Her punishment each time was to stand naked in front of all of them, a humiliation that Henry has found is a surefire way to make her behave.

"You're coming with us to HQ," he has told her. "So just relax and don't try any more of your tricks. They won't hurt you. They might keep you or sell you or ransom you, it's up to the chief." When she asked who the chief was, he replied with mild surprise, "Hud of course. Don't tell me you haven't heard of the famous Hudson, king of the bandits."

"But I want to go home," she wailed. "I miss my auntie and my cousin."

"Oh boohoo," he mocked her. "As if we don't all miss home as much as you do. Tough titties."

She contemplated this answer with pity as well as alarm. What these children must have gone through while she herself was growing up safe and sound in Tully! She has gleaned some idea. Bird, for instance, was abandoned at the age of seven by someone she called grandpa, the only adult caregiver she can remember.

But any sympathy she feels is usually surmounted by passionate regret or heart-pounding fear. Running off from Barrytown was delusionally foolish, and she can't bear to imagine what the future holds now.

Terra wakes abruptly to Rudi's harsh whisper.

"Get up, we got to get going."

She doesn't argue. She knows this haste means they fear reprisal for some petty crime. Sure enough, after they sneak through the bushes and regain the road, she glimpses pumpkins in the wagon. Bird is missing for a moment, then comes running after them lugging something that turns out to be a book.

"What the hell!" yells Rudi. "What you want with that thing!"

Henry is stern. "Bird, you know you're not allowed to take things without permission. It can get us in trouble."

Bird starts to cry, hugging the book tenaciously. Her sounds are high pitched and hysterical; she reveres Henry and receives his slightest admonishment like the end of the world.

Henry's too focused on their getaway to insist. "Never mind, Birdie," he says, "stuff it under the blanket. You can keep it."

Later that day they make a more organized camp, within sight of a lake that looks blue rather than the usual green, so Henry decides they can safely boil the water for drinking and cooking. Behind a wall of vines they have discovered a broken building with the words, "Cust...er Se..v…" written across the top of the entrance in flaked paint that may once have been red.

Henry spells it out. "Custer Sev. What's that?"

"Customer Service," Terra guesses.

"A good name for a home," he guffaws.

Inside, remnants of the original purpose are long gone, but bones and charred wood show the place has been occupied within the past year or so. Bird starts sweeping at once without being told, wielding a broom fashioned from twigs and twine. Yola and Rudi set off in search of firewood and whatever food they can scare up. Henry heads for the lake with buckets and a fishing rod, and Terra is put to work digging a hole at the entrance for a fireplace; she's to follow that task with "fixing the pumpkins." She gets nowhere telling him she knows how to fish.

"Yeah and you swim fast too, I bet," he scoffs. "You're not going anywhere."

Terra is tied by the ankle to the door jam with an ingenious knot she knows better than to try fathoming. She's squatting, jabbing at the dirt with a rusty trowel in angry frustration, when she hears Bird singing. Without thought, she suspends her work, lifts her head, and closes her eyes, to take in the unearthly, ethereal sound. Bird's voice is like rippling water, like bees humming, high and rich and unspeakably gentle. It's so beautiful, Terra doesn't dare turn around to look, fearful of its ending. Instead she gazes out at the bare tree branches above, melding her eyes with their curious shapes, tracing their crooks and turns, listening to—or rather drinking in—the child's song. "Row, row, row your boat," Bird trills, making it sound glorious. For a suspended moment Terra's outside herself, unified with sky, tree, air, music.

When the song stops, she turns. "Sing some more, please."

Bird, who's just gathering up her pile of debris, shakes her head, letting her long dark hair straggle over her face.

So feigning indifference, Terra starts singing her favorite song from Tully. "Morning has broken, like the first dawning, blackbird has spoken, like the first bird." By the time she's finished, Bird has crept over to sit beside her. When Terra starts singing it again, Bird joins in, their voices together soaring past the twisting branches into the gray cloud of sky.

The pumpkins are a disappointment. They're rotted on the bottom and puckered dry on the top. Only the seeds look appetizing. No wonder they hadn't been very carefully guarded. But Terra salvages what she can, using the trowel to hack into chunks what might be used to flavor a stew. Bird, having learned Terra's song by heart, goes on singing it, over and over. Then she lugs over the book she stole, holds it out wordlessly. It's a beautiful old book, though the pages are browned at the edges and the binding ravaged by mold. There are lovely pictures, of delicate fairies on lily pads, giants, dragons, maidens lost in the forest.

"Once upon a time, there lived a princess who was lonely," Terra reads.

Bird sits so close she's almost snuggling. Terra too, cross legged, gets lost in the cadence of the story. It's only when the silence around them is sharply broken that she realizes what a precious peace they had briefly entered, she and little Bird.

Yola's screams reach them first. But it's Rudi who appears, running like lightning, clutching a limp bloodied animal of some sort, maybe a rabbit or a squirrel. He's just starting to hide it in a bush, when Yola comes screeching past, tackles him. Their faces and clothes are spattered with blood, they roll on the ground grunting insults. Rudi finally extricates himself, dangling the corpse at Yola jeering, "I got it, I got it!"

"Give it to me, it's mine. I caught it."

"You didn't do anything to it, you stupid bitch. I got it."

"I set the trap."

Yola has her fists up, doing a boxing dance, ready to pounce again.

"Set the trap, set the trap," Rudi mocks. "So what, so what. I got it."

"Give it to me. Terra, Birdie, tell him to give it to me. Tell him."

"They're not going to tell me anything, stupid bitch. You lost."

She makes another dash at him, but he jumps aside and she falls down. She sits there on the ground, dusty and bloody, glaring up at him. The she picks herself up slowly, smoothes her hair, and says with a cold simper, "I'll let you see my cunty."

Rudi drops his hand holding the trophy, and considers.

Terra has been through a gamut of reactions from scorn to amusement, but now she starts to worry about the effect on Bird. She reaches out to put an arm around her, but Bird angles away, stands up and inches forward for a better look. Is this silly panorama about to turn ugly? Two skinny disheveled kids splashed with blood and dirt confronting each other. Yola's missing a shoe, Rudi's shirt is torn, the disputed mangled animal dangles.

Rudi replies, "I want to use it."

"You're not using my cunty, just because I let you once. No, but you can see it, I said. You can have a long look."

"That's not good enough," Rudi taunts, waving the bloody corpse at her.

Yola spits on the ground, furious. "Keep your stupid cat. It tastes crappy anyway."

"Just a minute," Rudi exclaims, seeing her turn away. "How long a look?" Yola pulls down her overalls, revealing a white belly and black pubic triangle. "You got to bend over, I can't see it that way. I can't see anything. Bend over."

"Nope, this is it, you look as long as you want, the cat is mine now."

"Crap and bullshit. That's no cunty, that's just the outside."

But Yola stands there, swaying her hips a little, a triumphant grin playing at her lips, clearly enjoying her power. Rudi has dropped the animal and reached into his pants for his penis, begins to pump it. But Terra has jumped as far forward as she can, the tied leg extended behind her, yelling.

"Cut it out, you two. Stop, stop!"

Rudi is startled only an instant, then leers. "Watch this, Terra, you're gonna like it."

But at the same moment Henry appears through the bushes and bellows, "Rudi!"

In an instant, Yola's pants are back on and Rudi's penis disappears. Both kids look sheepish and a little scared.

"We were only playing," Rudi whines.

"That's it, that's all I can take. I didn't bargain for this shit when I took you two on. Do you want to go back on your own? How did you like starving, Rudi, how did you like slavery, Yola? You want it again? Huh, huh?" Henry is pushing and prodding them, punching their shoulders and backs. "What am I going to do with you? What do you think I should do with you? You want to break the rules all the time, you're more trouble than you're worth."

"Sorry, Henry, sorry," Yola mumbles.

Now she and Rudi are on the ground, abject, Henry prodding them with his foot, shouting down at them.

"We got a lot of firewood," tries Rudi.

"Where?"

"I'll show you."

So Rudi and Henry end up tramping off together, Henry calling back, "Yola, you and Terra clean the fish."

After the boys have left, Bird picks up the dead cat, brings it to Terra.

"Will we be eating this?" she asks.

"I've never eaten cat."

There's not much left to recognize, but tufts of gold fur still cling to the body, which hardly has enough meat on it to consider. She thinks briefly of her beloved cat Cloud, purring and soft, but food wins.

She says, "If we soak it long enough, that will make it taste milder, and anyway the bones will add flavor."

9

The river glitters in bright sunset. The children have made their camp for the night far from the road, here in the crook of a sloping hill. They've been traveling west again, and have made good time since the beginning of February. Terra already has a fire started, Henry's hauling buckets of water, and Yola and Bird squat over potatoes, scrubbing and chopping. They're all getting nervous, because Rudi has been gone for an hour and he was only supposed to sneak up on chickens belonging to a wimpy-looking family it would be easy to outfox. The chickens, three of them, were in a cage in a wagon just in front of them on the road. They'd followed it, salivating and plotting, for a good five miles.

"I hope he doesn't try anything crazy," comments Yola.

"He'll be fine," grunts Henry, putting another bucket of water on the fire. "When Rudi's focused…and anyway he's faster than lightning."

"When he's focused," sneers Yola. "*If* he's focused you mean."

Into the first pot of boiled water, Terra throws turnips and onions and leftover squirrel bones. She would dearly love chicken parts for this measly stew. She hardly thinks of the family they'll be robbing. They looked like a placid crew, an aged man and woman and one skinny kid. Terra always tries not to look much at their intended victims. Hunger's pain and weakness have become too familiar for scruples, and she's still not used to it. She remembers only once in Tully not having enough to eat. It was after the snowstorm of the decade in '74 in the middle of September, in what was a heat wave one day and a frigid tornado the next. All the crops died. Even the root vegetable harvest was puny and all that winter they had to subsist mostly on salted fish and pickles. Her grandmother was ill for months, so it was Fair who scrounged goodies for young Terra—bean sprouts, baked apples, dried plums. Fair hardly ever shared these luxuries, simply sat smiling watching Terra gobble them up. I didn't question it, Terra reflects. I was grateful but it never occurred to me to ask what she herself ate. She briefly dwells on Fair's loving face, that worried look that so often irritated her.

What she wouldn't give to kiss her again, right now, hug her close. She would promise eternal obedience. But before gathering tears can spring, Yola jolts her out of her longing with a raucous cry.

"Hey! Here he comes."

Tearing along the ridge of the hill like a shooting star, Rudi zooms past without looking in their direction. In another moment, his pursuer appears, an ancient, burly man, but obviously athletic. They both disappear, but then suddenly Rudi pops out of a clutch of rushes in the river and throws them a dead chicken before vanishing again. Yola needs no prompting or second thoughts. She grabs the bird and starts ripping off its feathers.

"Hurry up," she hisses at Terra. "Let's get rid of this."

In no time the naked chicken is in pieces and submerged in the simmering pot. The ensuing delicious gamey smell is the only evidence of its existence.

Yola gives Terra her widest toothy grin, reserved for mischief. She has obviously enjoyed the tension of the hunt. Bird, on the other hand, can't stop trembling.

"I hope he won't catch Rudi, I hope he won't hurt him."

"Rudi?" Henry scoffs. "He'll never catch Rudi."

But the sun sets without Rudi's return. The children finish their meal anxiously, watching the reflection of firelight on the water. The river is shallow, running fast over large rocks, so orange flickers leap and prance. On the other side, more fires flame here and there. Beyond, all is black, shadowless as a vacuum. Tucked up in her blanket, Terra watches the water bubble and sparkle, misting the cold air with an earthy, moldy odor. A snuffle and a squirm at her side signal that little Bird has come for comforting. Henry has forbidden it, but he never seems to notice. Terra opens her blanket and cuddles the girl in the crook of her arm, kisses her mass of tangled hair that smells like seaweed, salty and mossy.

"Go to sleep, Birdy. Everything will be ok."

"Can't you stay with us?" queries Bird in a singsong voice. "My grandpa left me."

"Don't worry," Terra says with a hug. "You'll still have Henry. And when you grow up, you can come visit me."

"Where?"

It's a chilling question. Terra usually replies, "Barrytown, of course," and goes on to lull the child with promises of meeting Auntie Fair and cousin Orion and sleeping in a real bed. But of course she has no idea where she will be, what will happen to her after Henry turns her over to his chief. She has stopped trying to escape, though there's never been a minute when she didn't want to get away, and she's almost used to this harsh life, nearly two months of it now. She's fond of Bird, with a reluctant protectiveness, and while resenting Henry, has to admire him. But they'll reach their goal within a week. Henry pointed it out on the map this morning. They have crossed into the Albany enclave, though on the old map it's still marked Boston territory.

"Albany pushed Boston out of here five years ago," Henry bragged, ramming a grubby fingernail along the faded borderline. "It was easy. Now we run this whole area, including the Westfield River. Look here, fifty miles worth we grabbed from you. Bunch of wimps."

Terra dares to challenge him. "So you're proud of being bossed by that Sanmart crew?"

"Hey, Hud's a hero and a genius. He doesn't take orders from Sanmart, they listen to him. You'll see."

Soon Bird's soft breathing indicates sleep, mingles with the gurgle of the river. The fire fades to a glow of red embers. Before she lets her eyes close, Terra dwells on the memory of her eighth birthday, when Orion gave her a fishing rod he'd made himself. She can see his proud grin, that mix in his eyes of amusement and affection, can hear herself cry, "Orie! Oh, Orie!" Fair is there, and her grandmother, both of them laughing as if nobody ever had a care in the world.

She wakes to a sharp sizzling sound. It must be a dream: that can't be rain spraying the fire. But she hears Yola whooping, sits up to see her and Bird doing a frantic joy dance, mouths open to the sky graying with dawn. Henry stands palms open, grinning up as the water streams over his face.

Terra calculates how long it's been since she saw rain. The last time was in that spastic storm just outside Boston Bay. She throws off her soaking blanket, shouts and chants along with the others, though her ankle is still secured to a boulder. Their ecstasy lasts minutes. Then the cold gets to them, and shivering they grab shelter where they can. Bird crouches under the wagon, Henry and Yola huddle under a tarp. Yola is begging him to set up the tent.

"Hey," calls Terra. "Can somebody please untie me over here? I'm drowning."

But Henry hardly glances in her direction.

"Look," he reasons with Yola, "Rudi's not back yet and that could mean trouble. We need to pack up and get out of here."

"In the rain? Can't we wait til it stops?"

"No, we can't wait until it stops," Henry retorts disgustedly. "You know better than that. Why haven't we ever been caught? Because you do what I say."

But he doesn't move. Clearly he's reluctant to abandon Rudi. He tells Yola to untie Terra and she joins them under the tarp. They munch dejectedly on cold remains of stew and stale bread.

Sometime later, maybe an hour, maybe two, just when Terra thinks she can't stand another second of shivering wet, a pedicab appears, bumping along following the riverbank. In it are Rudi and two men in black and gold uniforms, they and the driver protected by an awning. Rudi is leading them here, finger pointing. Terra begins to let herself hope that with authorities comes her freedom. But Henry, instead of leaping to his feet to denounce Rudi and vehemently deny wrongdoing, stands up smiling.

The rain has weakened to a heavy mist, the air itself hanging damp, sunlight already shafting heated pathways. The ground runs rivulets of mud but there's still dust underneath.

"Greetings," he says to the men in a pompous voice, mingling graciousness with a touch of arrogance.

Where has he learned to talk like that, how does he dare? Rudi steps out of the cab trying to look nonchalant, but obviously smug.

"Henry," he says, "my friends here need proof of our mission. I told them it was no problem."

"Of course," Henry nods.

He digs into his backpack to produce a wrinkled roll of paper that he politely unfolds, hands to one of the men, the taller and more weather beaten of the two.

The man looks over the document and gets out of the cab, shakes hands with Henry.

"Lieutenant Judd at your service. Can we give you a hand?"

In an unreal sequence of events, Judd radios, a van appears, the children and Terra are installed with warm dry blankets and hot cups of cider, and the van careens off up the hill onto the road. Behind it wobbles the pedicab towing their wagon. Terra's gratitude is corroded with new fears. There's something about these black and gold clad men that presages much more danger than wily Henry and his gang.

10

Terra sleeps fitfully in a large room lined with narrow beds, one of about two dozen women. She knows they're in a sprawling mansion, she could make out that much when they arrived last night. With a grandiose entrance, wings extending on either side, brick, gabled like fairy tales, it sprawls just below the lip of a rolling hill. In the van, the feral children gasped excitement at the sight of it. They rode up a long curved driveway, so there was plenty of time to be dazzled. The front door was tall, in two parts, with brass knobs in the shape of lions. Over it arched carved wooden figures; all the windows were aglow behind gilded blinds.

"This is H.Q.," announced Yola importantly, awe in her raspy voice. "I've been here before."

"It looks like a castle," breathed Bird.

But then they bypassed the glorious entrance, drove around to the back, and pulled up by a distinctly unglamorous, ordinary door. Inside, a smell of too many people and rancid food. Henry and Rudi went off to the men's quarters. Bird was not allowed to stay near Terra, but had to bunk at the other end of the room with the younger girls. It was all very regimented, though not threatening. They were fed and given identical nightdresses with yellow flowers on them. For a while Terra could hear Bird sniffling in the dark, but a curt voice put a stop to that.

Just after the lights went off, Yola from the next bed hissed, "You'll be processed in the morning. Then you'll see."

Terra did not ask just what it was she would see. She tries to attribute Yola's malicious jibe to her usual crude animosity. But she's frightened, maybe more than she's ever been. During the time travelling with Henry's little band, she could feel older, superior, confident in the boundaries she set. Here, adults are in charge, this operates like some kind of institution, ominous even in its comforts. She has no power here at all. Terrible stories she's heard in the past rise up to haunt her: children sold into slavery, starved, beaten, raped, killed. Why should she assume, as she always has, that for some reason these things could not happen to her? She can taste the fear, acid in her throat.

Dawn starts at the small, high windows, presaging not sunshine but stolid, unwavering gray. In the gathering light, the long room evolves lines of sleeping forms. Terra closes her eyes again, conjuring her Barrytown home where Fair is lying in the next bed. Soon they will get up and bathe and slurp yogurt and tea and laugh and go off to work. Terra finds in this fantasy a few strands of sleep.

A tolling bell, resonant as a gong, sharply wakes her, still groggy and exhausted. She imitates the other women, throwing off their covers and standing at the foot of their beds. A plump woman in a billowing dress looks on, smiling in a rigid sort of way, hands on hips.

"Good morning, ladies, here we all are," she observes mechanically. "Don't hog the toilet, move along."

In groups of threes the woman take turns filing out to the bathroom, where the toilets have no walls but at least you can sit. Terra's grateful to then be offered a basin with soap and water and a chance to wash. Back in the dorm room, everyone's still standing in their nightgowns, silent. Then they are paraded into the next room, where they'd been fed the night before. Each woman is handed a bowl of oatmeal, and when another gong sounds, they all start eating and talking at once. Terra turns to the girl beside her, small eyes in a broad brown face, says hello.

The girl looks her over coolly, replies, "You'll be ransomed I bet. You look like you have folks with money. I'm going to be sold."

"I'm so sorry," Terra says lamely. "How do you know?"

"Got processed two days ago. Auction coming up next week. I'll go to the highest bidder. Hope I get a nice owner."

"Where are you from? Where's your family?"

"No family. Never had one that I remember. I'm good at cooking. Hope I get a place as a cook, that's what I'm hoping. Don't expect I'm pretty enough to have to serve in one of those harem things."

"But this is against the law," Terra gasps, even as she says it knowing how ridiculous it sounds.

The girl doesn't laugh, though. "That never stopped anybody."

Still wearing their nightgowns, Terra, Yola, and Bird are ushered by the plump manageress up a steep flight of concrete stairs. Behind a large desk in a bright, tall-windowed room, an officer with a black eye-patch and very small blond moustache gestures at a row of straight backed chairs. The girls sit. The room is not large, but the high ceiling, drapes, and soft carpet, plus the shining mahogany desk, suggest elegance. Yola's smug glances at Terra are not mitigated by the grandiose surroundings. She's been here before, it seems. Sure enough, the officer greets her familiarly.

"Well, it's our Yola."

"Thank you, Sargeant. Glad to be back."

"You did some good work. We've already had Henry's report."

"We did, we did. Look at this female we brought you."

Yola's grimace at Terra is a flaunting gloat.

"Is this little girl the one called Bird?"

Bird is trembling white, her voice a whisper. "Yes, sir."

"Henry seems to think you like being on his team."

"Oh I do, sir, I do. Please don't make me go away."

The sergeant studies her for a moment, with his one bloodshot eye, in a mix of disbelief and dismay. "What are you good for?"

Before Bird can burst into tears, Yola intervenes. "She's very useful to us, I promise, Sargeant. She fits through fences, she sneaks up under wagons, and also she hardly never eats anything."

Terra leans over to put her arm around Bird. The officer's gaze directs sharply at Terra.

"Stand up," he orders her.

Terra stands up. She hopes her face expresses pride and calm, but in addition to her fear she's acutely uncomfortable at being cross examined in a nightgown.

"What do you have to say for yourself?"

"I would like my clothes back."

The sargeant is electrified by this response. "What a devil!" He gets up and saunters around her, examining all angles as if ogling a foreign object. "What could this be? A feisty lady, eh?"

"Oh, yeah," snickers Yola. "All kinds of trouble, that one."

"Well, well."

Bird pipes up, "Don't say that, Yola. Terra's a good person."

"Well, well," the sargeant repeats.

64

Terra tries to meet his eyes with confidence, falters, struggles for indignation.

"I would appreciate it, sir, if I could get dressed and go home."

His laugh is genuine, and lengthy.

"Yola and Bird, go. You'll stay for a few days rest, then your team heads out again. You've done great."

Bird is prevented from embracing Terra by a yank from Yola, and they're gone.

Terra stands there, the sergeant musing at her face.

"You're quite a beauty, too, aren't you? You'd better bring a good price, or the boss might want to keep you. I think we'll put you in the bride brigade for now."

"I have important connections in Barrytown." The break in her voice takes the challenge out of her words.

"Do you now? What do you think you're worth to them?"

But she's using all her strength to control tears, and besides she realizes he's only toying with her. So she's silent, looking beyond him at map-covered walls, out the row of windows to the broad drive where uniformed officers stroll. They seem to be chatting amiably, for all the world like peaceful guardians, giving the lie to her stomach-clenching dread.

The rest of the morning is unnervingly bland. She's taken up some stairs, along a mirrored hallway out of some old picture book, with portraits and rugs, into a pretty room with three beds flaunting fluffy pink coverlets. On her assigned bed flops a stuffed pink teddy bear, absurd in its neutrality. The one thing about a teddy bear is that it's your own, she reflects bitterly. Terra is then shown a spacious bathroom where she bathes gratefully in a hot tub. The clothes she's offered are a choice between her old garments, now tattered and faded from months on the road, and new ones that are quite charming and comfortable. The skirt is a little short and the blouse a bit low necked, but nothing suggestive. She's glad to put them on, dignity restored. Lunch is served in a smallish room where half a dozen girls and women gather around a square table draped with a garish red and yellow cloth. Some are sullen, some seem overly cheery, but the whole impression comes off as routine.

The olive-skinned girl next to her comments, "You're the new one. You're in our room, with Trudy and me."

Terra tries to smile, gives her name, toys with her food. It's a delicious looking mushroom omelet, but her throat is tight.

"Welcome, Terra, I'm Gina."

Terra looks around at the others, who are eating calmly as if at home.

"What is this," she dares to ask. "Is this the bride brigade?"

Gina giggles. She looks a bit older than Terra, but her manner is decidedly girlish. Her long thick hair is pulled back into braids.

"Goodness no, is that what they told you? Only wanted to scare you for fun, I'll bet. No, we're getting ransomed. We won't have to be brides unless our families don't have the money."

Terra begins to smell the food and suddenly is ravenous, takes a bite. For drinks they have cranberry juice, her favorite. Of course she'll be ransomed, Fair and Orion will turn Barrytown upside down to rescue her. No problem. She even begins to plot how she can turn this into a spectacular story for the News Center when she gets back.

After lunch a guard comes to fetch her, leads her along more fancy corridors into a long room plush with sofas, voluminous drapes, gilt-edged tables. The same style floor-to-ceiling windows look out on the same broad drive, but there are eight windows here. The view extends to rolling lawns, and beyond occasional leafless trees, to a fenced area where horses graze, hills beyond. The pale gray sky is laced with sunlight pulsing through. There's a subtle perfume to the air in this soothing room, like vanilla perhaps, or honey. Well fed, dressed, reassured about her status, Terra has regained almost all of her bravado, and studies the charming room with interest. She has never seen anything like it. The subdued sense of luxury is mesmerizing, a fantasy or a dream. Even back in Tully, the proudest room compared to this was rustic, flat. A group at a corner table breaks, comes toward her.

At once she notices the tall tawny-haired man wearing a brocade jacket. He's about fifty, with a bright and easy smile. Something about his face makes her think the word beautiful. Everyone else now departs except for a balding blonde man with a sizeable paunch only partially concealed by his purple vest.

She takes the chair offered to her. Now the three of them are gathered around the small scalloped-edged table. The men are politely attentive, keeping their intense examination of her respectful. A glass of cranberry juice is brought to her.

The man in the brocade jacket introduces himself as Hall Hudson, his companion as Armand Jones. These are names she has heard somewhere, and as she struggles to remember, Hall starts talking about Boston, how much he admires its history and restored charm.

"A place we all revere as the cradle of democracy as they say." His voice is not deep but melodious and somehow soothing. "Had some difficult times there back in the 50s. But all's well now."

"Having some new blood in," chortles Armand. "I hear the old regime is out."

Hall waves his glass at his friend. "Perhaps our guest would care to comment on that. How about it, Terra?"

She wants very much to prove her intelligence, batting away a warning to herself that nothing here is to be trusted. It doesn't matter that she's being questioned by her captors; what matters is the beautiful room and the beautiful and amiable man. For some wild reason, she wants to impress him.

"Barrytown is peaceful and quite pretty," she comments, in what she hopes is a sophisticated and judicious tone.

The men's eyes consult each other, but she can't fathom their expressions. They are used to these interviews, of course, she reminds herself. They must examine a dozen girls every week. It's pointless to try to outfox them.

"What about the shakeup in Boston?" pursues Hall.

"I believe there's a new governor?" Then she tries to sound knowledgeable with, "Barrytown seems quite stable to me."

The men laugh jovially, neither mocking nor teasing, but as if rewarded for some bet they made.

"You do have a head on your shoulders," comments Armand.

"Proof that educating women only adds to their charm," Hall chuckles. "You're invited to take a glass of wine with us this evening. Would you like that?"

Terra wants to say yes, but asks archly instead, "Will I be permitted to go home soon?"

Armand shrugs, notes, "Your future is yet to be determined."
His tone, ice behind velvet, chills.

She acquiesces, "Of course," acknowledging their power. But she wants to also make it clear her will has not been consulted, their charm notwithstanding. So she adds firmly, "But I think you would be wise to let me go."

"Spitfire," comments Armand neutrally, nodding to Hall as if having taken her full measure.

The rest of the day is busy with activities that further intrigue and frustrate Terra. She and Gina are allowed to go outside to stroll in a walled garden that's already sporting shoots of green and a clutch of delicate snow drops. There are winding gravely paths, wooden benches, a cylinder of birdseed with sparrows chattering about it. This could promise to be a lovely little refuge in a month or so. But it has a weary, eerie tinge to it. A stunted willow tree in one corner looks like it may never bloom again, and a row of bushes have been cut to the ground as if in a last resort to revive them. Where the surrounding stone wall is broken, it's been repaired with scrap metal, formidably secure but blatantly ugly. Still, it's refreshing to be in the open air. The sky this afternoon is springtime blue, its only clouds lazy little puffs.

"I used to have a garden sort of like this," boasts Gina, "back home in Albany."

But Terra is already tired of stories about Albany, which she's beginning to suspect of great exaggeration. Uneasily, she has concluded that not much Gina tells her is quite true.

Instead of responding directly, Terra tries, "I wonder what's become of my traveling companions. Do you know if I can go visit them? I'm worried about my little friend Bird."

Gina replies, "Oh, don't worry about them. They'll be rewarded for bringing you in, especially if you get a good price. I wouldn't call them friends if I were you."

"Bird is different," Terra insists.

"Around here, you'd better concern yourself with yourself. You never know what could happen."

Terra glances at Gina's somber profile, hearing ominous overtones in the not-so-girlish warning.

11

"Tell them the truth, Orion. You're one quarter. That'll sell them ok."

Finch's whisper comes out guttural with his mouth full. He's chewing on bread as they sit over breakfast in the canteen, dozens of men pressed together at long tables. Finch is half Mohawk so he's been assigned to the highest scaffolding of the project. He's convinced this will make it easier to plan an escape, and wants Orion to join him. They've become close buddies in the weeks since Orion's arrival, their shared heritage a bond.

"My father was half Mohawk," Orion has told him. "My other half's as Irish as they come."

"Never mind. That makes you red enough," urges Finch. "They don't care. They need our talents. How are you with heights?"

"Always been fine with them, climbed to the top of trees as a boy. Scared the shit out of my poor mother."

"See? Close enough. Want me to tip off the teach?"

A pan of fried eggs is passed along to them. They taste greasy but the food here is generally nutritious. More reason to hope the plan is brainwashing and not murder. Orion nods agreement to Finch, a skinny, wiry man of thirty or so, with a thick head of raven-black hair on a small head, deep-set little eyes and a long nose, like a beak. Finch grins as he swallows, jabs Orion's shoulder with his elbow.

"We're out of here," he promises.

Orion eats heartily. He's adjusted to the grueling physical labor required from dawn to dusk. The prisoners are not beaten and are allowed enough sleep. They have classes every day, meaning pep talks, and once a week a couple of hours to socialize, or read publications selected for them. Saul has been assigned to a team at the other end of the miles-long construction, but Orion has been able to communicate with Roddy during rest time. Roddy goes from depressed to enthusiastic about the possibilities for advancement that the instructor has hinted to him.

Orion's work assignment entails repairing steel support beams on the west side of the cavernous structure, where the old mall withstood the most damage. The panes in the giant dome are missing, but its intricate network of triangles is mostly intact. As more and more volunteers show up every day, the structure takes on its restored shape with impressive rapidity. A few machines appear, their curious roar pulsing the air, and it becomes clearer how the mall is being expanded. With May come a few days of intense heat, presaging yet another suffocating spring. On one of these mornings, Orion is ordered to join the team heading for the highest beams, some forty feet off the ground. He finds himself side by side with Finch, far above the frenetic action below. Off to the southeast they can see the Merrimack River glinting silver winding through countryside still mostly brown, here and there a flash of green. To the north the mountains gently undulate.

Fitting a glass pane into a steel triangle, Orion comments, "Can you believe all this fancy construction back then just for shopping?"

"What they did best," Finch snorts. "Citizens were called consumers."

"It's huge. I'd guess about a mile across. How long, d'you think?"

"Could be three miles, from what I've been able to gather."

"What's it for?"

"Joy," replies Finch with a grimace.

Finch wears a ratty bandana around his forehead to catch the sweat. It's already soaked, his pointed, ruddy face slick. He's balanced precariously on a girder, wielding a wrench with gusto. Their exchange is cut short by the proximity of a guard, who cautions them to silence. He wears a mean-looking cudgel at his belt, though makes no suggestion he might use it. The guards are sparse up here, for the obvious reason that most of them would get dizzy. So now and then Orion and Finch steal enough privacy for their plans. Finch teaches Orion some Iroquois words, especially "ohonte," meaning green, which is to serve as their password.

One day the bloody corpse of Orion's rebel buddy Saul is found in the barracks courtyard. The captain calls a special session to announce the find. He explains that in all likelihood Saul angered loyal Sanmart volunteers by insulting their dedication, implying they were coerced. Orion bitterly reflects that Saul no doubt told truths and was targeted by the authorities to serve as an example. Poor old Saul, one of the best and bravest.

"So his fellow workers were naturally enraged against him," intones the captain shaking his head sadly. "We don't condone the violence, of course, and we will identify and chastise the offenders. But who can blame them, folks, decent hard working citizens like you, proud to labor for All Joy."

The corpse is left where it was tossed, far longer than for any imaginable reason, except to serve as a warning, which it certainly does. Nobody wants to look too closely at the vicious wounds.

Some days later, while Saul's fly-blown stinking body is still lolling in the courtyard, Orion and Finch get their first hint of a viable escape tactic. Wildfires have been reported to the east, and from their lofty perch the friends discern the spiraling black smoke in the distance. They have the same idea at the same time, exchange glances.

Finch whispers, "Just the distraction we need."

"The wind's moving the smoke fast this way. Let's go for it."

"Ohonte. I'm in."

They've already staked out a dilapidated shack about a mile to the south, near the river, as their rendezvous, assuming they must escape separately. Their backup plan includes heading for the Boston border, hoping to reconnoiter near it, in Merrimack.

Finch succeeds. Orion sees the last of him clinging to a rope swinging out over nothingness, disappearing. But Orion is spotted by a guard as he starts the same maneuver, and has to drop precipitously in a different direction, straight onto the roof of a guardhouse. He crouches under an overhang, waiting for the shouts to come nearer, for certain capture. But apparently it doesn't occur to them that he'd be hiding right there, and they all hurry past, fanning out everywhere else. When he dares to stir, Orion finds an opening into some kind of attic, drops inside. After the glare of sunlight his eyes gradually adjust, making out piles of ammunition and sacks of flour. Extra supplies, so this room will be visited periodically. It's unbearably stuffy. But now he stands a chance.

Later in the day, faint from thirst, Orion discovers a tube leading from the rain cistern and is able to divert enough to drink, though it tastes rusty and stale. He falls into a nervous sleep, hollow with hunger. He wakes to voices in a room just below. Two men are exchanging monosyllables. A gray dawn wavers through the slat serving as the only window. Orion finds a good place to put his ear, so he can hear them, but it's only two guards making small talk as they get ready for their morning shift. Orion is dismayed to learn that he's trapped in a place so central to guard activity. His stomach hurts from hunger and also from the bad water he's had to drink. He eases an opening in a bag of lentil flour, faking the kind of tear a rat's teeth would make, and crafts a disgusting pancake which he eats ravenously, further annoying his stomach. He is not in a good situation. How the hell will he get out of here?

Three days pass, with Orion more and more discouraged. He'll have to try some kind of escape, but his churning stomach has weakened him, and anyway all alternatives are fraught with danger. He thinks of Saul's mutilated body, concluding such a fate must be in store for him as well.

Then, bingo! On the fourth day around noon, the conversation below takes on new meaning.

"The underground level's pretty shallow, Boss."

A grunt of assent. "Won't need it for much. Storage mostly."

"Right. I understand the inside climate is so controlled, there'll be no need for refuge from it."

"You got it, Hud my friend. Flip of a switch. Hot or cold, whatever you want. Including Morgala, should you desire an orgy."

Hud chuckles enthusiasm. "Proven in the prototype?"

"Proven in the prototype," Boss replies smugly. His voice is high and edgy, while Hud's is smooth, throaty.

"Congrats, Boss."

"Not really. We've got a long way to go. Why I wanted you to see this, why I got you to travel here with me all the way from your comfy Berkshire headquarters. Look over there. A bunch of men hauling a slab of concrete on makeshift planks. That's what I'm talking about. We need to double the number of volunteers and get us more horses until we can manufacture some oil from coal, or frack it up from those shales like they used to, so we can get a couple more machines in there. We were supposed to be closing over the north end by the end of this month. But we've had to move the deadline to June."

"We won't be on schedule? What are your plans?"

"My plans are for you to speed up your abductions."

Hud pauses for a deep breath. "We're doing our best."

"No, Hud, you're not. You're good. But you're having too much fun."

The two men laugh, albeit tensely, and begin to chuckle over some incident the evening before. Something to do with women.

"Shied like a horse," crows Boss, as the two of them leave, guffawing in brotherly camaraderie.

Orion's nerves vibrate in full alert. These men clearly are in charge, especially the one called Boss. In fact, in all probability it's Armand "Boss" Jones, the infamous leader of the Albany enclave. The two of them visiting here means this vast undertaking, this gigantic dome big as a town, is destined to play some significant role for Sanmart. Orion yearns to find out more. That night, after long listening to total silence below, he creeps out the attic door, down narrow steps, into the guard room. There's just enough moonlight to make out shapes, table, desk, chairs, cloak rack. He takes off the telltale orange overalls, dons somebody's uniform. He rifles through the desk drawers, comes across a map of the All Joy structure, pockets it, finds and shoulders a backpack with a few Albany dollars and a canteen in it. He stuffs the overalls under a pile of flour sacks. He has a new sense of urgency, fearing what this dome might mean. His foreboding isn't specific but in it lurks a threat that hardly bears thinking about: could it be that Sanmart plans to duplicate Earth and leave the real planet to its fate? He's ready to risk flight.

12

As soon as she gets Terra's ransom note, Fair goes to see her friend Zed. He's in his lumber shop as usual, behind a work table piled with planks of various sizes, sanding down an old board. The light from the store window dances with sawdust motes. He grins a mile when he lays eyes on her.

"She sails forth to see her man," he begins with his usual banter, but shuts up after one good look at her face. "What the hell's the matter?" He hurries to put his arm around her. "Come, sit down." She mutely lifts both her hands, displaying a lock of Terra's hair, and he mutters, "They've got her, I knew it."

She lets him soothe her, sits by him behind his counter, sipping cool tea. Her relationship with Zed is fraught with ambiguities. He admires her openly, even ventured to kiss her one evening. She responded too warmly before pulling away. The incident hasn't been mentioned since, but has ringed their friendship with alarms. She's shocked to find she doesn't think of Miles in this context, as if her life with her husband in far-off peaceful Tully is more a dream than this intense and perilous real world. Zed has been particularly mellow about Orion's disappearance. He's always insisting, "The boy's fine, depend on it. The Sans just want to shake some sense into him."

As Zed reads the note, Fair moans, "Thousands of Boston dollars. Where will I come up with that?"

"It's a lot of money," Zed concedes. "But at least we know she's safe. They'll be keeping such a valuable possession well and healthy."

Not for the first time, Fair is appalled by his casual response. "How can you talk like that! She's a prisoner somewhere, treated like an object. God knows what they might do to her. Zed, you drive me crazy."

She ventures a glance at him: curly gray hair, short neck, heavy shoulders. She wishes she could tell him all her fears, needs his mix of jest and reassurance, but she's confided in him too much already. He knows her far better than she knows him. When they first met she thought him superficial. After all he runs a business—his mind doesn't stray far from practical matters. But the more she knows him, the more complex he seems. He studies people, and his insights are often remarkable. Above all, he's tuned in to her, in a soul-mate kind of way that makes her physical attraction to him all the more acute. Sometimes she thinks she might stop fighting, just have an affair with him. Miles would never know. But she holds back because she doesn't have any more emotion to spare. Whatever strength she has left over from her private struggles with hopelessness, she devotes to worrying about Orion and Terra, still children to her, children she feels impelled to guide and protect.

"What do you want me to say." He shrugs, pats the top of her head, resumes his work. "I'm not going to lie to you."

"Don't be so goddamn calm."

"Okay."

"I'm going to get her."

Zed gapes, drops his tools. "What are you talking about?"

Fair chuckles faintly. "So now you're not calm."

"My lovely, sweet, adorable friend…"

"Oh, cut it out, Zed. Flattery will get you nowhere. I am going to rescue my little girl, she's like a daughter to me. I'll keep in touch as well as I can, so when you hear from Orion, you can let him know. He has contacts that could help. I think I'll leave Tuesday, gives me a few days to round up all the stuff I'll need. If it's ok I'll borrow your larger pack…"

Zed has her by both shoulders. "Stop it. We'll think of some other way."

"What, what? You've got nothing to say about it."

"You're not going anywhere. Much too dangerous."

She looks up at him, sorrowful and annoyed. "Shut up."

He pulls her to her feet, holds her. But she wriggles away.

She says, "I'm sorry. You're a good friend. But I must do this."

"Truce." Zed drops his arms, pleads with his eyes. "May I cook for you tonight?"

"Now I can't ever resist that, and you know it. My place. Will you bring groceries?"

"Six o'clock."

Out in the street, Fair is obstructed by a parade loud with drums and trumpets. Flamboyant parades are more and more common these days, but this one features not military might, but a fleet of Zorian priests, resplendent in their milk-white robes, riding standing up in a wagon pulled slowly by white horses. So here they are. She's heard the rumors and announcements, but this reality stuns her. Hartford and Boston are gearing up for an alliance, and this is the proof. The Boston enclave, which proudly routed the dominant priests some twenty years ago, now stoops to embrace the enemy. Next on the agenda is a summit with Albany, when all three enclaves will become a formidable Sanmart monolith. And the bandits who took Terra are known to cater to them, providing funds with extorted money, slaves and so-called volunteers. How could this have happened? People are so scared, they'll accept anything that promises stability, survival. "Sanmart cares" is mesmerizing to believe. Look at them, cheering and waving flags at the ridiculous white robed fanatics. Anything to forget fear.

That afternoon at the Medical Center, Fair's foreboding about Orion and the political crisis, plus her continuous agony of worry over Terra, are all erased by a wagonload of refugees. Fleeing the wildfires engulfing the northern Hartford enclave, they're in various stages of exhaustion, many with respiratory problems. The air in Barrytown is far better, but a warm spring had already brought some stultifying days, and any strong wind wafts clouds of soot from the south. The affected children are put into a sealed room kept fogged with steam, and there they lie, their little faces puckered with pain and fear even when they can breathe more freely. Their ribs ache constantly, and even in some cases have been broken from the violence and persistence of coughing. Fair's herbal expertise has impressed the staff here. Whenever there's a treatment dilemma, someone says, "Better ask Fair about this." But some of the twenty people who arrived today just need feeding and calming. They all need lots of water. "We're out," announces one of the assistants. He's an angular man somewhere around thirty, with a long face made longer by a bushy drooping moustache.

"Out of water? Again?"

Fair's dismay is tinged with panic. She's already been once to the water officials to beg. They did not smile, parroting stiffly, "The

Medical Center already owes a substantial sum for water. The governor opposes subsidizing outsiders." One added with special animosity just for her, "You'd better think again before you take on any more refugees."

She won't go back there. She knows that as Orion's mother her status has changed from welcomed to suspect.

She says to the assistant, "Do you mind going down to the governor's office, maybe try some sweet talk?"

He looks back at her sadly, shaking his head. "I can try, but you know it won't work. They are right. The time has come, we knew it would. The Sans need to control the water because they take care of it for us. They should be paid."

"Lock the doors? Keep people out who need help? You can't mean it!"

"It's logistics, not morality."

"It is morality, yes it is. If they weren't charging so much we could do it."

He shrugs, turning away. "There's a lot of ifs in this world, Fair."

She glares after him, bursting with anger that has nowhere to go.

But she's saved from betraying her conscience, because later that day a squad of black and gold uniforms arrives to round up the refugees. They are not treated roughly, simply helped out of their cots and deposited in a large wagon pulled by two hefty farm horses. All twenty patients are crammed in together, coughing, disoriented.

"What are you doing?" Fair tries not to yell.

"Transport," says a guard. "Taking them up the coast. They have more supplies there, they can get better care."

Fair knows this is a lie. She wants to scream into the man's face, hit him over the head. But what good would that do? She has to be satisfied by killing him with her eyes.

He returns an equally insulting glare, takes satisfaction in adding with exaggerated solicitude, "You won't be troubled with refugees any more. They're being stopped at the border now." He puts on a wide grimace of a grin to let her know that he knows how this pains her.

The whole thing is so low key that no one passing quickly in the street could imagine there's a problem. Sanmart always operates this way, in exaggerated calm, as if everything is being done in the interests of "peace and prosperity for all," true to their motto. Only deviously, only by trying really hard, can people discover what has happened, that day or the night before: someone taken from home for no reason, meetings broken up, new restrictions on education, a sentence of sedition and hard labor passed. Everything is done in the name of law and order, everything is done paternally, for the common good. Who would not want to believe in their beneficence? It's so easy, so logical and reassuring.

So as Sanmart was able to creep in unnoticed, Barrytown has been a victim of its own virtues. People began to relax. Peace had continued with Hartford's priests and Albany's Sanmart bosses, neither of which had threatened them for a long time. Boston's fears concentrated on the ferocious vicissitudes of climate, and related problems like crop failures and disease outbreaks. It never occurred to them that their enemy would strike from within.

Besides, communication outside the northeast is spotty. A few areas still have some form of computer, but the parts for them are more and more scarce. News comes in over radios wherever towers still operate, sometimes clasped to a pigeon's leg, or more often delivered by messenger on horseback. Reports from elsewhere—the cult-ridden Atlanta enclave, the drought-shriveled west, Canada's devastating typhoons—feed fear but also enhance Barrytown's sense of invulnerablity. Amid chaos all around, the Boston enclave shimmers stability like a mirage.

The transition from messy, unpredictable democracy to beneficent paternalism necessitates significant increases in the Excell Security Force, only temporary of course, but welcomed by many as providing jobs. Many young people have admired the discipline and authority of the new police in their handsome black and gold uniforms. It feels good that you, your sons and daughters, can be a part of this peaceful, dignified order. With only a gentle suggestion from Gov. Monty, people start wearing gold ribbons on their sleeves.

Considering all this that evening before Zed arrives, Fair feels feverish and helpless. She washes her hair, brushes it to a shine, puts on her best dress, reddens her lips, drinks a glass of wine. Nothing she does seems to work out. Maybe she just shouldn't try any more, maybe she can't. Fair never stops torturing and blaming herself for Terra's kidnapping. And now Orion might be in danger, too, despite Zed's reassurances. So she throws herself into her work, work that makes her proud, and what happens? Her patients are taken away right under her nose, with not a thing she can do.

"You look beautiful," says Zed.

But he stands in the doorway, a bag of groceries in his arms, more flabbergasted than wowed. She laughs at him, pulls him in, takes the groceries.

"You found carrots!" She hears the hysteria behind her voice, hopes he does not.

But no, he's relaxed, smiling affectionately. "Yep, friend of mine tipped me off. And look at this stalwart looking celery root, how about that?" He accepts wine, starts slicing potatoes.

While slicing the vegetables, they chat about the planting that will start next week. A brief spate of rain has been reported to the west, in the Albany enclave, offering a hope that hovers over them like a blithe spirit. Zed entertains her with stories about his customers.

"I make them happy," he chuckles in his low key, ironic way. "I say, take a look at this antique rocking chair, the kind your grandmother used to cherish. Not, don't look too closely at this old wreck I just barely patched together. They need it, they want it, why not make them feel good about it."

"Here, pass me that celery root. I need to scrape it first."

He hands her the vegetable, their hands touch. Pause. She looks at him, his eyes are warm. She gazes past him out the window, where sunshine lingers bright, gilds the little room with fairytale tinsel. Just don't look too closely. What good advice.

The corn oil sizzles, they toss the rest of the vegetables into the pot, Fair stirs briskly with a wooden spoon while Zed adds the broth. Leaving the stew to simmer, they rinse their hands and pour more wine. But the mugs sit untouched side by side on the table graced with her best pink and green cloth, while beside it Fair puts her arms around Zed's neck, his arms encircle her, and their mouths meet. They have not kissed since that one evening they'd agreed to forget. But Fair has remembered it many times, at first guiltily, then hungrily. Here's his tongue again, more intoxicating even than she has dreamed, finding hers like a lost friend. She presses against him, trying to drown in his bulk, sounds, smell, muscle, desire, as if she could disappear into him, never rise to consciousness again. But rage and sorrow get the better of her.

"I'm tasting tears," he murmurs. He pulls back to study her. "What's wrong?"

"Wallowing in my misery." She tries to smile.

"Of course, you're frantic about Terra."

"It's all my fault."

"What can we do to cheer you up?"

She gazes at him. "All my defenses are down."

But it's a plea, not an invitation. He nods, gently leads her to a chair, pats her back.

"Don't worry," he says.

And she knows he means not only comfort, but also assurance that he'll keep to her boundaries.

They eat their rich stew slowly. Sitting across the table from her, from time to time Zed grasps her hands in both of his, listening to her fears and memories. Then he tells her for the first time about the girl he loved in his youth, who was raped and killed in one of those rampages in the late 40s, during the stampede north. His eyes are dry but so haunted that Fair is stabbed with his pain. Then he loses words, and she has no reply, so they sit silent in the wavering light of descending evening. Zed's brave shoulders are slumped, his wry persona stilled.

Fair murmurs, "Orion's father Seth was shot on a mission trying to get asthma medication for Tully's kids."

She offers this helpfully and hopefully, to show she's entered his terrible place, is with him.

He raises his head to meet her eyes. They stand up and move together. No passion accompanies them to the bed. They only lie down in each other's arms, spent, lulled to sleep by each other's breath.

13

Terra gazes over the most luxurious room she's ever seen, not even in pictures. Or yes, in that stack of ancient magazines her grandmother kept in the back pantry for school projects. As a young girl, her princess fantasies always took place in surroundings like this. Here's the same call to touch: underfoot a rug so soft it feels spongy, quilted chairs, a deep sofa proffering silken pillows with braided tassels. The smells are dizzyingly refreshing, a hint of mint.

The room is lit with just the right amount of muted solar lamps strategically placed, plus a row of beeswax candles on the mantelpiece. May's heat has been interrupted by a cold snap, so there's a low fire in the brick fireplace, kept just at the glowing point by the expert ministrations of a discrete aide. Terra is standing in a circle of girls being entertained by a jocular Armand Jones. He's in fine fettle; obviously this part of his authority is a favorite role.

"Some people are born leaders. You can't just up and decide to be one." He chortles and the girls join in the merriment.

His father was the famous Boss Jones who twenty years ago helped Boston resist the Zorian takeover, throwing out the priests for good. Terra has enough sense to see the irony: as Boss Jones Junior, Armand is part of an autocratic force in some ways as insidious as the priests of old. Plus he's now actively soliciting the priests' support to help Sanmart bully Barrytown. But her outrage fades to vague annoyance when she catches sight of Hall Hudson, chatting with a group to her left. She moves in his direction. He looks wonderful in a brocaded velvet jacket, trousers of fine black leather. His solid form, tending toward heavy, somehow elegantly carries off the exotic outfit, regally. Before she can break from Armand's bevy and join Hall's, she hears Armand remark, "I'll be taking a few of you back to Albany with me. Be prepared for a treat."

Terra slips into the circle around Hall, who is explaining in a cheery, fatherly way why ransom is excellent policy.

"It's an important form of income for our operations," he says. "Everybody wins. Folks like you get to go back to their families, and we can continue our liberation efforts."

One girl pipes up, "Have you heard from my father yet?"

Hall grins down at her benevolently. "In fact, my dear, we have. He promises the money by next week. You're on your way home, I'm sure, my dear."

"Thank you," she whispers, but she looks worried. How will he afford it, she must be thinking.

"You will miss us," Hall says. It's an order, and she nods vehemently.

Terra works her way closer to him. His back is to the fireplace and he's holding a large elaborately decorated cup in one hand. His hands are strong and pale, lightly freckled.

For a while he continues indulgently explaining how they should all be proud to be a part of Armand's mission to remake the world, to "save it from itself" as he puts it. He recounts his recent trip to New Hampshire, where a fabulous project is taking shape, which will "prove that the best is yet to come." He becomes aware of her intense interest, turns to smile directly at her.

"Please," she dares, "could you tell me if my ransom money has come yet?"

"I'm afraid it has not. But, Terra dear, you cannot be entirely sorry, can you?"

She's so upset by this remark that she wants to retort rudely, but to her own shock she says nothing. In fact, she simply returns his gaze. In that moment, a log falls in the fireplace illuminating his face in a flash. She finds herself looking into amber eyes, eyes the exact same color as her own.

She steps back with a gasp. All her life she has been looking for these eyes. Before she can stop herself, she breathes, "Were you a priest?"

His face darkens with anger, but he returns her stare. "What a question!"

The other girls in the circle move away from the two of them, in a fearful huddle.

But Terra is in a trance, hardly aware of her dangerous impertinence. "Were you a priest in 2065? In Boston?"

He signals an aide, briskly says, "Take her to my office."

Grasped hard by the elbow, Terra must make the best of an awkward exit.

He is a long time coming. She sits in near darkness in a big plush chair, looking at a desk piled with rolls of parchment. Along one shelf is a jumble of odd, ancient electronic gadgets. The shadowed walls are spread with maps. She is scared, but her main emotion is excitement. Is it him? Could it really be him? Or some relation, his brother, perhaps?"

He arrives with lamps, nobody with him. This is a good sign. She stands up, goes to the middle of the lamplight.

"Look at me," she says. "Look at my eyes."

But Hall Hudson instead sits heavily in his desk chair. "I know," he says.

"What do you know?"

"I know you have my eyes. I know you could be my daughter."

"My mother…"

"I wouldn't remember your mother," he says, "There were so many of them."

"Too many?" But her bravado has failed her. She slips back down in the plush chair, in acquiescence. "I actually know very little about it," she adds in a small voice. "I wish you'd tell me."

He looks across his desk at her. His shoulders are slumped, he looks defeated.

"What are we going to do with you?" He sounds as if he's really consulting her.

"You are my father."

"I probably have many children."

"But do you know them?"

"No. For the most part, no."

There is long silence.

Terra finally says, "I've been looking for you for a long time."

"You are beautiful. You are intelligent. I am proud to be your father. I hope you won't hate me. We thought we were doing the right thing. I was a very devout young man."

"Please don't feel bad." Is she actually trying to comfort him? Terra knows she should be angry, condemn his violence. But she's mesmerized by this treasure she has finally found, her very own father. She doesn't like to see this princely man brought low. "I mean, you were just very young, confused…"

"I think," he finally breathes, sitting up straight, "we had better forget this ever happened. Your ransom will come through soon, I'm sure, and you can go home. No one will be the wiser."

"Is that what you want?" Terra feels tears smarting behind her eyes. It would be stupid to cry now. She presses her lips hard together.

"Don't look so sad," he says.

"I want to see you again. Can you come to Boston to visit me?"

He smiles. "I very much doubt it."

"At any rate, can we see each other alone now and then, before I leave?"

He shakes his head as he gazes at her, as if he can't believe what he sees or feels. "I don't know."

But she can tell he's faltering. Her heart is soaring with something close to joy. She's not an orphan any more.

Part II

1

By the time she gets to the mouth of the cave, Fair can hardly see through the freezing snow. As soon as she wipes her eyes with the back of a sodden mitten, her hood drips down more icy drops, half snow half ice. She's been walking blind for some time now, having parted ways this morning with the last wagon that gave her a lift. The storm came on without warning around three. A May cold snap had given way to resumed heat with all the signs of continued drought, and then suddenly two days ago the temperature dropped to freezing. This morning, heavy gray sky hanging low, a tang in the air, but nothing alarming. Fair even congratulated herself on the travel-friendly weather. And then, without any preliminary flurries, the sky opened up at the same time the wind rushed from nowhere. Folks around her on the road ran for cover. Fair struggled on, determined to get to Three Rivers by nightfall. There's a Steward pal of Orion's there who can help her. But she didn't have a chance. She fell once; that was enough to bring her to her senses.

Inside the cave, she finds a well protected nook. A quick look around reassures her she's not sharing with anyone, but in another moment she hears a snuffling sound that has to be animal breath. She stops right away her too-comfortable nesting, lights a lamp, lifts it high. The cave walls are black dirt studded with ice patches. She goes deeper as it narrows. All at once her light catches the creature: a big Husky dog, behind it a pile of four puppies squinting up at her in fear overcome by curiosity. The adult is at full attention, growling warning. Could it be a wolf? Fair doesn't think so. She knows dogs. Not only is Tully graced with many, but her best friend on her escape to Maine from Canada years ago was a wiley and heroic black lab mix.

How to reassure the mother? Fair is not about to go back out into that killing storm.

"Hi, Mom," she says softly. "How ya doing. Beautiful babies you have there. Don't worry, I won't hurt them."

She keeps on cooing, backing away. The dog doesn't waver in her aggressive stance. Fair retreats to her own corner, sits down on her half-opened sleeping bag, returns the silent stare of the animal. After a long time, the mother licks her lips and sits down. Relaxing a little, good. As Fair's metabolism slows her own alert, she realizes she is so tired she may just fall asleep before she even decides to lie down. What will this perhaps wild dog do with a vulnerable sleeping human? Deciding peace must be made, she digs into her backpack for remnants of lunch, which she had planned for dinner if nothing better came along—a soggy eggplant sandwich. She breaks off a piece and throws it underhand along the floor. At her gesture the dog at once again springs to attention. But her nostrils are quivering and she eyes the sandwich with great interest.

"You can eat it, you can have it," Fair sings quietly. "Go on, your babies will love it. Feed your babies, go on, Mama…"

The dog's ears point forward listening, Fair continues her soothing litany. The puppies have untangled themselves from their protective pile, and come to peer out from under their mother's legs. They are at least six weeks old, probably more like eight or ten, healthy looking furry bundles.

"They must be a chore to feed," Fair commiserates.

She takes a bite of the sandwich. In spite of being icy cold and mushy, it tastes delicious. She unpacks her cheese and apples, the last of her food supplies. Dogs like cheese, so she throws a chunk in the animals' direction. One of the puppies darts out and snaps it up, at the same time the mother barks danger and the other puppies rush to tumble over their reckless sibling. The cheese is gone, and the pups back behind their mother. After this drama, Fair and the dog sit looking at each other, wariness palpably dimmed. Fair can't help it, she finishes the sandwich, watched avidly through every bite.

After a long time, in a self-conscious amble, the mother goes over and sniffs the bit of sandwich, nibbles at it. Testing. Then she picks it up and delivers it grandly to her offspring, who fight and howl over it, devour it instantly.

Fair climbs into her sleeping bag and the next thing she knows, she's waking out of a deep sleep. It's still snowing but it looks like dawn. Nestled in the crook of her legs is one of the puppies, looking over at her with groggy little bright blue eyes.

She greets it melodically. The mother watches nearby, but continues lying down, not disturbing one of the babies that's nursing. Spread out in front of her are the remains of some small furry animal, probably a rabbit. So the dogs have had breakfast. The scene is so peaceful, Fair closes her eyes again, willing away thirst and hunger.

She's warm inside the sleeping bag, really toasty where the puppy lies against her. Dozing, she lets her mind flow, tries to picture Terra healthy and cared for. Strategizes her approach to rescue her. She wonders again if there's time to get word to Tully, on the remote chance that Vita and Miles could come up with the ransom dollars or at least some better plan. She's well aware that Zed is not imagining things when he deems her inadequate to handle the whole outlaw organization by herself. Maybe she is acting rashly. Well, it won't be the first time.

She opens her eyes to the curtain of snow outside the cave entrance, which looks like it might be turning to sleet or rain. Her sleeping companion yawns at her fully, pink tongue vibrating, and scrambles over to stick his nose in her face. He's white with black markings, black circles around his eyes. She reaches out to pet him, velvet.

When she goes to the cave entrance to gather snow to drink, she can tell that by the time the sun is fully up, it will be pouring rain. This doesn't brighten her outlook for travel, especially with the wind picking up rapidly. It's really ugly out there. She returns gratefully to her nook, decides to light a fire in spite of fears it will spook the dog. But on the contrary, the dog seems to accept the fire as normal human behavior, so now Fair is sure she was once a domesticated animal.

Fair finishes all her food, eyeing a chestnut tree down a craggy slope not twenty feet away. It looks surprisingly healthy. With luck, there will be edible nuts nestled in the ground around it. How hungry will she have to be to go out into that punishing storm?

She sits side by side with the puppy who has adopted her, both of them warmed with the contact. She names him Sparky and consults him often.

"What shall we do about this, Sparky? What do you think?"

Sparky shifts against her, looks up into her face as if anticipating her wish. Sometimes he smiles, sometimes looks forlorn, but always seems sympathetic.

The sun when fully risen is not visible, hardly lightens the angry clouds. The wild wind drives the rain sideways. For a time, thunder and lightning add to the frenzy.

What will Orion be doing right now? He'll have the same weather, or worse. She pictures him being forced to work very hard, hoping he has decent food and shelter. She doesn't buy Zed's insistence that Sanmart may be building something great and wonderful. Zed is altogether too accommodating to the dictators' boasts. But she has to believe Orion's okay.

She drinks quantities of hot water flavored with chicory, but hunger eventually drives her to collect the chestnuts. Plentiful, as she had hoped, but now her clothes are soaked. She takes off most of them to dry, but she's running low on firewood. With the last embers she roasts a pile of chestnuts, which are so delicious even Sparky tries one.

She curls up in her sleeping bag and dreams disturbing images of Terra in a prison, weeping like a baby, stretching out her arms for help. She wakes up trembling with fear and resolve.

"I have to go," she tells Sparky. He accepts her lips on his forehead.

It's probably around noon when she pulls on her damp clothes and sets out, heading west.

2

O rion moves fast. He ditches the uniform as soon as he makes it to the treeline, arrives at the shack around noon. He escaped detection by a hair's breath, rightly counting on the changing of the guard at five a.m. when both shifts were sleepy. After all, they've been looking for him for almost a week now, assuming he's long gone. He chuckles thinking of their outrage if they ever find out he was right there under their noses the whole time. But his flash of self-congratulation is submerged by numbing fatigue. When he stops for a few minutes to eat some of the food remnants he brought, he catches himself falling asleep in the middle of a bite.

To make travel harder, a freak snowstorm a few days earlier has left mudslide piles across the roads, ripped fencing, wagon wheels, protruding tree roots and branches, now and then a dead goat or chicken. The temperature has catapulted back into the 90s, enervating, suffocating, frying roadside mixtures of cracked mud and browned grasses. A farmer here and there stands immobile, shoulders slumped, wondering what happened to the crops he'd just planted, washed out, leaving ridges of heat-whitened mud in the desolate fields.

When Orion gets within sight of the shack, he creeps around the edge of the clearing, waiting motionless for a long time, listening for signs of life. He lets himself believe Finch made it but would not have stayed here even a couple of days, would have moved on, surely. Hopefully.

Sure enough, when he finally does venture inside, slithering rat forms are all that greet him. He makes a quick search, locates a scratch in the boards left by Finch saying, "Plan B ohonte," and curls up in a corner for deep slumber.

Even before he opens his eyes, Orion senses night, in the cooling of the sweat coating his body. Consulting the stars, he figures he's slept more than eight hours straight. He feels refreshed and encouraged—this is the perfect time to travel.

He heads south, keeping away from settlements as best he can. He has great hopes for Plan B, locating Finch in Merrimack. At any rate, there's energy just in progressing towards Boston, going home to Silk and to Fair. He speculates whether Fair has heard from Terra, and if so, what. The beautiful girl he likes to think of as his sister is now a prime target for countless evils, in a world dominated by unfettered greed and lust. But he takes heart in the certainty of her courage and intelligence, if not her level-headedness.

His hopes cling to his fellow Stewards, secretly growing in strength every day, though the Sans seem to have eyes and ears everywhere. It continues to astound him how much they know. He suspects spies in innocuous places: innocent-looking boys, grinning grannies, the street vendor, the janitor. He makes a mental note to warn Fair about Glad, the ancient little crone in her building who has befriended her. He tries not to worry, but it's been months now since he was abducted, so how could it have become anything but worse for Barrytown? Sure, his mother is tough and wily, but she's no match for Sanmart. And her impetuous, impertinent manner could be her undoing. As for Silk, she's pretty safe in her usefulness at the News Office; when he dwells on her, it's with warm longing, flushed possessiveness.

His new knowledge of the All Joy venture has added a sickening lurch to fears for the future. What if this powerful Sanmart force succeeds in taking its domination to the limit? What's the meaning of the June deadline Boss Jones touted to Hudson? Orion can hardly get his mind to go where that implies. He must get to Finch and the others with his fears, rethink their tactics in this ominous light. The monolithic Hampshire Project looms invincible.

Near dawn Orion stops for a few more hours of sleep. Then as morning breaks, the fiery May sun streaming across the flood-pitted road and ashen fields, he comes across a group of travelers gathering up their baggage from an overnight stay. Their skinny donkey is hitched to a rickety wagon piled high with everything from blankets and pots to a pitchfork and a chair. They offer grainy coffee heated at their smoldering fire, and even some bread, which he gratefully accepts.

He has realized he'd better concoct a story to explain where he's going. Even the most innocent looking bystander could be pumping him for the Sans, and if he's too reticent it will look suspicious. So, bushy beard already well on the way, he becomes a businessman heading for Barrytown to open up markets for his fishing boats. He even concocts a sales talk about how his small, sturdy boats are also useful for floods. In this role, he joins in the group's gossip, learning that people trying to escape the alternating wildfires and floods to the north are massing at the Boston border, in a vast makeshift refugee camp. Boston is not letting anyone through without documentation or an escort from the Excell Security Force.

With help from wagon rides here and there, Orion arrives at the refugee camp outside Merrimack at dusk. In all his thirty years, Orion has certainly seen some terrible things, but nothing quite like this. Destruction, epidemics, grief, panics, near starvation, yes, but not this massive despair. Tully Island, tucked away in Vermont's Lake Willoughby, has always been a sanctuary from the wild chaos of the last half century. Orion knows how lucky he was to grow up there, where peace and plenty still echoed, where children still went to school, learning mutual respect and historical perspective, where adults ruled with egalitarian fervor, and where everyone sang gratitude and allegiance to the Earth. As a result, courageous and tough as he is, he finds tears in his eyes when he looks around. Here, in the valley on the Hampshire side of the border, hordes of tattered people and their makeshift dwellings crouch in the blasted dusk—no visible sunset, just awful heat still oppressing, fragments of soot in the gray air.

He's hungry and wants to bathe, but both needs are already luxuries. He relieves himself in a stinking pit that serves as common latrine. To one side, a woman is having a baby, surrounded by caring people, but no sign of comfort or sanitation. He helps a girl carrying water to them, averts his eyes from the scene. How can anyone be born into this? What kind of life? Orion heads in the direction the girl came from, soon finding the water source, a muddy trickle that was once a river. He washes as best he can, careful not to swallow the water even though he feels parched with thirst. He empties his canteen, and that's it until he can boil more. He sits on a log and munches drearily on an apple that has seen better days. He forces his mind to concentrate on the journey ahead. How long can he linger here without worrying about being tracked down? Very soon he must find Finch, plot a ruse to cross the border.

"Mister, have a bit of bread, mister?"

A grimy boy about seven stares at him, at eye level, sooty little face alive with hope. Orion stares back, guiltily chewing, hands the child his apple core. The kid grabs it, eats it up too fast, coughing. Orion pulls out a piece of bread crackling with age, offers it. This too disappears with remarkable speed.

"Some for my sister?"

"That's it, my friend," says Orion. "Where's your mother and father?"

"Dead I guess." His tiny shoulders slump now, his eyes stop shining. "My sister's hungry too."

"Stick with me, let's see what we can find."

Orion knows this is foolish, he doesn't need another mouth to feed, but he can't help it. The boy directs him to a small rickety wagon where a skeletal girl sits brooding. "Can you start a fire?" Orion asks.

She looks away in silence, but her brother pipes, "Sure can. We have some wood for it too."

He sets about digging out a little pit, arranging sticks in it. His faith in Orion's ability to produce something to cook is disconcerting. Orion tells them he'll be right back and goes off to try his luck.

The paths between the tents and other makeshift shelters are yellow dust. Kicked up by dozens of feet, the dust joins the sooty fragments wafting from distant wildfires, making all the air dense and gritty, smelling too of unwashed, unhealthy bodies. The largest tent by far is marked "Medic Tent," and from it come unbearable sounds of suffering. No doubt many patients are victims of the new HK154 flu, coming to be known as Atlanta Fever. Like the many epidemics before it, this illness drags on for weeks and is usually fatal.

Many groups Orion passes are hunched over small fires, cooking something, or maybe only boiling water. He finally stops where he sees an opening and senses a little energy. An old woman and a younger one, and a broad-shouldered man probably around forty.

They are ladling some sort of stew from a pot. Orion greets them, keeping his distance. Everyone is at the same time suspicious of strangers and aware they all share the same fate. Growing rumors of the spreading fever add to wariness. He wants to make it clear he respects their space.

The old woman replies, "How d'you do, sir. That's a mighty impressive pack you've got there."

Orion had not previously considered how whole and new his pack must look in this place. He shifts it on his shoulder, smiles, replies, "Better days."

"Amen," groans the man, nodding cheerfully. "What can we do for you?"

"Could I buy some of that food?"

"What've you got for money?"

"Albany dollars."

The old woman shakes her head. "Haven't you got any Hampshire dollars?"

"Sorry, no."

The younger woman nudges the man, comments in a low voice. "We could barter some of his stuff. I like the canteen."

"This is only rat stew," the man shrugs. "You can make your own."

"I'd have to catch 'em first," Orion says, "and I haven't seen a single one yet today."

"We ate 'em all," cackles the old woman.

In the end, they accept Albany dollars for a bowl of stew and he goes off to share it with the children, who produce two small bowls of their own and gobble it down. No need to tell them what's in it. They no doubt know. Besides, there are also remnants of tasty root vegetables, parsnip or turnip. He beds down for the night near the children, among other folks camped in the shadow of a rusted overturned van, all wheels missing. The children's cheer after being fed is contagious. Things could be worse. His belly is full, or full enough for now, and he's had a chance to boil some water, fill his canteen. He sleeps well, head on his pack.

He wakes in grey dawn to the blast of a trumpet, sits up to see a clutch of Zorian priests supervising the construction of a platform.

The campers have hastily made room for them, and now are gathering around to form an obedient audience. Orion has never seen a Zorian priest, though he knows all about them. They used to run the Boston enclave back in the 60s. But they were defeated in a historic battle, and now control only the Hartford enclave, sending out missionaries like these to make converts with their message of punishment and doom. His first impression is of pudgy bodies and grim, somehow petulant faces redeemed from ordinariness only by the flamboyant snow white outfits.

"Just ignore them," Orion advises the frightened children.

But their eyes are wide. "They have ways. Watch out."

The priests, white robes flailing impressively, mount the platform and circle around an enormous black box, where folks are told they must put their donations. Another trumpet blast.

"People, fall down and worship the great Zoria. Pregnant with Jesus Christ, she will bring him to us when we have repented enough. At that time, the Earth will be restored to health," drones a priest. "Come, give them all you have, for your salvation, your path to Paradise. Otherwise, you burn in Hell along with the accursed planet. Come one, come all."

Orion chuckles and shakes his head. He knows that the original Zoria died some time ago and was replaced by another extremely fat woman. Supposedly somehow embryonic Jesus was transferred from one womb to another. How gullible would you have to be to swallow all that? But he knows enough about human nature to realize the comfort it offers to folks with nothing left except fear. What solace to believe that a blessed outsized lady will give you a redeemer!

The refugees begin lining up to make their offerings, anything of value from a watch to a hammer. But then one man rushes forward carrying a tiny baby, and the priests stop in their tracks, gesture him to the platform. Orion hears a wailing scream from the crowd and sees the woman he saw giving birth near the latrine being held back with her arms outstretched. Clearly it's her newborn that's being donated. Another child to be brought up as a devoted Zorian from birth. The priests especially favor infants for their indoctrination schools.

He begins to gather his things, shoulders his pack. "I think I'll sneak off before they decide I have anything they want."

"Good idea," says the boy. "But we got to stay and be careful."

Orion puts out his hand, solemnly shakes hands with both children. "Best of luck."

"Thanks, mister. You're okay."

When Orion looks back, the kids are kneeling piously.

3

For a whole day, snowfall blanks out the views from the grand windows at Headquarters. Wind whips it into swirls, so they can just barely make out the white grounds and hills beyond. The staff runs around excitedly, making sure the water tanks are ready, and locating whatever other containers they can find to collect it. By noontime they have already purified enough to offer extra drinks at lunch.

Terra picks at her food in a trance. She is glad about this break in the drought, but unable to relate it to herself or any experience she might care about. She has found her father. What now? Will her whole life change, as she has always imagined? She knows she's not thinking straight, but there's this little bright edge of happiness that curls around everything she sees and does. This morning she finally confided in Gina, who now treats her like a foreign object. Sworn to secrecy, Gina nevertheless pulls away, seeks out the company of other girls. And truth be told, Terra does feel far different now from the others, as if lifted to some sacred realm, or at least admitted to high levels of power.

But her father does not seek her out. He has just returned from a week in the New Hampshire settlements, where he had some very important business everyone is breathless about: a grand project called All Joy. She glimpsed him a few times today, but he has not tried to contact her. She waits, almost holding her breath, through all the chores and activities the girls are ordered to perform. She gets no preferential treatment, to her chagrin. Now and then she has a flash of fear that her father will simply ignore her. Why should it matter to him whether he's found one of his offspring?

After lunch, she has to help clear the tables and prepare them for dinner, then she must join an exercise class, and get her toes and fingernails manicured and polished. Then she has to help mend clothes. Then all the girls have to put on nice outfits and gather in the great room for pre-dinner drinks and snacks. This is when they are on display, and they know it. The senior officers arrive to have a look at them, as well as Hall Hudson and any of his guests. This is also when the ransoms are usually announced. Terra anxiously anticipates her own reprieve. She's just as eager as always to be freed. But does that mean she has to leave right away? Not before her father has made some promise to her, surely.

But her ransom is not announced, even though several others are, to much applause. Everybody wins. Even the relatives forced to raise the sums of money, in most cases meaning deprivation, will be thrilled to have their girls home again. No mention is made of the captives in the basement, who will probably all be sold at the auction, or shipped off to volunteer for the project in New Hampshire. The mood in the elegant room is jolly, the snow outside now turning to sleet making the cozy fire and warmth all the more appealing.

Hall gives his usual short cheery speech about how together they are all contributing to saving the world. Then he makes a beeline for Terra.

"I can't say I'm sorry you won't be leaving us soon," he tells her.

Terra basks in his warm gaze. Other girls in their circle look puzzled and perhaps a bit jealous. Hudson is a striking looking man, and in complete control to boot. His bandit operation serves Albany's Sanmart, but here in his HQ, he's king. Who would not want his favor? From across the room Gina is staring at her with a mixture of disbelief and pity—where did that reaction come from? Terra drinks some wine, which she hitherto has refused, drains the glass, laughs too loud.

"Thanks for the compliment. But I'm sure my money will be coming soon."

"Oh, no doubt, no doubt." Hudson concurs, but he doesn't look convinced. He examines her. "I will see you in my office after dinner," he finally announces.

For the first time, Terra acknowledges the possibility that for whatever reason, Fair and Orion will not be able to come up with her ransom money. It's a disturbing, chilling scenario she doesn't want to contemplate. She dismisses the ghastly thought before it can take hold of her imagination. Instead, she revels in Hudson's attention. He wants to see her after all. Her father wants to spend time with her. They will get to know each other.

When she gets to his office later that evening, a guard greets her and leads her through a side door into a small, over-furnished room with stuffed chairs and paintings of horses on the walls. There's a salty, slightly stale smell overcast with the odor of ashes from a little glowing stove.

"Welcome to my den."

They both sit in big chairs on either side of the stove. The guard brings them coffee and goes away, closing the door. Terra finds herself nervous, feeling too small in the oversized armchair, awed by the man of her dreams beaming at her so casually, as if this were all normal. It's so far from normal, she can't imagine anything more bizarre. And yet, at this moment, she would not want to be anywhere else in the world.

He mentions the welcome drama of so much snow mitigating at least temporarily the acute drought problem. He goes on a bit about how important it is to control the water supply. He tells her has heard from Henry, whose little band is doing well, as usual. Then he stops talking, just looks at her.

She sips her coffee, says, "I'm having trouble believing this is real."

Hall laughs deeply. "You are a sweetheart, aren't you? Am I what you imagined, at all?"

"Yes, you are. Father. Shall I call you Father?"

"Please."

"Father, you're as wonderful as my dreams." He laughs again, very pleased, and she adds, "I just wish I could take you home with me. I'm sure everyone would love you."

"Everyone? I doubt it, my dear. They say I'm an outlaw, you know."

"Surely that can be fixed? I mean, you could convince folks, you could explain your goals and mission. Wouldn't they understand?"

"Do you?"

For a moment Terra is unnerved. "I want to learn more about it," she finally replies.

"Is that so? I'm glad to hear it. I think you could be of use to us. A bright, brave, beautiful girl like you, educated, experienced in different ways of the world. A writer, too, Henry told us."

"What else did Henry tell you?"

"Everything, of course. That's his job. He does it well."

Terra feels exposed, angry with Henry. "What purpose does that serve?"

"Can't you guess? The more you know about people the more power you get over them. Power is always a good thing to have."

Just above the stove is a particularly large canvas depicting uniformed men riding horses in formation with a brilliant sunset illuminating the action. The horses are galloping, muscles protruding, flanks damp, teeth bared, eyes wild, their physical magnificence the major feature. Terra looks back at the man who has spoken these words, sees her smiling father who has just been complimenting her, not only directly, but by addressing her as an intellectual equal. She feels her answering smile fill her whole face and soul.

"Power is a good thing," she replies, obedient to his pleasure.

Unwillingly, even as she says these words, she hears Fair's snort of scorn way in the back of her dazed brain. Though it's not a welcome reminder, it packs enough muscle to make her waver in her adoration. To calm her fevered heart, she makes a conscious decision to suppress her own old self in favor of enjoying the magical present.

"You see," he continues kindly explaining, "people need direction. They need to be shown the way, they need protection. Considering the challenges we've all had to face in this whole crazy century, it's no wonder. We believe we have the answers, in the best interest of all. We're trying very hard to fulfill that mission."

Terra doesn't ask why that has to involve kidnapping. She notes the thought, but dismisses it as counter to the magic of the moment, and says eagerly instead, "People do need help. It's wonderful you can do that. I must say I don't think they appreciate it as much as they should."

"You're quite right, my dear. You see, some of us are destined to be in control. Not chosen by Jesus, as the Zorian priests proclaim. I used to believe that myself. Back then, twenty years ago, the Zorians seemed to have all the answers. I was ardent, preparing to become a priest myself. But it was too easy. Leaving it all up to Zoria's Jesus. No, no. Though I am willing to give the priests lip service, because they do have such a rapport with common people.

It's actually men like us, like me and Armand Jones, and Governor Monty, men tried and true who know the score. Terra my dear, the thing you need to understand most of all is, without Sanmart's leadership the world will just fall apart. Look around you, there's proof everywhere."

Terra hesitantly suggests, "What about voting? We always learned that deciding things by popular vote is the fairest way."

"Fair to who? Think about it. Do you want folks who are stupid or ignorant or just plain twisted to be deciding your affairs?"

"No," she readily replies.

She looks at him, at the wonderful smile he blesses her with, his strong white hands poised in mid air open with emphasis. Of course, he's mistaken about voting. She knows from all her Tully schooling that it's the only way to make just decisions. But he can be excused for his enthusiasm, the conviction that lights up his dear face. It's just that he cares so much. He's a very fine man, anyone could see that. Does he talk about what he needs, his own desires? No, it's always what's best for others. So she is almost ready to accept his next words.

He says, "What would you like to do? If your ransom money doesn't come through? How about staying on here, working for us?"

"My aunt and my cousin," she starts, but stops. What about them? Is it possible they won't or can't come up with the money? How could that be? Orion must have plenty of clout in Barrytown. "They're not really my aunt and cousin," she finds herself confessing.

Hall Hudson, with only a spotty background from Henry, wants to hear the whole story. Terra rather enjoys dramatizing her orphan-like status, her unaffectionate grandmother, the rescue role Fair played in her childhood. She even sketches briefly her one encounter with her mother, so devastatingly impersonal.

"She was beautiful," Terra says, "at least to me, child that I was. But her face was very angry when she described your eyes."

Hall Hudson looks grave. "I think I remember her. Blond. A fighter, even with the drugs. But otherwise you wouldn't have been born. So you see…" He stops, then adds in a tone almost contrite, "If it helps, I didn't know at the time that the girls were drugged. I was young and I was devout. I was convinced I was doing the right thing."

102

Terra is torn, not for the first time, between a horrifying inkling of her mother's ordeal and the passionate need for her father. She wrestles with an image of the beautiful girl in frenzied resistance— disheveled, screaming?—drives it away with her impervious need.

"Well," she finally says, "my mother's experience was so bad that she never loved me."

He turns away, leans to ring the small bell on the table, and waits in silence until the guard appears.

"Bring in some sugar biscuits," her father orders him. "And cranberry juice."

Stung that he thinks he has to bribe her, Terra blurts, "I never loved her either. You're my first real parent."

"I understand," he responds. But there's just the slightest chilled edge to his voice that she becomes desperate to dissipate.

"Please, I'm sorry," she pleads. "I know it was long ago and a different time for you. What matters is your mission now. Don't worry about me. I'm confused. I'll get over it. I am over it. My life's been good after all."

He contemplates her, watches her nibble on the biscuit, which is fresh and delicious. She longs to see again the warm embracing glow in his admiring, perhaps even fond, face.

So she says quickly, "How can I help you?"

4

The sign reading "Welcome to Three Rivers" is crooked, dilapidated, and almost illegible. The browned vines half choking it look whipped and tortured by floods and heat. As Fair continues into the town, she's unnerved by the barren fields on either side. Surely they should be planted by now, but they don't even look plowed.

She plods along the narrow, mud-pitted street lined with very small cottages made out of ancient castoff materials like car hoods and rubber tires. Now and then looms a lopsided, patched-up wooden house from former times. The people she passes don't give her a second glance; they're attired as shabbily as she.

Sparky pads along beside her. She'd waved goodbye to him when she turned to look back at the cave entrance, where he was sitting with cocked head wondering at her departure. It wasn't until a few hours later that she realized he had followed her. She heard a sound behind her, and there he was. It was too late to order him away. He was ready to leave his mother anyway. And he simply gave her no choice. He joined her as naturally as if it had always been ordained.

But the boy who answers the door is not so clear on the subject.

"What's a dog doing here?" About ten, he has a shaggy cap of blond hair and big worried eyes. He's holding a frying pan still sizzling with something that greatly interests Sparky. "We eat dogs in Three Rivers, that's what we do with them. I wouldn't want to eat your pet. Is he your pet?"

"You won't be eating this dog," Fair says decisively. "Is your father home?"

"They took him away."

"Jed Trist?"

"They took him away." This time the child's voice wavers.

"May we please come in?"

He hesitates. "I'll have to ask Gran." He goes away, returns promptly. "Come on. The dog too. What's his name?"

"Sparky. My name's Fair. What's yours?"

This friendly conversation brings them to a nook behind the stove containing a bed containing a tiny old lady. The boy helps her sit up farther on her pillows and she stares suspiciously at Fair before wheezing, "What do you want with my son?"

"Your son Jed? I'm from Boston. My son Orion told me about you."

Orion's name has an instant effect on both the boy and his Gran.

She says to him, "Is the door closed?" Holds out trembling knotted hands. "I'm Letty Trist. That's Jed's boy, Van. We met your Orion once. A fine young man, a leader, what we need in these terrible times."

Van, still holding the frying pan, is now staring up at Fair with awe and admiration. His grandmother tells him to finish cooking, that Fair will be joining them for supper, and motions her to a chair.

"I'm afraid you shouldn't have come," says Letty. Her frail voice is surprisingly muscular, urgent with a will that won't fade easily. "Of course, how would you have known? We didn't expect a thing."

"When did they take him? Do you know where he is? My Orion is doing forced labor in New Hampshire, though they call it volunteering of course."

The old woman splutters with scorn. "The Sans are behind that, they're behind everything. They call themselves our saviors. They call everything the opposite of what it is. Volunteers! Ha!" She gives out a wild angry cackle. "They have a lot of folks fooled, but not yours truly!"

"But the Sans, Monty's guys, just sent Orion to Natick to oversee boat repairs there. I don't see why they'd worry about him."

Letty stares at her with large dark eyes surprisingly clear and penetrating.

"Don't you know anything?" she finally says. "The Sans are closing in."

After supper, Fair insists on cleaning up, while Van and Sparky play outside in the fading light and Letty knits in bed, keeping up a long monolog of information and advice. Fair has been allotted a cot in their second room, which also serves as pantry and storage area. As far as she can tell, Van's bed is a bunk above the cupboard in the main room. Before fatigue entirely catches up with Fair, she brings a cup of sage tea to Letty, thanks her once again for allowing them to stay.

"My poor Jed would've welcomed you far better. I'm afraid we don't have much to offer. Did you like the chicken-liver omelette? We'll have yogurt for breakfast. And how about that bread? Van's learned how to make such good bread."

Fair asks gently, "Do you hope to hear from Jed?"

"It's been five days now. You can be sure they didn't tell us where they were taking him. We have no idea. Maybe it's not about the Stewards at all. Maybe it's just that we stole some water a while back. Taking water is a crime now, so I don't know what to expect either way."

"Can you and Van handle things?"

"Oh, we can manage." But Letty's hands stop knitting, fall to her lap. "As long as I don't go and get any sicker."

Fair feels her forehead, finds a low fever. "I saw that you have some apples. I can make you up an excellent brew. I'll do it first thing in the morning."

"You're a healer?"

"I learned from my husband's mother, in Tully Island, where we're from."

Tomorrow she'll tell the old woman about Tully, about the trip with Terra to visit Orion, about all that's gone wrong since— Barrytown's corruption, Terra's flight and imprisonment. But now she's about to keel over with exhaustion.

"Good night, my good friend." And she kisses the dry, wrinkled forehead.

Letty falls back with a sigh. "Some things are still good." She has several teeth missing, but her smile is wide and sweet.

Letty persuades Fair to stay another two days to wait for their neighbor Fred to take her in his wagon as far as the foothills. So the next evening Fair is chopping carrots and potatoes at the kitchen table when Van stomps in with a bag of groceries, fish, flour, and milk. Behind him through the open door some of their chickens wander in from the porch, clucking indignantly when they spot Sparky. The street beyond is churning debris in dry wind.

"The floods didn't stop the drought," Fair notes.

From her bed, Letty comments, "We've seen worse."

"But Gran, what if the crops can't grow?"

"Stuff will grow. It always does. Stop worrying and clean that fish."

Van sighs, clearly relieved to be ordered back to everyday tasks. But Fair and Letty exchange a look agreeing on worry.

This morning before she got up Fair vowed only one more day of waiting. It's impossible to know what Terra's going through, but not fun to imagine.

While Van was out, she'd confided in Letty.

"Poor Terra, not even eighteen, spoiled by being brought up in quiet, safe Tully, lost on the road, kidnapped by who knows what goons, locked up in some basement or barn like an animal. Oh, Letty! And my brave son, coerced by some authoritarian boss, and mixed up in who knows what kind of dangerous plot. Probably in the hands of the Sans!"

"They're both adults," Letty remarked calmly. "I know how you feel, but get over it. You have to plan, not fret."

"No, I have to act," Fair retorted. "I have to go. Three Rivers is what, about fifty miles from the Berkshires? A few days travel?"

"But where in the Berkshires? You can't just go wandering around in the hills. You need a plan."

"Never mind. I'm going tomorrow. Anyhow, Sparky and I are eating you out of house and home."

Letty wails, "You are the most stubborn person I've ever met."

"So they say."

Now Fair throws chopped onion into a pot, vigorously stirs as it browns, then sweeps the carrots and potatoes from the table into the stew pot with the onions, releasing a pungent smell that makes Van remark, "Yum!" as he flops the fish down and whacks off its head.

"Just caught," he assures his grandmother. "I met Steve coming from the river. They're easy to catch with the floods, he says."

"Too easy," says Letty. "There'll be a crowd of them now, then nothing. And we can't preserve them in this warm weather. We'll have to salt and dry some. Have we got enough money to buy a few more now, while they're fresh?"

"Steve says he'll take chicken instead of money."

"Good. It's time to kill the speckled one anyway."

"Not Sally."

"I told you not to name them, Vanny. It only makes it harder."

"I won't kill Sally."

"Then Fair will do it, won't you, Fair?"

"Sure, if need be," says Fair. "But Sparky and I are leaving tomorrow, so it will have to be soon."

"Not leaving!" Van, already close to tears over his favorite chicken, now bursts into sobs, made worse by his manly shame at such weakness. "I don't want you to go! Everybody's always leaving!" And he runs out the door, followed by a sympathetic Sparky.

5

On May fourteenth, Terra is dressing for dinner while Trudy sobs on her bed. Trudy just learned this morning that she's been sold to Armand Jones, and will be leaving Headquarters with him tomorrow. Terra is torn between sympathy for her roommate's misery, and her own effort to look her best for the gala farewell this evening. She briskly brushes out her just washed and dried hair, grown out now to below her shoulders, adjusts waves over her forehead. Gina will soon be departing as well, her ransom fully paid. Terra will have this room to herself, a great privilege. But then, she has become accustomed to special treatment since being acknowledged as Hall Hudson's daughter and assistant. Everyone knows by now, and she is proud of it, scorning the hostility and jealousy of the other girls.

After several attempts, Terra finds the perfect perch in her hair for a white flower, clips it in place. Her dress is white with cherry-red trim, cleverly scalloped at the neck to reveal just the suggestion of her breasts, cut just above her knees. This dress was not issued to anyone but her. Because of that, she loves it as a gift from her father. She will be honored again tonight with a seat near him at the table.

Trudy wails, "I don't believe they couldn't find the money, I don't believe they didn't write to me, send a message. It's all lies. That creepy lecher Jones has been leering at me since day one. My mother would never let this happen. She'd sell her soul first. I'll probably never see her again, never see my mama again..."

Terra comes to sit beside her, arm around shaking shoulders. "Shall I ask my father about a message? Maybe there was one."

"Oh, would you? Please?"

Terra nods but adds, "You're old enough to leave home, Trudy. You're a woman now, almost nineteen, right? You can have an exciting life in Albany if you are nice to Mr. Jones. Why don't you try to look at it that way?"

But Trudy pulls back and cries, "What are you talking about? I have to be his whore! We can't all be like you, so fancy free and special." Her red, swollen face bulges with fierce animosity. "You make me sick. Playing along with those dictators. What are you getting out of it I'd like to know."

Terra stands up, gazes down at the distraught girl with sad pity. "You'd better wash your face and make yourself presentable. Mr. Jones does not like crying."

Then she tosses her hair and gives another glance in the mirror.

There's a guard outside their door but Terra knows it's not for her. She makes her way confidently to the luxurious part of the house, the east wing where Hall lives. The dinner is even more sumptuous than ever. Cream of mushroom soup, goat pie, sweet potatoes, cranberry pilaf, roasted carrots with chestnuts, apricot brandy. Armand and Hall are jovial and brotherly. All is going very well in their campaign for Sanmart's dominance. Most of the clean water sources are now strictly controlled, and glorious All Joy is nearly on schedule. Hartford has recognized the advantage of giving them Zoria's blessing, and is sending a coterie of priests to seal the deal. Over dessert of cake and whipped cream, sipping brandy, they congratulate each other.

"You've been doing a fantastic job with volunteer recruitments, I must say," beams Armand Jones. "We're almost back on schedule."

"Same to you. Team work, you and me." Hall raises his glass. "To our team."

Armand clinks glasses, takes a swig. "What I admire most is how you're communicating our idea. You put it right up there, up front: Sanmart for all."

"Sanmart for all. Sounds good, doesn't it? Folks are starting to see the light, I agree. But it's not just my golden tongue and lucky breaks. We owe a lot to Albany's models and military might. And the ESF, more and more efficient. It's crucial to have the muscle in plain sight in case of any treasonous complaints or tricks. When you've got them by the balls, they fall in line real quick."

"Damn straight. Glad to help. My generals are a topnotch crew."

"That's putting it mildly," chortles Hall, pouring himself more brandy.

The guards and servants have all left the room; seated around the table with Hall and Armand are only two officers and Terra. The tall windows are shrouded in gold-colored velvety drapes. The light is subdued, partly from surrounding lamps and partly from scented candles along the table, in slim silver holders. Terra is not sure what the men are talking about, uneasily evading the awareness that they're plotting some power grab. Though they now trust her to a point, they don't care much whether she's following the conversation. Her role is as always to be beautiful and attentive, and intelligent when called upon.

Over the last few weeks, Hall has been truly affectionate with her and earnestly proud as well. They've held several work sessions, when he avidly seeks her advice. He's been very interested in Barrytown and Tully. Someone has usually been taking notes when he interviewed her about them. It made her nervous at first when he started quizzing her about Orion, but what harm can it do? Orion works for the Barrytown government after all. But she's conscious of censoring her replies a bit. For example, why tell her father about Orion's tirades against the takeover of the water supply? She certainly doesn't want to get him into trouble. He's just an impetuous young man, a friend she has loved all her life. So she portrays him as a dutiful and responsible citizen, which of course he is. But she's glad when these particular work sessions end, the recording secretary is dismissed, and she begins the exciting sessions where Hall explains to her his mission, philosophy, and dreams. He waxes especially eloquent about the mission of All Joy, the Hampshire project that will exalt the chosen ones, herself included. The second of these meetings, just yesterday, as they sat companionably in his study by the stove, touched on ideals like safety and freedom and obligation.

"You see," Hall explained, "Being in charge means having a big responsibility. Most people just don't know what's good for them, so they have leaders to guide them."

"Will this help heal the Earth?"

"Oh, yes, that's happening already, wherever the Sanmart team is in charge. Didn't you taste the vegetables at dinner? Those carrots and potatoes are straight out of our greenhouse complex. And of course All Joy will provide the best for everyone."

"Tully has a greenhouse, too." Hall leans forward so she continues, "It's hidden underground so nobody can spot it from the lake. The top is all glass."

"Where did you folks get the glass?"

"Oh, we go on raids to the mainland. We collected enough old glass in just one excursion. And nobody got caught."

She's still grinning from the memory of these brave episodes from Tully lore when she remembers she'd been sworn to secrecy as a child not to reveal Tully's clever ruses to deceive the outside world. Terra has already told her father about the hidden fish pond and orchards, so the damage is done, if any. His glow of approval melts her qualms.

"Smart people, your Tully Island. Your leaders must be good, stalwart folks."

"Oh yes, they are. Fair's husband, Miles, is one of them. We're hoping Orion will come back. He's a terrific leader, too."

"Is he."

It's a comment, not a question. Her eyes drift to the painting above the stove. She asks, "Do you like horses, Father?"

"I love horses, Daughter. I shall take you to the stable soon. Tomorrow, if you like."

He starts entertaining her with stories about his favorite horse, and the evening drifts on in another dreamy timeless trance. But before she leaves him he asks again if she'd like to work with him.

He's standing while she's still sitting, and his large beloved presence feels a bit overwhelming. She doesn't answer right away.

He adds a little sharply, "I'm afraid your friends aren't going to come up with your ransom after all. It's been weeks now since they got our message. They've had plenty of time to respond."

"I can't believe it."

"Believe it. By the way, I should tell you that Armand Jones wanted to buy you."

"What!"

"Oh, very much. He offered to pay your ransom and more." She can only stare at him in horror. "Don't worry, Terra my dear. I told him you are not for sale."

But he's not smiling. She looks away, down at her shoes, his shoes, the plush purple rug. She wills his eyes to love her when she raises hers again. And yes, they do. His face is soft with amusement and affection.

"Poor Terra, don't fret. You're not an orphan any more, you're not a vagabond any more. You've come home." He pulls her up and hugs her tight, kisses her cheeks. "Nobody can hurt you here."

112

6

May has brought no rain, so the floods have slowly receded. From Hudson's headquarters on the hill, Terra can see the muddy fields below where nothing has been planted yet this year, the dry riverbed now trickling with brown water. Downed trees are scattered where the floodwaters dragged them. Young and old trees both, roots weakened by drought. People are out there already in high boots claiming them for firewood, sawing, chopping, hauling. Their horses are having a terrible time in the deep mud.

The auction had to be postponed, but is about to take place this weekend. Terra catches a glimpse of the basement prisoners being loaded into a couple of vans. Many of them will be shipped to the Hampshire project, but also many sold. She can only watch for a few minutes before feeling nauseated. Many of the distraught faces are familiar, from her short stay among them. What would it be like to be sold like a slave? Her father has assured her that this kind of transaction is only a temporary measure until things are brought under civilized control. He points out that these people will be taken care of, fed and sheltered, perhaps better than they had been when free. She turns away quickly nursing the comforting thought that a man like Hudson will soon make the world right.

Her days here are happy. She loves being in charge, having officers obey her requests for anything from a snack to library access, loves the sessions with her father and his cronies discussing philosophy and visions of progress, and the sacred mission of All Joy, loves most of all the tête-à-têtes with him. He has given her a mare named Audrey, and they've gone riding together twice. She's proud that she learned from Fair how to ride well. Fair herself learned in Canada, where her family migrated back in the 40s. Terra, stroking Audrey's copper-brown nose, gets a stab of homesickness so sharp it stops her breath. What she wouldn't give to be hugged and kissed by dear Auntie Fair just for a minute! And she used to get so impatient with her shows of affection, concern. Terra missing Fair thinks she has learned a thing or two about love.

Towards the end of May, events begin to disrupt Terra's idyll. It's rumored and then confirmed that some renegades have escaped from the Barrytown prison.

"I feel sorry for them," she tells her father.

"And so you should," he replies sadly. "Poor demented creatures, easily manipulated."

They are riding along the dried riverbed running with a muddy trickle. Peaceful, pleasant splashes under the horses' hooves. It's early morning, with mist lifting to a sparkle, at least an hour yet before the breathless heat descends. He rides ahead, upright and at one with his black and white stallion, Terra following on Audrey. Far behind, well out of earshot, saunter two guards. Hudson has exchanged his signature brocaded jacket for velvety forest-green; she wears a matching outfit. She's acutely, smugly aware of what a striking pair they are. The beautiful horses, the grand and handsome man, she with her cascade of auburn hair offset by the perfect green of her perfectly fitted costume.

Terra is not afraid to ask, "Manipulated? You mean by the rebels?"

"Precisely. Those sad people who do not, will not, see the light."

"I feel sorry for them all."

The riverbed widens here, and he slows until she's beside him, looks at her with benevolent pride.

"You have a soft heart, Terra my child. Maybe we need to toughen it up a bit."

"I'm strong, Father."

"The world out there is a dangerous, tricky place, my dear. Much work until we bring harmony to it. I may not live to see paradise achieved entirely, but you, Terra, you will live to see it, I promise."

"So will you, Father!"

Terra frowns up at his solemn handsome face a bit flushed from exercise, trembles at the very idea of his passing.

Smiling indulgently, he guides his horse up the riverbank and she follows, Audrey making the climb in dainty, precise steps.

He stops and she pulls up beside him. Ahead of them, perhaps a mile away, looms the impressive edifice of Headquarters—the once elegant mansion half intact, half haphazardly repaired, with an additional low concrete structure mostly hidden by dense bushes. Tall trees, a few of them old enough to look venerable, lean protectively over the house, branches furred with spring green. Many clutches of guards are sprinkled around the hill and winding drive, wagons, even some machines, but none of that seems more than comfortable and natural. Father and daughter pause together to admire the sight.

Hudson sums up the problem by explaining, "Our enemies are these goons calling themselves Stewards, planning to rise up. They will use force!"

Terra hears steel in his voice, is both inspired and worried.

"People will get hurt," she says lamely.

"They will. But daughter, this is one more reason we have to build All Joy, so that the chosen people have a haven, yes a haven like a heaven! Then the evil ones will wither and drop like the rotten fruit they are. This is foreordained. So don't worry, you are coming with us."

He takes off at a canter. Audrey's pace quickens willingly. The fine fresh air whips at Terra's face, and she can't help smiling into the wind.

After lunch that day, when everyone is relaxing and escaping the afternoon heat, Terra hears a loud commotion coming from outside the main entrance. From her room, looking down at an angle, she can see gesticulating guards surrounding three couriers who have just arrived. Fragments of shouts: you can't come in this way, emergency, Chief Hudson, take them away, let them in, listen, and something like horror or horrible. In another moment the couriers are pushed along through the door. But the shouts continue from the remaining guards, yelling to each other. Without waiting to adjust her clothing, and disobeying siesta etiquette, Terra rushes down the nearest stairs towards her father's office. That is how she discovers who is with him.

The guard usually at his door has joined the others inside. Half-dressed, Hudson leans over an aide furiously trying to fire up the old computer. Squeezed tight against her father, his arm around her, half-dressed too, one whole shoulder bared, is Silk. Orion's Silk.

Shock and confusion overcome Terra's fear at whatever else might be happening. To one side, someone has cranked up a radio, which finally begins to bark information. "Storms…tornadoes…hundreds." She makes out the words amid ear-shattering static.

"How long do we have?" Hudson's voice is strained.

No one seems to notice her, so Terra sinks back against the wall, palms against it for support. It looks like her father and Silk have some sort of intimate relationship, but how can that be? What is Silk doing here?

Silk looks beautiful even now, disheveled and anxious—her creamy skin, her scintillating rich blond hair. Terra puts quick fingers to her own hair and clothes, trying to become at least presentable.

"We've got maybe two hours before the first winds," replies the guard at the radio.

At the same time, a grainy picture flares up on the computer screen, jostled video of broken buildings, trees, vehicles, and people either fleeing or falling.

"Thousands of tornadoes crossing up through the Pennsylvania area," someone cries. "Heading straight for us."

"Serious business," comments Hudson. He pulses Silk against him, kisses her hair. "Don't worry honey," he tells her. "We'll be fine."

In the same moment that Terra's stabbed with searing jealousy, he turns to see her.

"Terra my dear. Good." He smiles. "I was going to send for you. We need to get ready." Reading her paralysis against the wall and her stunned expression, he shrugs, almost abashed. "You must be surprised to see your friend Silk here. I meant to explain it to you tonight. But there's no time now. Go up to your room and pack a few things. We may be in the bunker for a few days, it looks like."

As for Silk, her face reflects unmitigated hostility, even as she tries to appear nonchalant. She says, "Hello, Terra," in a voice like cracking ice.

"Now, you girls will have plenty of time to catch up when we get settled," Hudson chides briskly. "Go on, Terra." He turns to an aide, "How many left downstairs?"

"Just the three from the last raid. And the women upstairs whose money hasn't come in."

116

"Those women will have to go downstairs. Put them all in the inner room. We need the rest of the basement space to shelter the servants and guards. You know the routine?"

"Got it."

Hudson has let go of Silk, who's still staring archly back at Terra, who's paralyzed. Finally Silk lowers her eyes, slowly pulls filmy cloth up over her shoulders, says softly to Hudson, "See you," and is gone.

Terra's heart battles her brain for another horrible moment. Then she forces her muscles to move. In the corridor, people are running to and fro, whether pointlessly or purposefully she can't tell. The din of shouts is deafening. In her room, she gathers underwear, a change of clothes, a book. She's never been to the bunker, is not even sure where it is. Clearly it's for the elite, and before this she would've had a spasm of pleasure at the thought of being shut up anywhere with her father. But Silk has changed that.

Terra sits waiting on the edge of her bed, her bundle of belongings beside her. From here she can see out the window to distant rolling hills under a deepening gray sky. Ordinarily a few birds, crows or sparrows, cross this view, but right now not one. They must already know what's coming.

Betty comes to fetch her. Terra's so grateful that it's not a guard, she looks at Betty with new eyes. Betty has large teeth and would have a magnanimous smile if a front tooth weren't missing. Her hair is half black, half white, and her body loose and blowsy, though always neat in her crisp dark maid's uniform. Terra suddenly realizes that Betty's the only person she ever talks to on this floor, and that's only because she gives her orders. To her horror, Terra finds herself clinging to the woman stammering, "I'm scared."

Betty is not immediately sympathetic. She's never had anything from Terra except requests and distant thanks. Realizing this, Terra cries, "I'm sorry, Betty!"

Betty pats her lamely and waits for the outburst to subside.

"Of course, you're scared," Betty finally says, pulling back. "We all are, believe me. But you'll be safe. I promise."

"Come with me," Terra begs. "I don't know anybody else."

"Of course you do. There's your father. And this Silk lady's from Boston, isn't she? Too bad all the other girls are ransomed or sold, they might've invited some of them along."

"Why is Silk here?"

But Betty isn't telling any tales. She's instantly all business.

"Let's get going. Here, I'll carry your things."

Terra must comb her hair and wipe her face, and put on a dutiful expression.

It's an amazingly short walk from a side door in her father's office down a dozen steep steps, through the bunker door, thick as a vault. Terra's heart sinks at the sight of the space, more like a hospital or dormitory than a place to spend time. Bunks line the walls, curtains ready to be drawn for a modicum of privacy. There are three doors, marked Hudson, the name of the chief guard, and Hudson's top aide. Betty secures a bottom bunk for Terra, deposits her little bundle, and backs away from a hug.

"I'll see you in a day or two," Betty says. "Just relax."

"Where are you going?"

"Over to the basement. Most of the servants shelter there. It's fine."

And then quickly Betty's gone.

Terra notes with alarm that male officers are claiming most of the bunks. A few female senior managers or junior guards take the others. The atmosphere is comparatively calm, almost routine, but there's a strange spark of excitement in the air. A long table in the middle of the room is set with plates of food—hardboiled eggs, cheeses, bread and jam, olives, grapeleaves, pies. The only chairs in the room are those around the table, high-backed and rather stately, hardly for relaxing.

The door to Hudson's room opens, and Silk drapes there, wearing an aqua satin dress that could be a nightgown. But it doesn't matter because it clings to perfection to her willowy form. From behind her, Hudson's strong white hands come around her waist, run down her belly. He nuzzles her neck before he steps past her.

"Almost ready," he smiles. "Servants, dismissed."

At once the servants scurry out and the door clangs shut. Then Hudson booms, "Time for our Morgala Moment."

His aide uncovers a porcelain vat covered with an intriguing ceramic design, a mixture of cupids and lions in variations of red—pink, rose, maroon, purple, violet. The aide, a thickset morose looking man, fills a champagne glass from the spigot and presents it to Hudson, who puts it by his place at the head of the table.

Hudson claps his hands, and everyone starts grabbing a glass and lining up at the spigot. Then he comes over to beam down at Terra. "Get a glass of Morgala, my dear, and sit down near me at the table. We don't have much time." He doesn't see the usual admiring obedience in her face, so he adds, "This is all too much for you, I know."

"Why is Silk here?"

"Oh," he replies easily, "she just arrived last night. She's on an educational mission."

"She's the partner of…she used to be…"

"You haven't had news from home for a long time. This will all become clear." He holds out his hand. "Come, we will drink the first Morgala together."

"What's Morgala?"

He laughs delightedly, as if she has just lisped, "why is the sky blue?"

"You will love it, my dear. It's an elixir that puts us to sleep for a few days. We can drink it, or we can choose to inhale it in steam. When we awake, the storm is over. We sort of hibernate."

"It's a drug."

"Such an ugly word. But yes." He is guiding her gently to the table. "First you feel fuzzy, though your sensations are acute, then gradually a delightful veil settles over your brain. This is how we avoid all unpleasantness, pain and worry. There's no such thing as catastrophe here at Headquarters."

Hudson himself places the delicate glass in her hand. The mixture is pinkish and warm, fizzes a little. She looks around the table at everyone, seated, glasses raised expectantly. Silk, next to her father on his right, holds up her glass, smirks in Terra's direction.

A gigantic crack and crash muffled from afar indicate that the storm has begun its devastation. Hudson drinks and they all follow. But Terra puts down her glass. She eats along with them, some cheese, a couple of grape leaves. The food is doubtless delicious but she hardly tastes it. She listens to the terrifying noises from above, remembers the shocking video. Remembers a tornado that touched down near Tully years ago, when she was about twelve. Everyone cowered in caves or root cellars. Fair held her close. What she wouldn't give for Fair's arms around her now!

Terra watches the drug take its effect on each person. Slowly or quickly, the effect is the same: silly grins, euphoric sighs, dreamy eyes, awkward coordination, louder voices. Some get up to replenish their drinks, staggering as they return. Hudson, whose glass has been refilled for him, raises it to Terra, encouraging her with a kindly and paternal gaze. She puts the drink to her lips. Tastes strawberries, a hint of champagne, something syrupy, tart.

Silk is pulling Hudson to his feet, laughing wildly. They are kissing with abandon, almost falling as they stumble to his room. The door closes. Many others now make for their bunks, where they lie emitting little groans of contentment like babies, grinning idiotically.

Terra feels mingled fear and distaste, plus a growing chill of loneliness. Still, she will not drink. The refusal is a conscious rebellion against her father. Beloved father, the hero she sought her whole life, who has betrayed her. With the woman Orion loves. While she's wrestling with heartbreak, she notices a young guard, cherubic and curly-haired, making his way a bit stealthily to the aide's door, which is ajar. The boy is instantly seized in hairy naked arms, and two male voices join in a duet of ecstasy before the door closes. Terra smiles grimly: there's one thing her father does not control.

Some kind of whirring, pounding noise, a series of crashes and cracks. It sounds like everything outside is being blown to pieces. Terra looks around the room, where most of the bunk curtains are pulled, everyone except her gone away to another world. She envies their coma, their dreams, their escape. She feels so alone she could be lost among the stars. She drinks her Morgala.

7

At the top of a hill, Orion can see the town of Merrimack below, a pitiful little greenish drought-depleted river running through it. He's just left the last encampments behind. Nobody would want to stay long up here: no refuge from the raging heat because all its weakened trees were ripped up in recent mudslides. He pauses to wipe his face streaming with sweat, calculates that it's about eleven o'clock. He takes a carefully small sip from his canteen, looks around for some kind of shade. There's a big old maple lying at some distance that just might provide enough, and he's about to explore, when he feels a steel grip around his neck.

"Just hand over that canteen," growls a familiar voice.

"Sure," says Orion. "Ohonte."

The grip relaxes and Finch is peering into his face. "Old buddy! Orion! Brother!"

And then the men are wrapped in an embrace, near tears with relief and joy. Finch is clad in a ridiculous mixture of clothes too small for him, including a woman's skirt, and rubber shoes that cover only half his feet. His jaunty bright yellow shirt has draping holes under the arms. His hat is sturdy straw but eaten away on one side. His beard is as big and bushy as Orion's. Finch leads him to the very tree he was headed for, where he reveals his little refuge of a tattered blanket and some supplies like a pile of nuts and a cup. Here in a patch of grateful shade, Orion hands his canteen to his friend, who starts to drink like a maniac, but stops himself quickly.

"We'll have to get down to the river soon," Finch says, wiping his mouth. "Hope they haven't got it fenced off trying to sell it. Damn, that tastes good!"

"Were you waiting for me?"

"Not really. I never could hope it would be this easy to find you. I just ran out of energy. And, I might say, hope too."

"It hasn't been that long."

"Where were you?"

"I only got half way out, had to hole up in a guard house for a week or so."

"I couldn't wait in the cabin."

"Of course, I know. I got your message there."

"Ah good, great. And here we are after all. Boy, you look gorgeous."

"You're not bad yourself. Love your skirt."

Finch punches Orion's shoulder. "Let's get going. I hardly have a bite left to eat, sorry, and I'm still thirsty as a cactus."

But they wait until after the worst of the noon heat, another few hours, so they have some leisure to exchange news.

Through the Steward grapevine, Finch has learned that Fair left Barrytown about a week ago headed for the Albany enclave. While Orion's still seething with wrath and worry, he adds, "Plus we found out that your cousin Terra has switched sides and is now working for Hud."

Orion snorts his disbelief. "Can't be true. She has more sense than that. Could be she's playing their game for a reason. Or they've got her hoodwinked. Poor little Terra doesn't know anything from politics."

Finch's expression is affectionate but skeptical. "Sure, whatever. Now for the worst news."

"God help us. What is it?"

"Your sweetheart Silk was seen in the vicinity of Hud's H.Q. It's rumored she's working with him."

"Rumors, rumors," groans Orion, "to hell with that. Her assignments often take her to the Worcester area."

"I'll bet," sneers Finch, but changes his tone when he sees Orion's face darken fiercely. "Okay, it's only a rumor."

Orion thinks about Silk with longing and misgiving. He pictures her welcoming him, her milky arms and thighs, but the image is stale and somehow ominous. Can she be in danger? He's convinced she would never betray him, but what if they coerce her, even torture her? His response to Finch's information is to worry all the more about her safety. And that of precious Fair and Terra as well. How are any of his women going to survive in this rotten new Sanmart world? It would be easier if the Sans would attack, could be confronted. But their insidious, saccharine Big Brother tactics are slippery and devious. Orion wants to take a knife to their throats and all he can do is sneak around and plot.

Like everybody else, Orion was taken by surprise by Sanmart's drive for absolute power, and even more at its success. When he first got to Boston five years ago, he was enthralled with its democratic energy, enthusiastic citizenry, well-organized well-being, almost jubilant plans for the future. Barrytown, the political and cultural center of the Boston enclave, had become a relatively pretty area: buildings repaired, vegetable gardens well tended, trees nurtured, the school, hospital, and spiritual spot kept up, the marketplace thriving. The area where the outcast poor used to be forced to live was largely either razed or rebuilt. Boston had made peace well enough with its old enemy the Hartford priests, and with Albany's Sanmart bosses, neither of which had dared threaten them for a long time. Boston's fears concentrated on the ferocious vicissitudes of climate, and related problems like crop failures and disease outbreaks. It never occurred to them that their enemy could strike from within.

Finch pats his slumped shoulder. "Brace up, brother. We're not helpless here, you know. Our Stewards are everywhere now. You and me, we'll be back in the swing as soon as we contact them."

Orion nods. Already he's turning shock into action, his brain scanning all immediate possibilities. He tells himself not to be impetuous and rash, always his tendency, pulls himself up and barks, "Right. So let's head west, not to Boston. Now listen, Finch, I've got news for you, too. Look at this."

He pulls out the map of All Joy that he took from the guard house desk, spreads it on the ground between them.

"Map for that old mall we were adding to," mutters Finch. "They've got a whole city planned for it!"

"I heard them talking, the guys who run Sanmart, Hud and Boss Jones."

"No kidding!"

"The round up of so-called volunteers, that's a well-planned operation including bandit abductions; this dome, it's meant to be a world of its own, for the elite. See, look at this."

He turns the map over to show writing on the other side. It proclaims, *Sanmart for All: Joyful Mission to Save the World, by Armand Jones.* There follow a couple of paragraphs of nearly hysterical rant, summarizing a chilling manifesto.

"'Inspiration for the new world,'" reads Orion out loud. "'…all meant to be, the suffering and confusion, wildfires, drought, floods, tornadoes, destruction of the old planet. Like Noah's Ark. So the chosen ones alone survive and prosper.'"

"'Led by,'" Finch continues reading, "'the great Armand Jones, greatest among the chosen ones, whose destiny is decreed.'"

"That dome," cries Orion, "that grotesque thing we were resurrecting, it's for him and his Sanmart cronies. It'll be its own world, nobody in or out, except forays by special forces outside to pillage for resources and slaves. Populace kept in control through restriction of water supplies. Plus, do you see this? To fuel it they plan to make oil from coal!"

Finch is shaking his head in disbelief. "Oil? Coal? Worse than I imagined."

"Than we ever could have imagined."

The two sit in silence, brave intrepid men as they are, overwhelmed.

8

Fair shares the last of her rabbit with Sparky. Not that he needs it—he hunts very well for himself. "Your mom would be proud of you," she tells him. Fred sits cross-legged peering at a map. Every once in a while he pours more corn whiskey into his coffee cup. He's a tall, spindly young man with lots of straw-colored hair, not only down below his shoulders but all over his long face in a bushy beard with fulsome sideburns. He's very good natured and goes along with almost anything Fair proposes, as long as he has his flask. Fair would heartily like to get rid of him. Because of the storm, they were holed up together for two days in an abandoned root cellar. And now they're lost, spending the night in the lee of a fallen oak. There's a river nearby, they can hear it, but the wind keeps deceiving them about which direction the sound comes from.

"Didn't we pass that sign that said Belchertown," Fred says. "It was something-town anyway. Remember?"

"Just so we're not too near the Westfield River. That's where we could get into trouble and really have to watch it."

"From there on, Albany controls the territory."

"They took over that area in the 70s, I think, if my history's correct. There's a rumor, a pretty substantial rumor, that Sanmart's bandit headquarters is located around there."

"Wooo…" Fred breathes with a shudder, takes a solid swig. "We don't want to tangle with them."

"Well we have to tangle with them," Fair says impatiently. "I'm betting that's where Terra is."

"I mean, without a good plan," Fred amends amiably.

Behind the rush of the river, Fair hears a sound that startles and alerts her. Quietly she throws dirt on the embers of their fire, gestures silence to Fred, and grabs Sparky's muzzle to warn him. But the horse and wagon remain a sure advertisement of their presence. Fair hopes that at least the horse won't get noisy.

The voices get louder. Whoever they are, they don't worry about detection. That's not a good sign.

"Look, right over here," cries one voice. "Can't you see the stupid rock?"

"Don't worry about the rock," comes an authoritative and condescending reply. "We stop here for the night. It's too late to travel now, moon or no moon."

"The moon is good. I vote for travelling by moonlight."

"Fortunately," comes a third raspy voice, "you don't have a vote."

Now the unmistakable sounds of camp making, though they don't seem to be lighting a fire. Sparky is growling at whisper level through her fingers, but she knows he won't be able to hold off his natural alarm system much longer. Sure enough, he twists away and bursts into a series of sharp barks. Consternation from the other travelers soon translates into the appearance of two figures in the gloom, holding off at a distance.

"Who's there?"

Fair replies tersely, "Who wants to know?"

One of the voices says, "A female."

The other one snaps, "Of course it's a female, you idiot."

"I'm here too," announces Fred tremulously.

"We're armed, don't make trouble," warns the taller man, coming forward.

He's only a boy, maybe sixteen or seventeen, but he's burly, and he's toting a gun.

Sparky's barking up a fury, making as if to attack. The boy sneers, "Call off your puppy or he gets it."

Fair whistles and cajoles until Sparky returns to her side, clearly unconvinced.

The shorter figure lights a lamp, holds it up over them. He's even younger, maybe thirteen, with a malicious grin. He says, "Just one old lady and a sissy guy."

"Shut up, Rudy." The older boy peers at them closely, lowers the gun. "What do you think we can sell them for?"

"You're not selling anybody," Fair snaps. But when she starts to her feet, the boy pushes her back down.

"Sit," he orders. "All you have to do for a healthy life is be quiet and do what I say. We won't hurt you."

Fair longs to retort, you sure won't, just a couple of kids, but she can't be sure there aren't a bunch more of them or even adults. So

126

she bides her time, checks for the hunting knife under her sleeping bag. Fred is trembling, trying to reach for his flask, but Rudy stomps on his hand. Fred lets out a yelp and the boy cackles.

The older boy yells, "Yola!"

The cry brings running a skinny teen-aged girl, toting a rope. She gleefully ties up Fair and Fred.

"The Chief will love us now," she crows. "We'll get good money for these two, plus the horse! Right, Henry?"

"Well done," says Henry. "We can use the wagon, too. Our other captive is getting sore feet. We don't want to ruin his feet now, do we?"

"No indeed," cackles Rudy. "Don't damage the goods."

The three children are all in a cheery mood as they hustle their prisoners off through the brush to their own camp. Huddling there tied up to a loaded wagon is a young man with matted hair and deeply dejected face, guarded by a little girl brandishing an axe, which she lets fall in relief at the sight of them.

"It's heavy," she sighs.

"Good work, Birdy." Henry pats her head. "Look what we found."

9

Terra sits numbly on a piece of the house. All around her are the remnants of her briefly luxurious life, a broken table, shards of a vase, muddied rugs and drapes, half a bed. Here and there strewn among them are objects from farther away: the shell of a farm wagon, wings of a wind turbine, corpse of a goat. Trees of every size prone and broken. On the far hills great naked swaths pockmark the green. Much of the mess consists of things that are unidentifiable—nobody will ever know what they once were.

The sun is shining ironically bright, but the air is damp and dank. Terra thinks she must be cold, but she's not sure. She's still confused from the drug they took some days ago, three days maybe? Morgala. The great Morgala Moment. Well, it's true that it saved her from experiencing anything of the storm's wrath. When she woke up it was over. She emerged from her bunk as glassy eyed as the others, and picked with them among the leftovers on the table.

But she's still haunted by the dreams, or rather hallucinations, that riled her sleep. Terrible images, like her mother's hate-filled beautiful face; wonderful images like her smiling father waiting for her in a sunny meadow, holding their horses by the bridle, and Fair running to her with open arms. She dreamed of Orion, too, fulfilling her desire to kiss him, feeling his strong man-smelling bulk, protected in his arms.

She tries to focus on the half of the house still standing, nothing missing but a few windows and doors, a siding of roof. Workmen are already gathering with tools and ladders, yelling instructions as if there's something worth doing. She herself is completely passive, without any motivation at all. Betty appears from somewhere, coaxing.

"Come on," says Betty, "we've got some warm breakfast for you. Oatmeal. You love oatmeal."

"I don't love oatmeal, Betty. And I'm not hungry."

"Yes, you are. Come along."

Before she lets herself be persuaded, she asks wanly, "Betty, what's going to happen now?"

Betty laughs. "You think anybody knows?"

Terra doesn't see her father until nearly evening, when she's summoned to the dining room serving as office. Some of the faces still look a bit groggy, now and then somebody yawns, but most of the dozen officers and managers crowded into the room are frowning with concentration. Her father looks angry. He stands at the head of the table, wearing his black and gold uniform which is rare, stiff with determination.

"I give you two weeks," he announces. "I want this whole compound in top shape again within two weeks. Got that? Now listen, we're going into emergency mode. All units will serve restoration around the clock, never mind other projects. I want this place repaired, re-stocked, and re-armed, pronto. We, your leaders, are bound for All Joy, but you who remain are also among the Chosen. You are meant to steadfastly hold this bulwark of order for the world to come."

Somebody asks, "What about the crops? Ours are mostly ruined."

"Find somebody's that aren't. I don't care how far you have to go. Take plenty of men, don't hesitate to use force."

"Chief, what about incoming bands with hostages?"

"Put them and the hostages to work."

"We'll probably be getting a lot of refugees passing through."

"Do what we always do with refugees. Pick out the ones we can use, chase off the rest. But no favoring pretty women this time. We need muscles and craftsmanship. Keep that in mind."

Terra is proud of her father. What a good leader he is, how brave and smart and competent. But there's a bitter edge to her pride: does he really belong to her after all? Silk is not in the room and Terra ventures to hope that she's gone for good. Though she certainly would like to ask her what the hell she was doing here, and in her father's bed. She has glimpsed a side of her father that distances her, it's sort of like an altered lens, and she doesn't like it. She longs to worship him as always before. She can muffle this little voice, but she can't turn it off. So she chastises herself—how ungrateful can she be?

Hud orders a full report of their situation sent to Albany. Headquarters there was spared destruction, but the tornadoes cut a devastating swath through neighboring towns, so they are occupied with their own emergencies. Not much help from that direction, for a while anyway. Then he announces a decision to recruit more volunteers within the Boston enclave. "Take all boys over sixteen," he says. "No coercion yet, but use the best persuasion techniques you have. Promise them anything. Especially for their families. That always works."

After several more decrees, Hud outlines an intensified public relations campaign. "And Sanmart plans to be taking over the schools very soon—that will help spread the word, with kids bringing it home. It's something Boss Jones and I discussed thoroughly when he was here. Folks need to see the light. We've had too much resistance to taxing water, for example. Ridiculous. We need real education. That will help as well with our military recruitment. In the near future we expect all boys and girls to passionately *want* to serve Sanmart." He pumps his fist for emphasis, chanting, "Sanmart saves!" Everyone in the room raises their fists, chants along with him. Even Terra. She feels a little awkward, but it's a thrill to join her voice to others supporting her father and his dream. He calls himself an outlaw, she thinks, but that's only out of modesty. He's actually a brave, resourceful and visionary hero for this troubled world.

At last he comes to her. After all the speech making, and orders declared, he dismisses most of the crowd. He unbuttons his uniform, leans back, summons her.

"Come here, my dear. Sit down next to me. How are you doing? Want something to eat?"

He looks tired so her reply is all the more tender. "No, Father, I'm fine. You should have something, though."

He gestures to a servant, orders coffee for them both.

"So now we've been through a trial together. We've shared a Morgala Moment. You're on my team, daughter. Welcome to the Sanmart elite."

"I don't care about that. I just want to be with you."

"And help me. Help us."

"Oh yes."

"Now, you wanted to know why Silk was here. Silk is your friend and my friend. What is wrong with that?"

"Well, you must know that in Barrytown, she's the partner of my cousin Orion."

"Who's not really your cousin."

"No, but a dear friend from childhood. I wouldn't want to see his feelings hurt."

"Silk is very fond of your Orion. I'm sure she wouldn't want to hurt him."

"But then, how…"

Hud smiles at her hesitation. "How can I say this delicately enough for your tender ears? Silk likes to give pleasure. Orion need never know."

Terra can't think of anything to say that's not a contradiction or judgment, so she is silent.

"I can see," her father continues, "that you're offended on some level. Understandable. You know little of the world. Someday you will be amused at your youthful opinion on this matter. Let's move on to more important things. Are your temporary quarters okay? It's only for a few days, until we can remodel the upstairs here for more bedrooms. Is the space too small?"

"Oh, it's fine, Father. I'm so grateful to have a comfortable bed. And Betty has brought over some of my things that weren't damaged. She even found my cherry edged dress, the one you gave me, remember?"

"Good, good. And how did you like our Morgala Moment?"

"It saved me from worry over the terrible storm. I did have some very odd dreams."

"Odd dreams, yes," he laughs. "It's a magical concoction, our very own mix."

Terra feels a compliment is in order, so she smiles. "It's a treat."

"So that's it," Hud says, standing and draining his coffee cup. "We're in for some uncomfortable days, I'm afraid. But we'll survive and prosper, as always. Soon we'll be on our way to All Joy, no worries at all."

So she's dismissed, and goes outside again to wander around the debris. She finds the remnants of the garden she so liked to visit, but not much left there except toppled saplings, bushes stripped by hail, and little bits of flowers strewn about like snow. Even the walls are hacked off in chunks. A bit further on, she finds the chair she used to favor in the library, perched all alone amidst bits and pieces of books, shredded pages, broken spines. Though it's still damp she curls up in it, swallowing tears.

10

Birdy inches closer to Fair, who is tied to a tree. Henry and Rudy have gone off to raid a nearby farm field, and Yola is busy with the fire. Fred is tied to the larger wagon and the other hostage is curled up under it in a desolate ball.

"I heard you talking to Henry yesterday," whispers Birdy. "You said you're looking for someone."

"Terra. Do you know her?" Fair looks closely at this pallid little thing. What could she know about Terra?

"I know a person named Terra."

"How?"

"Tell me about the Terra you're looking for."

Birdy's eyes are sly under her curtain of tangled dark hair falling over her face and down her thin chest. Not big on trust, this child. But Fair obliges briskly. Before she's finished two sentences, Birdy squirms with delight.

"Fair, you're her Auntie Fair. She told me about you. We sold Terra to the Chief."

"Oh my god. You? You're the bandits that took her?"

Fair is amazed, but after two days and nights with these children she's not incredulous. They are astonishingly efficient. With all her wiles and adult smarts, she should've been able to escape by now. But they haven't given her half a chance. They've made friends with Sparky to boot. The dog has decided that the whole band is now his pack, and he trots after them in a glory of possession. Right now he's sniffing around the campfire with Yola, who nudges him away from time to time, but speaks kindly if imperiously to him.

"We captured her in a pit," Birdy replies proudly. "She fell in." Then hastily, "She wasn't hurt."

"Where is she now?"

"The Chief has her. Waiting for ransom."

"Is she okay?"

"I expect so. I don't think they'll sell her. I hope not." Birdy looks distraught at this idea, which doesn't seem to have occurred to her before. She adds, "Didn't they contact you?"

"Yes, but we can't pay the money."

Birdy looks like she might start to cry. "Oh I hope they don't sell her. I wouldn't like to be a slave. I'd rather be a bandit."

Yola yells, "Hey, Bird, get away from that stupid old lady. What're you two jabbering about anyway?"

Birdy hastily scampers backward, but shakes her hair defiantly at Yola. "Not your business, Yola, so don't worry about it."

Fair feels insane with urgency. She has got to get Terra away from those people, the Sanmart conglomerate that seems to be everywhere and behind everything. She has no illusions about the possible fate of a beautiful teen-aged girl in their power. She remembers only too well her own abduction at age fifteen. Forced into the Baron's harem, she only escaped by starving herself almost to death. That her first sexual experience was with beloved Seth and not the Baron was pure luck. Well, also a good deal of pluck on her part, it's true. But Terra's chances of escape are bleak. She'll have to be rescued. But not at this rate! Again she eyes the knot around her ankle. Once she surreptitiously started to work on it, but Rudy sneaked up and swatted her hard. "Touch that rope once more," he hissed, "and you'll be very, very sorry."

"Okay, Rudy," Henry cautioned. But he was frowning thunder at Fair. He hadn't missed a thing. She learned her lesson. The knot looks formidable, anyway. She'll need a knife, but hers was discovered when they first frisked her.

Fair tries to gesture to Birdy behind Yola's back, but the child is studiously ignoring her now. Fair's brief hope that she might get help in that direction fades miserably away.

When Henry and Rudy return they are dejected and disgusted.

"Nothing left in that old field except bits," moans Rudy. He turns his sack upside down to tumble out a few withered carrots and some leaves of wilted chard.

"The storm took everything," Henry explains. He sits down on a rock near the fire and stares into it gloomily. "We'll have to boil up those husks, I guess."

"They won't be too bad along with the mushrooms," offers Yola. "And we can add on some bones from yesterday, still some marrow in them."

"Let's just kill the dog," Rudy proposes.

Bird gives a cry and runs to put her arms around Sparky's neck. He nuzzles her in return. Rudy cackles wildly, adding, "He's nice and plump, too."

Fair recovers from panic in noting that nobody takes Rudy seriously, including Rudy himself. The boy just enjoys teasing people, especially girls. Fair is almost fond of these bandit children, making their way in life as they best know how. They always give her enough water and enough to eat, and don't tie her hands any more. But Fred is in an agony of withdrawal from his alcohol. Fair is worried about that: after he begged Henry to find him some whisky, Henry's too intelligent gray eyes registered the whole story. It would not be hard to persuade Fred to do anything if you could give him a drink for it.

Lying in her sleeping bag later on as they all settle down to sleep, Sparky nestled at her side, Fair tries to concoct a plan. It's a comfort that they're headed for Hud's Headquarters—there's no secret about it—because that's where Terra must be. So at least they're traveling in the right direction. She's aware of the possibility of her own fate, which is not pretty, but she figures before she ever gets sold off she'd at least break a few legs or hopefully slit a few throats. Bravado. It's worked before. This pep talk fools her enough for a restful sleep.

11

The west wing has been repaired enough for Terra to move back into her old room. Gina's and Trudy's beds have been removed and a pretty little divan and desk put in, so the space is quite elegant. There's a lot of tumult on the floor above, however, where a suite is being prepared for Hud and his closest aides, as their luxurious east wing is scarcely more than rubble. But in any case Terra spends little time there—she's eager to help restoration any way she can. For the first few days she works in the fields, planting zucchini, green beans, beets. It will be months before new crops can be harvested, so dinners are odd mixtures of root vegetables and pickled fruit from the cellar and anything the foragers bring in. The food improves daily, though, as troops fan out and raid nearby farms and homes. Hud says this is a kind way to let them pay taxes, their contribution to the glory that is All Joy.

"The people recognize more and more that we are the chosen elite, and their duty lies in our survival."

Terra enjoys the physical labor, which reminds her of Tully, even though the sun blasts unmercifully. In the afternoons they all take siestas, so the working day doesn't end until almost dark. One evening, sunburned and dirt-caked, Betty summons her from the field.

"Your father wants to see you."

Terra pushes back her floppy hat, wipes her forehead with a muddy arm, blinks.

"Right now?"

"Looks that way. I guess you can clean up some, though. You're a mess."

Terra laughs but Betty does not.

"Okay, Betty. Set up my bathtub, will you?"

Betty nods and stomps off. Terra finds her in her room giving orders to a couple of servant girls trotting back and forth with pails of hot water from the kitchen. She slides deliciously into the tub, soaping, smiling at the girls pouring water over her.

Hud is sitting in his office but he gets up and gestures her to his private den. She takes her usual big armchair facing the dramatic painting of crazed horses in battle.

"We've both been very busy," he begins.

"How are the repairs going?"

"Oh, very well, very well. Look, my dear, I specifically want you to stop working in the fields. It's not appropriate."

"I don't mind the work. I like helping out."

"I know you do, daughter. And that's commendable. Just let's find something suited to your talents. How would you like to start restoring the library?"

"Oh, yes! Are many of the books salvageable?"

"Not many. But enough for you to start there, then we can get more as you wish."

Terra thanks him, truly flattered and excited.

"Now," Hud continues. "To business. First of all, Boss Jones will be paying us another visit, and I expect you to help entertain him in your usual charming way. After all, Sanmart is rooted in Albany, and the Boss is Albany's beneficent leader, guide to us all. You might say he's Sanmart incarnate, and All Joy his sacred creation."

Terra is not thrilled with this news. She finds Jones creepy and her father's deferential treatment of him uncomfortable. But she manages to nod and smile.

He adds, "Plus, he's bringing your old roommate Trudy with him. So you girls can have a nice reunion. Of course, she'll be sharing his rooms upstairs, but you're free to take walks and lunch with her, whatever. Would you like that?"

"Oh, yes," breathes Terra, not meaning it at all. She hopes Trudy won't wail and cry on her shoulder, and feels guilty for her lack of sympathy.

"Boss Jones is coming strictly on business. Albany was hard hit in some areas, so cooperation there is on the agenda. But in addition, there's trouble brewing in Barrytown and environs, with those Stewards and their rebel cohorts threatening to undermine all the great projects going forward with Governor Monty. They've had to jail some of them, and send others to be rehabilitated as good citizens. It's a sad situation. Just a few malcontents fomenting unrest and distrust among loyal Bostonians. A great pity."

Hud's words are melancholy but his tone is angry. Terra trembles to see him so upset. She's anxious to make him feel better, restore him to his carefree, expansive self.

But his next words kick her in the stomach.

"I've found out some news about your old friends that's most disturbing. Your so-called aunt has decided to take you away from here herself rather than pay the ransom. She's been heading in this direction for quite some time."

He stops, waiting for Terra to finish her cries of amazement and concern. He doesn't register sympathy, only patience.

"Calm down, my dear," he finally tells her. "Just listen. Then together we'll decide what to do."

"This can't be," Terra finally breathes, holding both hands to her heart. "Auntie Fair, how could she? Such danger, and hardship! Oh Father, Father, how can she think she might rescue me? Why couldn't they find the money? What about my cousin? What about Orion? Why isn't he stopping her?"

"Orion," echoes Hud. "That young man's in trouble. He's escaped from a volunteer job in the Hampshire settlement. It seems he's one of the rebels, the Stewards they call themselves. For all I know, he's already in jail."

Terra is starting to wonder where Hud gets all this information. She bets he does know whether Orion's in jail or not. He seems to know everything. He seems to be expecting her to repudiate Fair and Orion, but how can she do that? She's having trouble breathing. She stares into the rolling eyes of the foremost horse in the painting before her, and for the first time registers that the animal is in a frenzy of terror.

"But I don't want to leave here," Terra finally manages. "We've got to let her know that, before she does something rash. Can I write her a letter? Can you locate her? Or would you like to invite her here as a guest? I'm sure she'd appreciate that."

"Terra, dear, you're in a fantasy. Although I don't blame you for wanting your world to be harmonious and simple. The tough fact is, you're going to have to choose between your father and those people. I am your family, not them. You've said so yourself."

He's looking at her sternly, clearly willing her to be strong and responsive to him, but she's paralyzed with dread. She longs to

138

comfort him, she longs for the peaceful depth of love she felt for him only minutes ago, but all of her senses are submerged in a pit of foreboding. It begins to dawn on her that he won't take no for an answer. With a wrenching sense of loss, she decides to lie.

"Father, dear Father. Of course I'll do whatever you think best. I'm very fond of my old friends, and I'm sure they'll eventually see the light and join with us in making a new world. I can pretty much guarantee it, they are such fine people, intelligent and wise. They'll be a wonderful addition to our forces for the future."

Hud nods approval. "Well said, daughter. I'm sure you're right. So you really don't have to worry. Either they'll join us or…they won't."

His tone of smug satisfaction tinged with warning does nothing to warm the chill that has gripped her spine.

The next morning Terra is on her way to the back room where the library will be temporarily housed, when she hears a familiar sound. A harmonica is playing a tune she recognizes with a shock: "Walk of Life." The words of the old song come into her head as she stops short in the hallway to listen. She's known them from childhood. "After all the trouble and the double talk, you do the walk, you do the walk of life." It's Tully's favorite festival tune.

Who would know this song? Who would play it just like that on the harmonica? It can only be Fair. But how can it? Could she be here? Of course not. Hudson would have told her—but he did say she's headed here. If he doesn't know, and Fair is hiding, surely she wouldn't be playing her harmonica. Terra follows the sweet strains until they begin to fade, steps backwards to where they're strongest, just at the threshold. She looks quickly and guiltily around. There's a guard farther along the hallway. With a start, she realizes that he could be purposely posted to watch her. So she saunters on into the room, takes her usual place at the broad table spread with books in various states of repair. Finds a discolored volume of poetry from the 2050s praising some forgotten warlord, makes a good show of assessing it, turning browned pages reverently. The music is no longer audible. Maybe it has stopped. After a long tense time, she ventures back to the threshold. The guard is still there. So is silence.

Who else would be playing that song, in just that way? It's an ancient Tully tune, she's never heard it anywhere else. That's hardly proof, but Terra decides she must make sure. She contemplates confiding in her father. Surely, if she tells him her old friend is near, he'll be welcoming. But this thought never quite forms before it grows apprehensive little edges that gnaw at her confidence. Hall Hudson won't tolerate any violation of his rules and self-interest. And even if he did, Armand Jones would ruthlessly insist on protocol. And Jones is right here, not conveniently off issuing orders from Albany.

Terra continues her work. The familiar smell of mold and damp. The hopeless obliteration of whole sections, ragged remnants. The guard strolls by the doorway every now and then, salutes if he sees her notice. At one point she goes to the window. It looks out on the back of the house over fields and barracks. Nothing noteworthy, except that directly beneath her is the basement dormitory where new captives are kept, where she herself trembled in a prisoner's nightgown just two months ago. Which means, it actually is possible that Fair is there now.

Terra doesn't want to wait for a foolproof plan. Quickly she walks to the back door, hurries past two guards, hearing her own guard snap a warning to them, and runs out into the field. Nobody physically tries to stop her, but they're all yelling now. Ignoring them, she keeps going and suddenly falls over hunched figures toiling in the dirt. She picks herself up, whirls around to see the guards briskly approaching, and looks down directly into the mud-smeared face of beloved Auntie Fair. She and Fair gape at each other for a split second, then Fair shakes her head and dips it again, pawing soil around a budding plant, mumbling, "Later, not now."

Terra too catches the danger of the moment, stumbles away. When the guards catch up with her, she's nowhere near Fair. Instead, at her feet cowers little Birdy.

12

More wildfires follow in the tornadoes' wake, giving no respite. All across the northwest Hartford enclave, as soon as people emerge from shelters to confront the storm's destruction and death—remnants and ruins of fields and orchards, buildings and landscapes, corpses flung like weeds—word comes, hardly even a day before the smell arrives. The smell of heat, scorching, ashes. Then the heat itself, black clouds, the first distant sight of orange licking light. This time there's no escaping to underground refuges. Nothing to do but run.

Fair hears this nightmare firsthand from captives arriving the evening of the day she saw Terra. Ten of them, brought by fast wagon pulled by four horses, directly from the Litchfield area, traveling day and night. Most of them are very young, adolescent boys and girls who will fetch a good price no matter how they're disposed of. At once the boys are herded away, and the girls dressed in the silly standard flowered nightgowns, announcing uniformity and acquiescence.

"We could hardly breathe," cries one hysterical girl, whispering and choking at the same time, sitting next to Fair on her cot. Others encircle them, in the few minutes they have before lights out. "The air was full of soot. I felt the flames on my neck, I swear."

"We were easy to capture," puts in another girl. "We were sitting ducks, so scared, we didn't even ask who or why they were giving us a ride."

"But maybe that saved our lives," puts in another. "I don't know what's happened to the rest of my family. Except they took my brother too. But what about my mama?"

"The fire was so close, and so crazy, with a wind that whipped it on and on and everywhere."

Fair tries to reassure and calm them. "You're ok for now. You've had something to eat and you can have a good night's rest. Chances are the fire won't reach us up here in the Berkshire hills." But she feels a hypocrite trying to minimize the fate they face, fire or no fire.

Lying in bed later, her eyes continue to stare wide open into the dark. Terra's here! She looked wonderful—in that one absorbed stare they shared, it was clear she was healthy and well cared for. But Fair is helpless, something Fair loathes to be. She ponders yet again every possible option for escape, but each one has to be weighed along with chances of Terra's rescue, and all fall far short of any reasonable chance of success. For example, what if she sneaks out of here in the middle of the night? No, she's wearing the telltale nightgown and she has no idea where her own clothes are. Suppose she waits until she's dressed in the bland fieldwork overalls—she'd be much less likely to be noticed in that outfit. She could probably come by some weapon, a knife from the mess hall, perhaps. But as soon as she pictures herself creeping through corridors in a building she has never seen before, she knows that option is crazy. Then in a brief surge of hope, she imagines Terra plotting in her turn to rescue her. What opportunities might Terra have to get to her, with clothes, weapons, even accomplices, a secret exit? Dreamily contemplating this scenario, Fair is drifting into sleep when she feels a slight scratching on her arm. Without surprise and with only a little revulsion, she assumes it's a rat. But then her blanket is being lifted and a tiny hand rests on her lips. The light and bony collection that is little Bird curls itself against her.

Fair kisses her, shaking her head. This is so dangerous. How has Birdy made her way all that distance from her end of the dormitory?

"I climbed under all the beds," Birdy whispers. "On my tummy, like a lizard."

Fair holds her close, comforted beyond measure by the need and warmth of the child.

"Oh, Birdy, you must go back."

"I will. I wanted to tell you Sparky is ok. Henry told the soldiers that he's with us. So they let him be. I think he's waiting outside, as close as they'll let him get."

"Thank you, Birdy. I was worried."

"I also wanted to tell you I saw Terra."

"So did I."

At this point the door at the far end of the room opens with a shaft of light and the matron peers in. But she doesn't enter, closes the door.

"I put my pillow under my blanket," Bird says proudly.

Fair gives her a squeeze of approval.

"I think Terra lives here," Birdy continues, her raspy little whisper blowing on Fair's ear. "We went to give our report to the sergeant, and we saw her, just walking around like a normal person."

"You mean, not a prisoner?"

Birdy nods and Fair tries to wrap her mind around such a strange possibility. Can Terra have cleverly concocted some kind of deal? Hopefully not a service or sexual deal. Such a turn of events surely would improve their chances of escape. Now she remembers with new eyes the guards' reaction to Terra in the field. They had not touched her, merely exchanged words, nodding rather respectfully, gesturing persuasion. But why had she run into the field in the first place? The harmonica, she must have heard the harmonica!

Birdy snuggles. Fair kisses her again.

"We'll be leaving soon," Bird says. "Maybe tomorrow."

"Are they treating you ok, Birdy, and the others in your gang?"

"Oh, we're fine. We do this a lot. We get paid. You were quite a prize. The boss was very happy to get you." Birdy's voice is sad. "I wanted to say goodbye, Aunty Fair."

When tears smart Fair's eyes, she feels a fool. "Goodbye, Birdy."

"But I wish I could help you. I think they'll be selling you soon."

"I'm afraid you can't help, dear Bird. Henry and the others would stop you, if the soldiers didn't. You don't want that kind of trouble. But listen, when you're a bit older, come to Barrytown to visit us if you can. I know we'll be there. I know we'll be safe, Terra and I. Promise."

"Promise."

Little Bird kisses Fair's cheek, slips away to the floor, disappears into darkness, silence. The lack of her is cold as ice. Fair lies awake forever, contemplating the twist of events that features Terra as a possible free member of the household. Not free enough to run into a field without questioning, though.

Barely hours later it seems, a ponderous gong announces waking time. Dawn is just suffusing the small high windows. It can't be later than five o'clock; they must be in a hurry. Sure enough, the morning rituals are put into high gear, everything speeded up, the matron shouts urgency. They all scramble into their work outfits, rush through breakfast. As they emerge into the fresh light already soiled with a blackened horizon, they are handed shovels one by one.

"Today," yells the commanding guard, "you'll be digging ditches. Save your butts as well as ours. Firebreak."

They load into wagons that don't have far to go before glimpsing the first sight of ominous orange flicker in the distance. Down circling roads descending hills, passing wrecked trees strewn about, but also clumps of still beautiful and unfelled forest, here and there piles of stones or timber that were lately houses, ruined cropland looking like some tantrum toddler randomly smashed it. As soon as they catch sight of the mass of refugees contained behind barbed wire fencing, they're urged out of the trucks at a trot.

All morning they work without a break. Fair's back is killing her. Finally she begs the guard to let her rest. He prods her with the butt of his rifle, but looks more closely and grumbles, "Okay old lady, over here." So she sits for a time on a rock, looking out across the meadow to the mob whose loud complaints reach her on the breeze. They must be terrified. The fire is closer now. The area being cleared by the prisoners is twenty feet wide, and extends the whole length of the foothill. Fair gauges that it's enough to stop the flames, as long as a wind coming this way doesn't spring up. It wouldn't stop the refugees though, if they ever could break through the barbed fencing. She figures if the fire got close enough many would try, and most would die in the process—the guards are all armed with guns. Sanmart's black and gold uniforms no longer fake beneficence. There's almost an element of relief in that. Now the enemy is declared, clear and in focus. No more having to negotiate pretense and slimy, twisted rhetoric.

13

The atmosphere in Hud's study is not only chill, it's downright ominous. Terra is surprised to see Armand Jones there before her, sitting in her usual chair. Her father gestures her to a less comfortable, less prominently placed chair facing Armand. He himself sits stiffly behind his desk.

In her mind Terra examines every detail of her dress and appearance, acutely conscious that the men will read and judge it. She's still in her loosely casual library outfit: grey blouse and darker skirt, unalluring grey stockings. She knows there's mud on her shoes. She has combed her hair since her insane rush out into the field, had time before she was summoned to color her lips, but otherwise she does not meet the feminine standards of either one of them. Armand in particular stares blankly at her.

Her father's first words hardly reassure her. "Terra, you've been behaving strangely. What possessed you to dash out among the prisoners?"

Before she can reply, Armand barks, "Just what were you after, young lady?"

Terra decides not to answer him. She finds herself afraid, unable to summon her usual saucy daring. Worse, she senses that her father is afraid, too. That can't be.

Her voice is cracking when she finally says, "Father, I had no idea the field was worked by prisoners. I simply missed helping with the planting. You know I really enjoyed helping out that way."

This reply rings false to her and no doubt to them. Hud shifts uneasily in his chair. Armand shakes his head and laughs shortly.

"She's not as clever as we thought," he comments to Hud.

Hud says, "Terra, we are very concerned. Tell us what you were doing out there."

Terra lifts her chin. "I feel awkward with Mr. Jones here, Father. Forgive me if I seem to be holding back."

"Of course, my dear," Hud replies with something like sympathy. "We understand, but it can't be helped."

"Time to stop pussyfooting," Armand breaks in. The veins in his bulbous nose pulsate with indignation. "You are going to tell us everything or you'll be very sorry."

"Now, Armand," Hud starts. To her horror, Terra notes that his glorious white hands are trembling.

"Shut up," Armand rages, "I'm in charge here and we're wasting time. Listen, Terra my girl, you've had it pretty easy in the last few months prancing around as daddy's little pet, but that's over now. You're still our property, Sanmart property. Get it? Now here's the score. We know you spoke with one of our gang folks, a kid known as Bird. You know that's against the rules. Who else did you contact out there? Tell the truth, and tell it fast."

Terra longs to tell her father that she knows Fair is here, beg him to free her. But she certainly can't confide in Armand Jones. He's already treating her as guilty of something. So she decides to tough it out.

"Mr. Jones," she says in a voice almost hushed with respect, "I'm afraid I can't speak of certain matters outside my family. I hope you'll pardon us for a few minutes so I can speak to my father alone."

Armand stands up briskly. "That's it. Have her ready to go in two hours, directly after lunch, at 1 o'clock." He rings for the guard and snaps, "Take her to her room. Bolt the door. She's under arrest."

The guard looks at Hudson Hall, who slowly nods.

Terra locks eyes with her father but there's no encouragement there, only sadness and perhaps a touch of humiliation.

Betty is already in her room, packing things in a small suitcase. Her replies are more brusque than usual but at least she's not crowing. Terra wants to scream and cry but she can hardly even voice words, her heart is so tight with pain and fear.

"Whatever you want," she replies to Betty's inquiry about what to take. "I don't care." She watches the woman efficiently gathering her few belongings, excluding the stuffed animals, pretty pillows, fancy perfume, and jewelry that now it appears never were really hers.

Now Betty's gone and Terra sits on the edge of her bed with the suitcase beside her, looking out the window to the hills beyond, at what's left of the trees sporting their springtime yellow-green, at the great patches of debris, a whole roof on its side, a railing, a wheel, jumbled crazily together. She's not on the side of the house facing the fire, but the air is smoky, as if fogged.

The next time her door opens, it's her father. He stands near it, shoulders slumped.

"I couldn't save you," he sighs. "I tried."

"You tried?"

"Jones never liked my acknowledging you. He was always against it. He wanted to buy you instead. He was always angry about that. Now what you've done has given him his excuse. There isn't anything I can do. I'm in trouble enough already. He claims I've overstepped my authority. He threatens to replace me."

Terra realizes that he expects her sympathy. "Too bad," she says acidly instead.

He looks mournful. "I'll always be proud of you, Terra."

"Where are you sending me?"

"To Albany, my dear. You can have a decent life there. Armand will treasure you. And when we've been successful in our great mission, we will live together in All Joy. We can be father and child once again. Dear Terra."

"You're selling me to Jones after all?"

"No. I'm giving you to him as a gift. It's what he requires."

"What!" Terra is wild with disgust, outrage. "But you can't."

"Yes, I can. Or in any case, he will simply take you, so I might as well save face."

"But I haven't done anything! What have I done? What crime could deserve this?"

"You're too much of a risk, you see. I've always known that, actually. We know that you saw your friend Fair, you know she's a prisoner here. You would try to free her or otherwise mitigate her fate. But she's a rebel along with her son, dangerous characters both. With Sanmart it's crisis time. Which side you're on is a matter of life and death now. In fact, you are lucky that Armand so desires you."

Terra wants to throw up, gags. "My own father will do this to me?"

But instead of shame, Hud is condescendingly paternal. "Relax. Nobody's going to hurt you. I'll send Trudy in shortly to explain it all to you. Be a good girl, Terra."

He doesn't try to embrace her, goes quietly out.

Terra does not go quietly. She figures Fair will hear, or at least hear of, a full-blown tantrum, so she kicks and screams all the way from her room to the van waiting at the side entrance. She must make sure Fair knows she's leaving Headquarters. Besides, it feels good to destroy the illusion of obedience the bosses would prefer to convey. Trudy is traveling with her and maintains an enigmatic grin all the way down the drive, until Terra stops screaming and collapses back into her seat, panting.

She snarls at Trudy, "What's so funny?"

"You are. You have to admit." Terra glares. Trudy adds, "Daddy's little girl has fight in her after all. I'm impressed."

"How can you be so cold and cruel? Don't you understand what's happened?"

"Yeah, we're both Armand's whores now. Welcome to the club."

Trudy turns to stare out the window, her profile sad and harsh. The road is winding up and down hills in the opposite direction from the fire. The van is fueled with cooking oil and smells of fried potatoes. The window is soiled and the seats are hard. This is some kind of military vehicle, no luxury pretended. But Trudy produces a bottle of water, passes it to Terra who drinks gratefully. Though it's still early afternoon, the sky is shadowed almost like twilight, casting the bizarre countryside with its ruined fields strewn with rudiments of possessions in a mystical pall.

14

Trudy's not surprised when they stop to pitch camp before dark. "We'll be waiting for Boss Jones to catch up with us," she explains. "He had more business at Hud's Headquarters. Seems like your father took some risks setting you up as his heroine. The Boss has had to put him in his place."

"But my father's central to the mission," Terra protests. Depressed to the point of paralysis, she's lying on her cot. She argues half-heartedly, "He runs the whole bandit enterprise, brings in tons of resources for Sanmart. He's really good at what he does. He's one of the important leaders."

"Could be. But things are changing fast. The whole Sanmart works is gearing up for complete takeover. As soon as the water supplies are locked in, nobody will have much chance to resist. Looks like we'll be heading for this gigantic refuge called All Joy, that's going to save us, apparently. Lines of authority have to be clarified, that's the language, and you'll hear more of it. Listen, Terra, get over yourself. You were never more than a plaything, a potential pawn. There are more important things at stake than your comfort or virtue. More important than mine, too. As women we're just spoils of a war that's only beginning."

Terra perks up at Trudy's tone. The girl is talking like a politician, hard facts and persuasion. Terra pulls her tousled hair back from her face, sits up angrily, snaps, "I'm not going to be any man's spoils of war, or any other object. You watch."

Trudy grimaces. Yay for you. Getting mad feels good, but it will get you nowhere. Yeah, I'll watch while they beat you up and then have you gang raped."

"No."

"Terra, listen. We can get out of this. Don't do anything stupid. Play along with Armand. It's the only way there's any hope."

"Hope for what? Survival? I'd rather die. I want to die right now anyway."

"Oh god, you're insane. What am I going to do with you? You just don't get the situation. You think you're talking big, but dying is a real option if you don't behave."

"Behave!"

"Behave," Trudy repeats viciously. "That's right."

"Now you listen, Trudy." Terra stands up to face her friend, hands on hips. "I've never been a slave in my life, or even a victim of any sort. And I'm not about to start. You can do what you want. Maybe that's best for you. But don't try to tell me what to do. I'll see Armand or myself killed before I get in his bed."

Trudy does not look convinced, or impressed. "Bravo, Terra. Poor Terra."

At this point two guards come in carrying a tray of food and a flimsy gown they spread on Terra's cot. The tray goes on the little table between the cots.

One of the guards tells them curtly, "The Boss won't be here til late tonight. Eat and get ready."

Trudy nods acquiescence. When they've gone, she comments, "Looks like your showdown is coming sooner than I thought."

Sitting on the edge of her cot, Terra drinks from her glass of wine, serves herself unappetizing looking stew.

"My Aunty Fair," she confides proudly, "escaped from a situation like this. But first she faced down the baron who'd kidnapped her, started starving herself until they gave up."

"I wouldn't want to starve myself," Trudy notes, chewing voraciously. "I doubt it would help anyway. These guys can be merciless. Sometimes I don't think they're human."

"Of course they're human," retorts Terra. "That's what makes them so revolting." She contemplates Trudy for a while, dares to ask, "You mentioned getting out of this. What exactly did you mean?"

Trudy looks around as if for eavesdroppers, asks in an undertone, "You know who the Stewards are?"

"Sure, rebels."

"Right."

"Come to think of it, Hud mentioned that my aunt and cousin are working with them. It seemed he was very indignant about that. What does it mean?"

"Power, Terra. You may think Sanmart is an unbeatable giant. But giants have been beat before by hordes of brave folks. The Stewards are everywhere, and getting organized in all the enclaves, Hartford and Albany as well as Boston. They have power too, in numbers and in right."

Terra stops chewing in astonishment at the glow in Trudy's usually dull face. She takes a gulp of wine, murmurs, "You mean, they can rescue us?"

"I mean they can, yes, but I also mean we're small potatoes and there's other vastly more important work to be done."

"Well, how can we do it cooped up in a harem? And besides, Trudy, I'm not convinced Sanmart isn't right. My father explained it to me very well and carefully. The Earth is in terrible trouble, and only a strong authority can prevent complete breakdown. Average people need strong leaders and strong rules."

"Average people need rights and hope. The Earth needs caring average people, not guns and jails and elites."

Terra has heard this kind of talk before. It sounds exactly like Fair, and many other folks in Tully. She learned this rhetoric in school. She used to believe it. But her admiration for her father, and his faultless logic, and the chaos she sees around her, turned her mind around. She has come to see Tully as a sort of endearing naïve group more suited to an older generation.

She says archly, "My father's helping build a special refuge called All Joy, where we'll be safe. What's wrong with that?"

Trudy is gazing at her sorrowfully, as if at a sick child. "Look at you," she says slowly, "such a beautiful intelligent girl, so brainwashed. Pitiful." She shakes her head. Her curly blond hair is awry, her makeup faded. She has the tired air of a distracted mother. Terra is at once infuriated by her condescension and filled with odd tenderness for their intertwined female fate. She considers herself to have entered hell, and sees that this woman with her is not being mean, only kind.

Terra surprises them both by replying gently, "You're a good person, Trudy. Better than me, I think." She leans over to kiss Trudy on the cheek. "We don't have to agree. Nobody will listen to us anyway."

"You are brave, Terra." Trudy even smiles a little. "But please don't risk your safety rejecting Armand. The world needs women like you."

Terra thinks it over. "Maybe I should do what my father would want."

"Not for him. He let you down, Terra, he betrayed you. But for us, for the future. Tough it out for the rest of us."

"How do you manage to stand it?"

"I always think about how I will take revenge some day. I like best to think about Armand's throat cut, bleeding."

"That might work," Terra responds grimly.

After dinner is cleared away, Trudy goes laconically over to her trunk of clothes. It's a large container, opens sideways to show clothes hanging, including some of Armand's. Terra stares down unbelieving at the dress they expect her to don, with transparent panels and hardly any neckline at all. She grabs it with both fists and throws it on the floor.

Trudy pulls out a shiny lavender number. "Armand likes this one a lot. So do I, actually." She laughs harshly. "You see, I'm a survivor. I like to eat well and dress pretty."

In the moment Terra is stricken with the look of desperation and self-disgust on Trudy's face, Trudy screams, recoiling from the contents of the trunk. A guard comes quickly in, asking what's wrong.

Trudy cries, "A rat, I saw a rat."

The guard splutters contempt, goes out chuckling.

But Trudy continues to gasp, pointing at the trunk. "Terra, there's a child in there."

Terra jumps up. At the same time, little hands, then legs appear, then a whole Bird.

"Birdy!"

"You know this person?" Trudy's astonishment quickly turns to caution. She puts her finger to her lips. "Quiet," she whispers.

Bird nods agreement, rushes to embrace Terra. "We have to leave right away," she whispers. "Fair."

"Fair? Fair's here?"

Birdy nods vehemently. "With the horse and dog. Come on."

"Come on where? You silly little girl," growls Trudy. "You are just going to get us in a heap of trouble."

Ignoring Trudy, Terra holds Birdy tight, kisses her. "What's the plan?"

Bird reaches into her pocket for a knife, hands it to Terra. "Just in case." Then she pulls Terra by the hand over to the back of the tent, lifts the canvas, revealing a ditch just large enough for them to fit through.

Trudy says matter of factly, "You'll be killed."

"You're coming with us," Terra says.

"She can't," Bird counters.

"No," Trudy agrees. "I'd screw up whatever chances you have. I'll stay here." She turns to Bird with a touch of respect. "Would it help if I cause a distraction?"

"Oh, yes," Birdy breathes.

"You have to come," Terra insists, "I'm not leaving you here."

"I can best serve our cause here. Besides, I don't want to die yet. You can help me a lot by tying me up."

So while Terra stuffs a few things into her backpack, Bird binds Trudy's hands to her cot and sticks a silk scarf in her mouth.

Birdy says, "You can still make a lot of noise. Start yelling a couple of minutes after we're on the other side."

In a blur, Terra and Birdy are in the dirt emerging on the outside of the tent while Trudy sets up a horrific squawking sound that brings all the guards running in her direction. Somehow there are now dark bushes around them, they are crawling, it's pitch dark, and then they're running across a meadow to the shadow of a barn's remains. Fair emerges from nowhere, Audrey in tow, pushes Bird and Terra up on the horse's back, joins them, and Audrey takes off like the wind. Disappearing into blackness, under trees, around debris, over hills, through brush, the horse with its three fugitives, followed by a speeding Sparky, gives rein to the wild.

15

Fair says, "Hand me that spoon. No, the big one."

Bird hastens to obey, watches the pot return to a boil, her eyes huge with longing. "It looks awful good," she breathes reverently.

Never mind that she saw what went into it: a fish head, day-old squirrel parts, half-rotten carrots, tangled tree roots. She knows well what magic can be wrought with skill, desperation, and a mighty hunger. It will taste delicious.

Terra returns with an armful of dried twigs and leaves, banks up the little fire they've got going in a circle of stones. Nearby a stream gurgles, sounding for all the world like the river it once was. It even smells good, mud and earth and ferns. Darkness is curling around the edges of a cooling day. Sparky's lolling tongue shows enormous enthusiasm for the pot's contents. Audrey munches sulkily on dried grass—she still misses the luxurious fare back home in Hud's compound.

"I'll give you a good brushing in a minute," Terra tells her. "Cheer up."

"Cheer up," echoes Bird with a delighted laugh. "You silly old horse."

"Not so silly," Fair reminds them. "She's the reason we're here."

It's been nine days now since they fled Armand's encampment, riding in heart-choking terror all through the night. They only slowed when they came to remnants of a town recently obliterated, probably by tornadoes, where they collapsed into brief comatose sleep. The place had already been ransacked, but they came away with a few odds and ends like a jar of preserves, a frying pan, a blanket. The first few days they barely had enough to eat, Fair's pack holding only bare necessities, a bag of chestnuts, some utensils, a few herbal remedies. Terra came away with nothing but the flimsy clothes she was wearing, though she has since been able to barter for a pair of trousers; they are much too big for her but she rolls them up, belts them with rope.

As she finishes up her stew, sopping the remnants with stale bread, Fair notes, "We'll be at the lake by tomorrow night. Then we'll need a boat."

"We had that close call near Ticonderoga," says Terra, "but you know, we've been really lucky so far."

"And smart," comments Bird. She is tucked up in her blanket, already yawning. "Lucky and smart."

Terra gazes into the twinkling embers of their little fire. This time of evening always brings sad thoughts, about her father's betrayal but also his attention and affection, their happy times together. After a long day on the run, always on the watch, always frightened, this relaxing time allows awareness of her sorrow. Her life's mission accomplished, and gone again in just months. What more is there now? He's been found and lost. Fair is no help. She's determined to get Terra back to Tully fast, to keep her safe forever.

"But I don't want to be safe forever," Terra regularly protests.

Fair only looks back at her hard, unmoved.

Terra pushes on. "What about Orion? I thought you were so eager to help him save Boston. Why are we running away?"

But Fair just seethes. "Are you forgetting what happened to you? Come on, Terra. Your so-called father sold you to the highest bidder. Think about it."

"No, no. He gave me as a gift. He was forced to. He didn't want to do it."

"If that's what you want to believe. Tell me this, where would you rather be right now, squatting by a fire with us or in bed with old Armand Jones?"

This usually silences Terra, sulkily. Bird sometimes chirpes helpfully, "We love you, Terra."

Terra, brushing Audrey with the remnants of a broom, fondles her ears and gives her a kiss. Audrey's great brown eyes seem to caress her in return. Terra knows well that Fair and Bird risked their lives to rescue her from Armand. Escaping Headquarters, they'd endured hours of near suffocation in a wagon packed with corn husks, not knowing if they'd be discovered before the wagon got safely away. It was dangerous, but Birdy had begged to come, assuring Fair that since Henry was getting promoted and his little operation disbanded, she was sure to be sold. Then they'd had to brave the guards surrounding Armand's encampment. The story of how Bird got into Terra's trunk is endless entertainment.

"I just slipped by," Bird relates wide-eyed and proud, "under the table and whisk! Under the tent flap." She chuckles in her apologetic way, tossing back her hair from her glowing face. "They were arguing about something, stupid old guys. How can they call themselves guards?"

There's no extra blanket for Audrey, So Terra covers her with an array of clothes, a jacket, her overalls. The weather has grown hotter every day, June promising ferocity, but nights are unpredictably cool.

Fair studying a map says, "The problem is, I don't know if the border is still in the middle of the lake or not. I seem to remember that Albany expanded east and took over some of Vermont."

Terra says, "Crossing the border won't be easy."

Birdy breathes, "They'll be looking for us."

"For sure," Fair concurs, "you and me, and especially Terra. They'll be livid that she's outfoxed them."

"They don't like to lose," says Terra. "They're not used to it." But then she muses, adds, "Maybe my father is secretly glad for me."

Fair snorts, "Dream on, girl." She smoothes the map and traces with her finger."We'll have to move fast all day. Let's hope the weather holds." She lifts her face and nose to the sky. "Smells like rain."

Fortunately the rain holds off until they are almost there, within sight of Lake Champlain, looking down on it from the shelter of an abandoned shed on a hill. But their relief is clouded by Fair's condition. She's been feeling ill since morning, and finally she can scarcely walk at all. She throws up whatever's in her stomach and collapses in a corner of the shed.

Terra says, "I knew that damn stew didn't taste right."

"The stew was fine," pants Fair. "I think I've got a flu of some kind. Could even be this new Atlanta Fever. Look in my pack, find the cayenne and cloves. Cook an apple in water with the spices and give me just the water."

Birdy gets out the herbs while Terra puts all their containers outside to collect rainwater, and then rummages around the shed to find anything that will burn. After they've made the medicinal brew for Fair and covered her with blankets, Bird and Terra face a diminishing smoky fire and nothing but a little bread and a wilted cabbage to eat. For a time they worry about Sparky who has disappeared, but he returns with a bloody rabbit in his jaws, so they concoct a dinner after all.

"The good news is, we're here," says Terra. She glances over to make sure Fair's asleep. "The bad news is…"

"Fair is sick."

"I'm afraid so. Let's hope she's wrong. Let's hope it's just something she ate. It could have been that pumpkin shell she had for lunch."

"I ate it too."

"Well..oh, Birdy, if she really has that Atlantic Fever…what will we do?"

"It's very bad."

So they agree to wait until morning to make any decisions. It's a miserable night, with all the blankets covering Fair, and the wind roaring around the shed as if to knock it over any minute. Above all Terra is kept awake with fear for Fair. These fevers mutate and crop up unexpectedly all the time, and they are often fatal.

Terra rides Audrey down the hill for the last time. It's been over a week since they came to the shed, and Fair has finally gathered enough strength to put her foot down.

"We have to have that boat," she insisted last night and again first thing this morning. "You've spent enough precious time negotiating with those idiots, Terra. They want the horse, and they're going to get the horse, plain and simple."

Fair is still too weak to walk well, but she's threatened to take Audrey down to the lake herself with enough fervor to be convincing. She's sitting propped up in her comfy corner, sickly pale and voice trembling. But her eyes glow with life and it's clear she's getting well. Of course Terra is thrilled, but she is proud of having guided their little band through this trial and has gotten used to leadership.

"I found the boat, didn't I?"

"You did," Fair said gently, "and bravo. But face reality. How would we take a horse up the lake? You picture her swimming behind us? You're just hanging on because you're still a fool about that scum of a father of yours."

"No, I love Audrey."

Fair sputtered with irritation and started to cough so violently that Birdy came running with a cup of water.

"Never mind, Aunty Fair," Terra conceded. She bent down to soothe the shaking shoulders. "I know you're right. I'll go right away."

It's a cloudy day, cool enough as yet to be pleasant. The path through scrubby trees is narrow but that ensures little traffic.

"I'll come back for you," Terra promises Audrey, stroking her rough chestnut mane. "After this is all over, we'll bring you to Tully Island where you'll be happy forever. I promise." This scenario is pretty unbelievable, but it feels good to croon it softly, over and over, as if the chant and Audrey's trust could make it so.

The sailboat, with *Miranda* painted brightly yellow on its green hull, is about 25 feet long, with only one real sleeping space in the bow, but two benches below and two above, so that quite a few people could be accommodated if necessary. There's a little sink and stove, and a pull-out shelf for a table. It's quite solid and cozy and Fair will love it, but Terra's still flushed from her burst of tears at parting with Audrey.

As it turns out, they're living on the boat a week later as Birdy, who has contracted the fever, worsens. *Miranda* is tied to a dock but with her bow almost on shore, so she's hidden by overhanging willow branches. From the lake one catches only a glimpse of her stern, and from shore only a vague outline. Fair, now fully recovered, frets daily at their increasing danger from Armand's goons, bound to find them sooner or later, but this is the best they can do. Neither she nor Terra wants to forfeit Birdy's comfort.

The child lies in the sleeping area, no longer sitting up or asking to be carried outside, or asking for anything at all. Fair has confided in Terra her fading hope of recovery. The fever has gone to Birdy's chest, her cough is almost constant, harrowing. She cries that her ribs ache with every cough. She keeps bleeding and she's pale as snow.

"We're going to lose her," whispers Fair one evening.

She and Terra have finished washing up after their little supper, and are relaxing on deck in darkness deepened by the overhanging curtain of leaves. Through branches they can see a stretch of the carpet of stars in the clear spring sky.

"I can't stand it," Terra replies. "The most beautiful soul that ever was. Precious Birdy."

"But Terra," says Fair, hesitates. "Have you forgotten that tomorrow's your eighteenth birthday?"

"No… I mean, I didn't forget, but how can I celebrate with Bird so sick? And Audrey gone, and so much terrible sadness in our world."

Fair shakes her head, comes to embrace Terra in the loving hug that has so often comforted her. The water gently rocks the boat to the rythmn of their heaving shoulders.

Part III

1

June, 2083. It's been two weeks since they buried Birdy. That is, they wrapped up her tiny flimsy corpse, attached stones, and gave her tenderly to the water, which swallowed her in an instant leaving scarcely a ripple.

"Fly away, fly away with the gods, little Bird," Terra chanted.

Together she and Aunt Fair sang Bird's favorite song, "Morning has Broken," and Fair played "Listen to the Mockingbird," and "Walk of Life" on her harmonica. Then they launched *Miranda* immediately up the lake, in a good wind that sent warm spray to mingle with their tears.

For the past few days they've been docked just north of Burlington, celebrating having safely crossed the mid-lake border from the Albany enclave to the Boston enclave, not even questioned by a patrol boat. Now they must decide how soon to abandon *Miranda* for the tricky trip to the northeastern corner of Vermont, to reach Lake Willoughby. *Miranda* is well hidden in a reedy cove, so they've felt free to go ashore for badly needed supplies, food and water. They have a good supply of Albany dollars Trudy shoved at them as they escaped. But they're wary of strangers, and hurry back as soon as possible. For all they know, Boss Jones has traced them to the lake and the alarm is out, with their descriptions. Sparky is a sure-fire giveaway, so they have to leave him on the boat during their forays to populated areas, to his wounded indignation.

"You need to guard the boat," Fair tells him apologetically, stroking his silky ears.

But Sparky's eyes are all hurt. He knows he should go with her everywhere.

Tonight they finish their rather luxurious meal of fried carp and spinach pancakes, and some good local wine with a fine earthy bite. At nine o'clock dusk is fading over the water and the cattail reeds, birds calling evening song. They've brought the last of their wine up to the deck, where a cooling breeze defuses the steaming heat of the day. Fair sits in the corner of one bench, knees drawn up with Sparky asleep across her feet. Terra lolls on the other bench, against pillows.

"But we need to get much farther north before we go cross country," Fair insists.

"Oh, I'm sick of this boat. The wind's been crappy lately. I want to really travel. We can go much faster on land."

Terra knows she sounds impatient, but also knows Aunty Fair is used to that. She needs to be prodded, Terra thinks, light a fire under her old bones.

"Listen to me. For once," retorts Fair with surprising vivacity. "That kind of attitude will get us into trouble, and not for the first time. Tired of the boat! What kind of silliness is that? You may be eighteen, but who would know it?"

Terra grimaces. "Oh, and you're so wise."

But Fair is silent, and Terra knows this means compromise.

Soon they've agreed to travel up the lake as far as St. Albans, hoping for a decent wind. They're just starting to head below deck to get ready for sleep, when Sparky starts up like a lightning bolt, growling and barking mightily. Without a word, Fair grabs a knife, and Terra jumps behind her into the entryway. This will not be the first false alarm they've weathered. But Sparky won't quit.

Fair shouts, "Who's there?"

The figures that emerge from the darkness at first look like one weird creature with two heads. Both men have bushy black beards; one leans heavily on the other.

"Put the knife down, Mom," says Orion's voice.

Fair drops her hand with the knife to her side, but still clutches it in disbelief. Terra keeps crouching in the entryway.

Fair ventures, "Orie??"

One man is having trouble getting the other into the boat. When Fair hears a moan of pain, she rushes to help, followed by Terra. At last Orion half lies on the bench, breathing hard.

"His cut got infected," the other man says. "I'm Finch."

An hour later, after Finch has devoured quantities of food and water, and Fair has treated Orion's wound, they all sit around one candle below deck. Scraps of cloth that Terra has boiled for bandages are draped to dry. Orion lies on one bench flushed with fever. But he manages to grin.

"We're ok now," he sighs.

"You're not," retorts Fair.

Terra laughs. "You two are back to normal!" She turns to Finch, "You'll see a lot of tough love around here."

Finch chuckles. "I've heard all about you both. We're so lucky to be here."

"Tell us what happened," Terra begs.

But Fair says, "No, no. Don't tire them out now. Wait until morning."

"I couldn't be more tired than I am right now," smiles Finch.

They put Orion to bed in the stern, both women insisting that he take Terra's space, closing the little door panel. Then Finch in whispers fills them in briefly, from escaping the Hampshire Project, to their struggles across Vermont.

"How did you find us?" Terra wonders.

"We Stewards have contacts everywhere," Finch replies proudly. "No problem."

He refuses the inside bench, and goes to sleep on deck. Fair and Terra settle down in the dark.

"Aunty Fair," breathes Terra. "It seems too good to be true, Orion back with us."

"I hope it's not too good to be true," Fair replies in typical acerbic fashion. "Who knows what happens next."

In the morning the three of them take a quick swim, consume bread and cheese, and juniper tea. Orion when he wakes is still feverish, so they make him stay in bed. The women confer on deck with Finch, in cool green freshness, a gentle breeze. The June day will be boiling soon enough, but right now, with the sun just up, it's comfortable and serene. They brief him on their adventures up to now.

Fair stresses how important it is for them to get moving. "The Sanmart goons, Boss Jones and his cronies, are on our trail. They want Terra back, of course, that's a matter of pride. But also they want me for escaping, and now you guys are here and they're hunting for you too. What a bonanza for them."

"The four of us on the loose," Finch concurs, "are an insult to their power. But it'll take Orion a week at least before he can travel, right? And meanwhile, we made a promise to meet with some Stewards down near Burlington. I really should go."

Terra has taken an immediate liking to this energetic, devoted friend. She says, "We can try to help, can't we, Aunty Fair?"

Fair sighs. "Well, Finch, we've decided to stay with the boat a while longer, get farther up the lake. So Orion can recoup where he is. But even though this cove is excellent cover, every additional day here is risky, you can see that. What if we set sail today, get farther on, wait til he's better, then you can travel back to your comrades."

Finch's long face gets longer, his gleaming little black eyes droop. "I guess you can do that. But I have to fulfill our promise. There's an important mission coming up. I need to leave in just a few days."

They agree to let Orion decide, and troop down to gather around his cubby. He drinks quantities of tea and even keeps down a chunk of bread, thrilling Fair. She dresses his wound, pronouncing it "on the mend."

"Okay, I'll tell you what I want to do," Orion says, more vigorously than they expect. "First of all, Mom and Terra, you take the Steward pledge. Slam your right fist onto your heart, swear "in the service of the Earth, I fight for justice and equality." When the two women obey, he continues, "and now we can tell you our situation. Finch?"

"Right," says Finch. "Here it is."

He crosses his legs on the bench, leans forward, his long lean face dim in the shadows. The boat swings rhythmically against the shore, softly rocking. He starts with Sanmart, touching on its insidious takeover, so subtle that few folks took much notice until it was too late. The Stewards grew out of reaction to the first dismissals and jailings, gaining members very quickly in the past year. He and Orion contacted a couple of Steward cells on their way here, shared their knowledge and filled in the gaps. Membership and meetings are secret, because even though Governor Monty touts free speech, those who speak out disappear, many probably "volunteering" in New Hampshire.

"You see what happened to Orion. That's typical. Sanmart doesn't tolerate arguments, not any more. Same thing with me. I was taken from my home near Worcester right after I urged

166

some folks to resist paying for their water. Which brings me to All Joy. That's the cute name for the project in New Hampshire, an enormous complex that started out as an indoor mall back in the 20s, and they're adding to it. The result can house probably three or four hundred people. We've learned they plan to create an Earth replica, and seal it off. Everyone left outside will serve them, forced to continue polluting and depleting the planet for the benefit of the elite inside. Absolute control over all water supplies guarantees submission."

Fair, sitting opposite him next to Terra, chokes rage. "So that's what they're up to. The evil bastards. It's not enough to run the whole Boston enclave, Albany and Hartford as well. They want the whole eastern seaboard."

Terra queries, "But how can they control outsiders from inside their mall?"

"A complex combination," Finch explains. "Police force and brain washing, on top of doling out water only to reward obedience. It's amazing what folks will do for water."

Orion puts in, "They have a mission to justify it, all written up. We read excerpts."

"They preach their superiority," Finch went on to explain. "You see, they've been chosen by God to perpetuate the human race."

Fair splutters and Orion adds, "I'm sure some of them know the mission thing is all an excuse, but their goal is to convince everyone of their chosen place in history. That way, they might just get cooperation, with people too scared to think it out. Besides, dissenters will be dying right and left."

Terra asks faintly, "You can't think they'll succeed? It sounds crazy."

"It's not any crazier than the world has become already," counters Fair bitterly.

The four of them sit in silence. A bird warbles from somewhere, a breeze churns the water and rustles the reeds around them. Terra feels numb with shock and foreboding. Of all the dangers she's faced in her short life, from killer storms to marauders and bandits, none has left her with such a feeling of abandonment. She recognizes that her father must be mixed up in this inhuman plot. Boss Jones is the virtual dictator of the Albany enclave, and probably of Hartford and Boston as well, and Boss Jones rules her father.

Before she can bring herself to implicate him, Fair seethes, "The head of the bandit operation, Hall Hudson, is one of the chosen no doubt. I'm talking about Terra's father. The priest."

As they all look at Terra, she feels her face crumble in shame and grief. Orion reaches out to squeeze her shoulder, says, "Steady, Terra, it's okay."

"Now," breaks in Finch reassuringly, "let me tell you what we're going to do about it."

He outlines a plan of action through September. "After our first step, we've got to move really fast. They'll be on to us, and we're no match."

"We have the manpower," Orion adds, "but nothing like the fire power. They even have tanks."

"But what do the tanks run on?" Fair asks.

"On gasoline." Orion pauses for effect. "Yes, they're digging for oil and gas."

"No, no," Fair replies, "can't be. There isn't any more of that stuff."

"When you frack there is."

"Frack," Fair repeats, like tasting poison. "You mean hydraulic fracturing, blowing up rock to get at the oil? But that takes fuel too, to start with."

Terra is lost. She senses that something awful has opened up before them. She trusts Orion and Fair's judgment, but she can't picture the complete crisis, only fragments of it. And behind it all glimmers her father's face, handsome, concerned, admiring, still beloved. Her mind reverts to their horseback rides across the meadows, their affectionate tête-à-têtes in his office den. These sweet scenes persist in crisscrossing the dire pronouncements of her dearest friends, like warm currents in cold water. Her heart is torn in two.

"They're already getting oil from somewhere. We guess Canada," Finch continues. "But they need a lot more. So they've taken over an abandoned fracking site just east of the Green Mountains."

Orion says, "And we've got to stop them."

Fair can hardly get out the words. "You mean they're burning fossil fuels again? After all the agonizing and bans way back in the 40s? Can they be that crazy?"

"It's not crazy," Finch counters, "when they're creating a refuge where they'll escape the consequences. Hence All Joy."

Terra thinks, this is just the kind of thing Boss Jones would do. And yes, it would appeal to her father, with his convictions about superior people and glorious goals. Simultaneously she shudders to realize that in his eyes she herself would be one of the chosen elite. Of course he would include Silk, too, in his honored entourage. Terra gave Fair brief details of encountering Silk at Hud's Headquarters, but as yet they have not told Orion. Of course he needs to know, but she can't bring herself to be the bearer of such terrible news to her beloved, sick brother.

Orion, half sitting, his still swollen leg propped up, raises his palm in a stop signal and blurts, "Mom, we're got to get to that meeting, Finch and I. You can see now, from what we've just told you, it's essential."

"You're not going anywhere," Fair starts.

"Wait," cautions Finch. "Orion, you can't even walk yet. I'll go by myself. It doesn't take two of us."

"I won't let you go alone," insists Orion. "It's too dangerous."

He struggles to his feet, sways. Fair pushes him back but she's no match for his strength, weak as he is.

"I can walk perfectly well," he proclaims, and falls forward. Finch and Fair break his fall.

"Never mind," Fair says firmly, "I'm going with Finch."

2

Fair and Finch have been gone for three days. One morning Orion hauls himself out of bed and up on deck. He plops down on a bench grinning broadly at a stunned Terra, his grin widening as she hurriedly finishes pulling on her shirt, hair still soaking from her morning swim.

"You could have warned me," she scolds.

"Sorry," he laughs, not sorry at all. "I wouldn't want to catch you nude."

"Orion, that isn't funny."

But she's smiling too, gets up to pour him tea. "So, you're well now?"

"Just weak as hell. Haven't used my limbs for what, two weeks? But look at that." He displays his leg proudly. "A nice clean scar, that's it."

"Beautiful," she agrees, bending to inspect it. "Your mom is a magic healer."

"She is." Orion sips his tea, looks at her over the rim of the mug. "What do you think of my trying a swim?"

"I think it's nuts. You can hardly walk."

"Swimming is easier than walking. I just have to get myself into the water." He peers over the edge of the boat. "I think I can do it."

She doesn't try to stop him. Instead she offers her shoulder to steady him, as he stumbles down the gangplank. He falls when the water is up to his knees, but he's in and gives a whoop of joy, sets off at once with powerful strokes of his arms, his legs reluctantly following.

Terra watches anxiously, calling, "Not so far, come back to the boat."

The cool water feels glorious on his sweaty skin. He's had many a sponge bath from loving female hands, but he yearned for this immersion, rebirthing him. He looks back at the beautiful girl leaning over the railing, thinks how much he loves his little sister. But he catches himself noticing her breasts under the damp shirt, the curve of her tanned leg, and warns himself to protect her.

Doesn't quite make the connection until she jumps in the water to swim after him. Then he recognizes it: she's a woman, and he's attracted to her. This shocks him so that as she comes closer his face registers dismay.

"Are you ok?" she says, paddling round him. "Come on back, you've showed off enough."

"Terra."

"What?"

"How old are you?"

She starts laughing so hard she splutters. "Eighteen. What a question!"

"I'm almost ten years older."

"So? That doesn't make you wiser, if that's what you're getting at."

She splashes his face and dives under water away from him.

"Oh, damn. Okay, forget it."

He heads for the boat, feeling weak now, dizzy not so much with the physical effort as with the newfound discovery of his feelings for this woman he's always thought of as a little girl.

Eating breakfast. he fiddles with the fishing rod so he's not looking at her. It's been too long, he decides, months now since he was last with Silk. Although he did have a nice interlude with a sweet Steward girl at one point on his journey here. He'll have to find a woman, that's all there is to it; these sexual flashes over Terra just won't do. Silk. He has schooled himself to dim Silk's magnetism since he heard more rumors about her. Most recently, he was told she was spotted at bandit headquarters in the Berkshires. His initial attempt to dismiss this or somehow excuse it gave in to doubt. He's even allowed himself the wild idea that Silk is involved with the Sans. When such thoughts creep into his head he feels sick. He still dreams of her body, but he no longer hungers to see her again.

The day passes quickly amidst all their tasks. Orion catches and cleans a couple of fish, repairs a chunk of Miranda's hull, naps deeply in spite of himself, and wakes to see Terra arriving back from a foraging expedition with eggs, cheese, dandelion greens, blackberries, and drinking water. Each item is an amusing story, and she sprawls on the bench across from him describing the farmer's wife, the roadside trader, the other girls digging up dandelions, and the elusiveness of the hidden berry patch. She has piled her sumptuous auburn hair in a clump at her neck, but the tendrils escaping curl damp with sweat on her skin even though the day's heat has cooled in a merciful lake breeze.

Orion gratefully gulps water, washes greens and berries while Terra busies herself at the fire pit they've crafted on shore, a circle of bricks and stones. Sparky ambles back and forth between them, helping out with his enthusiasm. Eventually they're back on the boat relaxing over wine, a very good dinner consumed. The sun is low in a pale sky, the air almost refreshing.

"I think I might be able to walk pretty well in a couple of days, "Orion says, "so I can do the errands and give you a break."

"Weren't those berries delicious," she grins, licking her lips. "Let's try to find some cream to go with them next time."

"I'll do that," he promises.

"Or yogurt."

"That would be good, too."

Here he stops, frustrated with such an inane conversation in light of his illumination of the morning. He longs to say something significant, to document the change between them.

He blurts, "Terra, let's use this time together to be serious. Mom and Finch will be back any time now."

She doesn't offer the pert banter he expects. Instead, after a silence she says, "Well, I haven't told you everything about my imprisonment in my father's house. Shall I?" She leans back, her lovely orange-brown eyes worried. "It's about Silk."

"Is it true then? She was there?"

"You know?"

Orion adjusts his sore leg extended on the bench, replies grimly, "Tell me."

So she does. He can see she's making a huge effort to soften the blow. He loves her for it. But when she says, "…and Silk was there, in his room, half dressed," her own shock and disbelief carry the full horror. He feels tears smarting his eyes. She's at his side in an instant, arm around his shoulder, comforting, crooning, "Don't cry, Orie, don't cry. She's not worth it." She wipes his cheek, kisses it. "I'm sorry, I shouldn't have told you. Don't be sad, Orie dear."

He hangs his head, leans on her, takes her hand. "Thanks, Terra, I needed to know. I absolutely needed to know. I've been torturing myself." Then he gasps. "That's why she was with me in the first place? That's how the Sans seemed to know everything…She told them!"

Now he's angry, livid, clenches his fists. "The bitch, the bitch."

Terra pats his back. "Be angry, that's good. Be mad as hell, Orie."

The sun slips out of sight, shadows deepen across the water. The two old friends sit together in a long silence. Eventually Orion puts his arm around her.

"Do you feel something different, Terra? Between us, I mean?"

"Not really, Orie. We've loved each other like brother and sister ever since I can remember. That's not going to change."

"We're not related at all, you know."

"Not by blood. But so what?"

"It means I can love you in a different way," he says very carefully and quietly.

She pulls back and stares at him. "Is that a good idea?"

"I think it's a very good idea."

She shakes her head. "You're just upset about Silk. Let's talk about this another time."

The surrounding darkness yields soft noises, rustling leaves, slapping water. He feels her pressing into him, warm.

"Now's good," he says, and leans down to kiss her.

3

Nearly a week later on July 1st, Fair and Finch are pushing hard to reach *Miranda* before dawn. After they ran into some Excell patrols that took too great an interest in them, they stopped traveling by day. Their disguises are good—Fair dyed her hair black and Finch, now beardless, is wearing woman's clothes—but discovery felt close. Besides, daytime temperatures often hit the 100s, draining their energy.

So as the sky lightens, they've been on the road for six hours—and then suddenly there's the lake, reflecting new light, casting a watery breeze. They stop to reconnoiter, crouch behind some bushes. Finch takes off his heavy wig, liberating his own hair with a sigh of relief. Fair gulps some water, hands him the canteen.

"Hungry," he mutters.

"Same here. Hope they've got something tasty."

"I'll eat anything."

"As soon as we alert Sparky, get ready to board fast."

"But we don't want to scare them shitless."

Fair nods but notes, "Barks like a maniac. We don't want to rouse any curious campers."

"Okay. Say the word when you're ready."

Fair thinks, not for the first time, what a good buddy Finch is. When he first came to the boat she'd been prepared to humor a young man, but she learned quickly to respect his insight, loyalty, and courage. At one point, when an Excell security guard had them cornered and was asking too many questions, he pounced on the man, twisted away his gun, knocked him over the head with it, picked up Fair like a bundle, and took off into the bushes faster than a deer. When he finally set her down, she was out of breath, but he wasn't.

She takes a moment to savor the peaceful scene. *Miranda's* yellow and green merge nicely with the reeds, ideal camouflage. The firepit and surrounding trampled ground seem cozily reflecting their many meals together. The calm water scintillates with dawn's pink sunshine. She already feels her arms around her son and dear

Terra. As she signals Finch she's ready, steps out of their cover and nears the boat, suddenly she stops in alarm. There hasn't been a single sound from Sparky.

The sweet scene is at once ugly with danger. She exchanges a look with Finch and they drop to the ground, wiggle backwards.

"Something's very wrong."

"Sparky," agrees Finch.

The silence sweeps over them like a pall.

"I'll go," he says, pulling out his knife.

She nods, watches him creep towards Miranda, disappear below deck. When he emerges a minute later and summons her with a gesture, the look on his face sends dread scorching through her nerves.

There lies Orion, tied hand and foot; beside him sprawls Sparky, head covered with blood. Finch is shaking Orion, who slowly opens his eyes almost swollen shut in his bruised face.

Orion croaks, "They got Terra."

Finch unties him. Fair gets water to bathe his face, gives him a long drink. Then she leans over Sparky, and starts to groan sobs. The dog's skull is crushed. He will never bark again.

A few hours later, the three of them are almost ready to leave. Fair and Finch have grabbed a little sleep, Orion is practicing walking. He's convinced the Sans will come back for him soon.

"They only left me alone because they didn't have any orders about me. They were just after Terra, a special search team from Boss Jones. They argued about it. One of them convinced the others I might be wanted alive. So they'll be back." He's eating everything in sight while he's packing. "Sparky put up a good fight, Mom," he adds, patting her shoulder.

Around noon, when they've reached a thick patch of woods, they decide to rest. Fair is stumbling with exhaustion and grief. They snack on provisions, Orion lays out a blanket for her. She gives herself permission to cry, but she can't. The full catastrophe has her by the throat. Her beloved dog beaten to death, her precious little Terra once more in the clutches of ruthless and all powerful men. When she wakes she can't believe she slept. How could she? Lying there in the shadows, sensing Orion and Finch quietly busy nearby, she turns over, watches Orion whittling arrows, Finch testing their fit in an impressive bow.

"Hey there, Mom," Orion says casually.

Fair gets a jolt of strength from their calm and focus. With these two men, she can do much. They will rescue Terra again. They will rid the Earth of the Sans. Bring democracy back to Boston, strive to restore a healthy planet. She sheds despair like an old skin.

"I'm ready," she says. "Let's go get Terra."

When they reach the first safe house it's close to midnight. It's a small cottage of mud and straw next to a greatly diminished green pond. Fair and Finch stayed here just a day ago, so they feel confident knocking on the door. A decrepit old lady opens the door, takes one look at them, and straightens up to become a muscular middle aged woman. They all give the Steward sign, fist against chest.

"Good to see you again," crows Marion heartily. She whips off her tattered scarf, and a spasm of white-streaked hair springs out around her head. "But unexpected. What went wrong?"

She hurries them inside, offering mugs of water all around. They huddle with her at a table in the main room. The moon sheds a watery light, supplemented by one small bayberry candle. Marion presides like a rock: large, placid, and so acutely aware she seems to possess a hundred darting blue eyes. She grasps the magnitude of Terra's abduction without distress, only intense interest. On their last visit, Finch had already told her what he and Orion learned about All Joy, adding to information she and her neighboring Steward cell had gathered.

"You know about our September action," she rumbles, in a voice both hoarse and strong. "We'll be targeting the dome, that old mall they've restored. We're waiting to make sure we can disable it significantly, not just nick it here and there so it could be easily repaired. We aspire to remove it from the Earth."

Fair sees Orion and Finch exchange a look of total disbelief, but Marion pays no attention.

"Chances are your girl Terra will be taken there eventually. But we should try to find out where she's headed now."

"Could be Albany," Fair points out.

"I can find out tomorrow," Marion assures them. "Meanwhile, you need to rest up."

They bed down wherever they can in the tiny space. As she falls into a sleep solid with the certainty of safety, Fair reflects in wonder that neither Miles nor Zed has entered her head for days. Her muscles, her heart, her brain are knotted passionately into one focus. She's never felt so intensely her complete self, yet so fiercely inseparable from a multitude of others.

4

At the north end of All Joy where the egg shape is flattest, the grand entrance leads directly into a public square. All around it recently planted fruit trees—pear, apple, peach—are already leafing out. In the center of the square soars a grand stone statue of Boss Jones, Zoria's inverted cross in one hand, a pistol in the other. High above looms the vast round roof, formed by myriad triangles of steel into which solar panes are being fitted. Living units open onto three tiers of walkways rising on either side. Though palatial, the space still retains the feel of the gigantic commercial mall it once was.

When Trudy first saw Terra again three weeks ago, Trudy snarled and sneered. But Terra knew it had to be an act put on for the guards. Sure enough, as soon as they had a moment alone, Trudy whispered, "Don't tell them I helped you escape. It's ok, you'll get through this."

Eventually Trudy crafts some minutes with just the two of them, in the bath house, wrapped in towels. Other women who bathed with them have gone to dress for lunch, so they can linger, feet dangling in the water. Terra has been a prisoner here in All Joy for almost a month now and she still can't get used to everything being done in groups, everyone crowded together, space always hard to come by. What she resents most is being treated like a cog in a wheel, a machine part. Though she hasn't yet had to perform sexually, she's reminded of her certain fate by the urgent preparations for Armand's arrival. That glorious day is set for August 12.

When she realizes that Trudy has arranged this tête-à-tête, she rushes to ask, "Are you still in touch with the Stewards? How can we get out of here? I swear I'll kill him."

"Hush and listen to me. Yes I am and yes we will get out, but not for a while. You'll have to behave."

"Like hell."

"Terra, more is at stake here than your pride and virtue. Starting with me. I've been promoted to Manager. I've pretty much aged out of the primary harem. I've turned twenty, and I'm proven barren. Surely you don't want to get me in trouble? I have to be able to count on you. When they offer you the drug, take it."

"Morgala, I bet."

"That's right. It will help a lot. Just pray you don't get pregnant. Did you and Thad use protection?"

"Of course. What the…But okay, tell me what to do. I'll try."

"Just keep your tits up, as they say," quips Trudy with a wry grimace. "Now look, we've only got a couple more minutes before they miss us, so just remember tomorrow to be on the lookout for my signal—I'm going to show you the weak link in this damn monstrosity, where we can escape when the time comes. You'll be given an official tour. Keep your eye on me. I'll pretend to stumble just about where it's located. Got that? Now if something happens to me—I risk a lot on occasion to communicate with my outside contact—you need to take over my role. Shut up. You can do it."

"Other Stewards are here?"

"The less you know the better for all of us. But my precious friend," Trudy squeezes Terra's knee with a grim smile, "destiny is on our side."

Terra looks at the soapy water congealing around her ankles, up around at the makeshift pool where the water never seems quite clean, at the stone benches all around, some draped with towels, sponges, bottles of body oil or shampoo. The verging on messy that's everywhere here at this ridiculous terrifying so-called All Joy. People go around talking about it in hushed and reverent tones, but all Terra sees is the chaos of construction and the untidiness of indifference.

In the locker room they hang up their towels, dress hurriedly.

"I hope they don't give us algae again for lunch," snorts Trudy.

The next morning, Terra joins half a dozen other girls for the introductory tour. Leading it is Grozen, a wedge of a lesbian with a masculine voice and jutting jaw. Everyone is wearing the same flower-peppered smocks, though Grozen and Trudy wear red aprons as well, indicating their status.

The group first gathers around the Boss Jones statue, in the public square. Grozen calls their attention to the suite on the first tier towards the front where the Boss and his favorite cohorts live when they visit. The doors are decorated with dark blue velvet, with golden images of crowns and moons.

"Very soon, our blessed leader will be staying with us for good," Grozen announces with pompous fervor. "The great day of the Sealing is set for September. We just need to finish the roof. Look up! You can see those dedicated volunteers working constantly to get all the solar panels fitted, making us airtight."

Terra remembers what Orion and Finch told her about those so called volunteers. She finds herself so removed from this whole drama, she's hardly here at all. As often as she can, she brings her mind back to *Miranda*, to their sweet peaceful days there, to the new love that began to burn with Orion.

She's rudely returned to reality as Grozen describes the lovely room each girl will occupy in the Jones suite when it's her turn to serve. "It has to be the second week after your period, so the Boss gets the best chance to bless you with his child. He already has ten children You can see the little darlings in the Child Center, just over here."

The group is treated to the sight of children from two to seven, playing and moping in a fenced off area behind the public square. On one side of the kiddie park is a field of vegetables and on the other a fish pond. Every conceivable space has a purpose. Ahead looms a vast wall covered with vertical farms, vegetables grown in stacks, "using mist instead of soil," Grozen touts proudly. She points to the roof, where men in orange overalls are laboring to install glass panels into triangle shapes. "Our roof is already impermeable at the entrance—soon it will all be covered and we'll never feel weather again."

Just as Grozen leads them further back, away from the park and the children, towards the huddle of buildings she calls the military barracks, Trudy lets out a cry and falls to one knee. Terra at once looks around carefully to make note of their location. To the left is a clutch of storage boxes, to the right a line of uniformed men drilling with shotguns. Trudy's deft accident indicates a space between the boxes. She's already up and limping away, everyone's alarm subsiding. So that's it. Terra takes a quick look backward to memorize the route.

Grozen now brings them to a stop with a grandiose gesture at an enormous boxlike structure with machine parts. "Gaze at this, sweetie pies. This here's our Morgala magic. When our sacred leaders decide to reward us, we are treated to this elixir that brings us heavenly peace and comfort. It comes in liquid, like wine, or in the air as perfume that enters our lungs like velvet. See the knobs and arrows, how carefully the dose is administered to us, the blessed chosen ones."

After making sure the girls are suitably awed, Grozen hurries them on, but the group has barely reached the other end of the dome, where she's pointing out the servants' quarters, when the sun suddenly goes out. The sky turns black. Before they can reach the shelter of overhanging walkways, torrents of rain drench them. The rain is hot, pounding their skin in burning needles. They can hear the children shrieking in the distance, and most of the girls are screaming too. Grozen hushes them affectionately, with many unnecessary caresses, and herds them into a space that looks like a dilapidated dining hall, with rough and rickety tables, a dirt-trodden floor. Here they huddle, shaking off the water soaking their clothes. Grozen tries to distract them with more inspirational promises. Behind and above her the rain is so thick it obscures everything.

"Be thankful for the rain right now," Grozen chides, "as it helps to fill all the giant cisterns over there just outside the Western wall. Anyway," she croons soothingly, "we won't be victims of the elements much longer, as soon as they get all the panels installed." She roughly shakes wet spray from her cropped black hair, slicks it back with a devout smirk. "And what's more, along with Boss Jones, priests will be joining us, to care for our souls. We'll be building a small temple for worshipping the great Zoria and her unborn Christ. You are blessed with paradise, girls."

One brave and foolish girl ventures to ask, "After the Sealing, will we get to go out again?"

"Why would you want to do that?" Grozen replies brusquely. "I told you this is paradise. You're lucky to be here. The ones left outside, they will serve us and then die along with the planet."

Terra can see Grozen vengefully eyeing the girl, who's pudgy and flustered—destined to get in trouble. She quells her heart's urge to help. Only one thing counts now: stopping Sanmart's plan to abandon Earth.

5

Orion and Finch emerge from a small copse of trees into a desolate farm field where drought-withered crops have been flattened and drowned by the recent brutal rain. Corn stalks parched white, kale black, shriveled carrots and potatoes uprooted and strewn around. Four children are bent over, feverishly collecting the blasted vegetables. They look up only briefly. Behind Orion and Finch, still within the trees, Marion is holding her hand out palm backwards to halt the others.

"We could cross here," says Finch. "The Connecticut River can't be far, so the site must be just on the other side of this field."

"The kids are with someone," cautions Orion.

"We need to find out who."

They turn back to join Marion. Their party now numbers eight, including a few teens, all well equipped although dressed to resemble refugees. Fair opted to stay behind in charge of the safe house, because of Marion's close knowledge of the area. They've just crossed the Green Mountains, which loom behind pocked with mudslides. Their goal is the old fracking site in the valley, where Sanmart is said to be reviving the operation.

Marion says, "You two are wanted men. I'll do the reconnoiter. I'll take Sammy with me, play mother and son scavenging for food."

"But we're staying right here," says Orion. "Any sign of trouble…"

"Any sign of trouble, you don't do a thing," retorts Marion. "I can take care of it."

So hulking Marion and lanky fifteen-year-old Sammy wander into the field looking hungry.

One of the kids yells, "This here's our stuff." But he doesn't stop long, instead fills his basket even faster. Marion and Sammy start grabbing what they can. In a few minutes, an old man and woman appear, glancing very uneasily at Marion, and call to the children.

"Okay, that's good. Let's go. Come on, get in the wagon, step on it."

Soon the way is clear for all the Stewards to troop through the field quickly, to the other side. And there in the valley, the river glinting in the distance, lies the old fracking site with its machines still erect. The group huddles behind a ridge; there's definitely activity down there, even the rumbling of machines. This is their target but there's no mood of celebration. Danger tenses the air.

They pull back to a farmhouse that has collapsed but retained its foundation, where they share water and rations. It's nearly dusk, so they decide to bed down. They have a plan, but at this point it seems doomed. How can they be a match for the Sanmart construction team? Orion voices this fear, the others grumbling assent.

Marion answers, "We'll be using our brains. Brain over muscle any day."

"Way to go, Marion," cheers Sammy.

"We've got to be sure we get it right," warns Diego, a white-bearded elder to whom everyone looks for sage advice. "I don't much feel like being grabbed as a volunteer, or worse."

"Let me remind you," says Marion, "what fracking is. They blast millions of gallons of water along with toxic chemicals deep into the earth to shatter the shale where the oil or gas is located. The backflow has metals, additives, radioactive stuff. Groundwater's polluted forever. The gas is mostly methane…"

"Okay, okay, Marion," concedes Orion. "We know how bad it is. You're right. We can do it."

"They need this fuel to run their oh so joyful dome," notes Finch. "So we cripple it."

"That's good enough for me," Diego says.

But Orion's sleep that night is fitful and fraught with nightmares. The morning light, hot and gray, attacks his face with relentless force. He struggles to hold onto an image of Terra, lovely and sweet, in his arms. Her legs and arms are wrapped around him, her mouth seeking his. But she melts into ragged reality.

Someone hands him a cup of tea and a chunk of bread; they all share carrots boiled with tubers. Nobody has bothered to think up a spice for the dish, which tastes vaguely of dirt—they eat only out of hunger, not pleasure. The August day is oppressive, lacking oxygen, promising suffocating heat. Mudslides due to drought and downpour have formed wet brown hills all around. Finch voices hope that the mud has damaged the fracking operation. But when they gather at the ridge above it, clearly it has survived just fine. Today there's even more activity, uniformed guards in full view. Surely the workers will have lookouts, so they don't dare go any further without preparing for confrontation.

Marion, Orion, and Finch, along with elder Diego—the de facto leaders—huddle together to make a final decision for action. The others take shelter as best they can from the throbbing heat. The plan had been to disable the pipeline carrying water from the river. But Marion shakes her head.

"Pipeline's too well guarded."

Diego comes up with another plan, pointing at two enormous piles of sand to the left of the major pump.

"Sand's essential for their operation," he says.

"Because," Marion explains, "you have to mix it with the water you slam into the rock."

Diego adds, "Sand disables engines."

All are reminded that with his seventy years, Diego comes from the age of machines. The youngest stare at him: when Diego was their age, folks still rode around in individual gas fired vehicles.

"Stall their damn machines," breathes Finch. "What a coup."

"It will take weeks," chortles Marion, "to even dream of fixing them."

Diego gets congratulatory slaps on the back, and they all huddle close together, meticulously planning their moves.

6

All Joy resonates with glory. The Sanmart flag with its great white star on gold, and Zoria's with its inverted white cross on red, fly together on all sides of Boss Jones Square. The band plays inspiring music, punctuated insistently with resounding drums and trumpets.

Crowded to the railing on the second tier, Terra catches sight of a familiar face among the first ceremonial arrivals: it's Henry, dressed up in a black and gold uniform marching with some kind of honor guard. He looks smug. She's always been fond of Henry, his intelligent irony, his sharp grey eyes, his swagger on the cusp of manhood. She recalls his reprimands and disciplines as domineering but compassionate. She wonders if he's heard about Birdy. Those miserable days on the road with the feral children seem sweet in comparison to the bizarre distortions here.

Trudy pushes through to stand beside her.

"Magnificent," Trudy gasps, with her well-practiced enthusiasm. "Look, here come the blessed priests."

Terra's too nauseated to play the game. She only woodenly stares. Sure enough, a phalanx of white-robed men is flowing through the entrance, lugging their huge inverted cross, while the music gives special rein to trumpets. Now here comes Boss Jones himself, looking ridiculous in red velvet. Is he pretending to be some kind of king? But Terra's lapse into ridicule is short lived. Following close behind him, gloriously decked out in multicolored robes, is her father. The sight of him sends her falling into Trudy, who has to catch her, hold her up.

"Holy shit," Trudy murmurs. "It's him."

Terra swallows tears. Pulsing adrenaline, she clutches the railing with both hands. She had thought she was rid of him, safe from the love and the longing. But no. He looks so beautiful. She wants to throw her arms around him. Does he know she's here? Of course he does. That's why he's been re-instated as part of the inner circle. Look at him, surrounded by other dignitaries and flocks of guards. He's smiling, proudly, with perfect dignity. Suddenly she's no longer separate from all this poisonous pomp, but an integral part. Yes, mistress in the principal harem, future mother of little bosses, daughter to a valued advisor. She feels tainted, shamed, trapped.

Her inner voice calls up his betrayal—he traded her to the Boss in return for his own glory—calls up Orion's strong arms and devotion—their whispers and promises lying together rocked by *Miranda*. But her lifelong yearning for her father overwhelms her fight for strength. She slumps against Trudy, defeated.

Terra lies in semi-darkness, still smelling Boss Jones on her skin. He left her here hours ago, but sleep will not come. Nor does she want it to, pulsing with revulsion. What she wants most of all is to find soap and water and scrub herself to bleeding. The room is silent. She can make out the shapes of furniture in the shadows beyond the pool of light from the low lamp, outlines of the erotic pictures she has seen on the walls, a faint line of light under the closed door. No doubt someone waits on the other side, ready to serve her obsequiously, unless she makes any trouble.

There are no windows, so Terra has no idea what time it is. She was brought here after the welcoming feast, mind dulled with wine and Morgala, torn from Trudy's embrace, stripped and draped in some kind of silky material. Armand was not gentle, but he wasn't overly rough either. He was obviously puffed with triumph but a bit weary after all these young women. He didn't speak except to call her a naughty girl, and compliment her on her breasts. He didn't take long.

She wants to flee but at the same time somehow feels that if she stays exactly here, it will not have happened. Eventually the door opens, and a servant girl chirps cheerfully.

"Rise and shine."

After her bath, Terra is clothed in a soft pink garment indicating her new status. She even gets a dollop of gold colored metal to crown her head. She still can't get used to being treated like a robot. She feels like garbage, a crushed thing with no motivation for a will of her own. She's told that she'll breakfast in the Diplomats Dining Room on the third tier, instead of the usual refectory.

"Your father will be joining you," the servant says matter of factly. "The Honorable Hall Hudson."

Most of the dining room is not yet furnished, but in one corner there's a collection of tables with tablecloths and dishware and bowls of red grapes. Terra sits, toying with a cup of coffee but not raising it, hardly able to breathe.

In he strides, all aglow at the sight of her. He kisses her cheek, sits and tucks in his napkin. He's wearing one of the lovely brocade vests he favored at Headquarters. The better to enthrall her of course. But she can't help it, she's dazzled by him, his beautiful honey brown hair, his fond eyes, his resolute shoulders. She screams at herself about his betrayal, but after all he has never pretended to be overly brave. Why not grant him this flaw?

"My dearest darling daughter, here we are together again! Never to be parted, my dear, side by side always from now on."

At first she half-heartedly tries to convey her feelings about her revolting role here, but he smiles gently patting her hand, comments, "We all have trials to bear. Bedding the Boss is not much of an ordeal, my dear. You're a beautiful young woman, what do you expect?"

When Terra looks up above them, she can see the sky. Triangular glass panels in the domed top here have already been put in place. Perhaps by Orion. Yes, that could be. A surge of longing for him fills her heart, a source of strength she can nurture. It feels good to know her real self is still in there somewhere. But she doesn't even know for sure if her captors left him alive. And could they have ambushed Fair and Finch as they returned to *Miranda*? She remembers brave Sparky being clubbed, his piercing cry. Mocking her fears, peaceful white clouds are sailing about in bright blue, for all the world as if everything is fine.

Her father shares his awe and pride in All Joy, pausing frequently while consuming a pile of blueberry pancakes to wave his fork about for emphasis.

"And, we now have the Zorian priests on our side. They bring God and holy Zoria and her unborn Christ along with us into the future. The glory is complete. Do you see?"

Has he detected disbelief in her face? She remembers his rejecting the Zorian line in the past. She quickly smiles, replies, "I do see that having God and Christ on our side is helpful. Oh yes."

"The great prophet Father Karl will be addressing our community this afternoon. I'm sure you'll be impressed, my dear. And Zoria herself is said to be already on her way from Hartford in time for the Sealing."

Terra nibbles on grapes, forgives his mind-numbing rant, enjoys his glow of enthusiasm, his happiness, his earnest desire for her complicity. The moment is magical, bewitched.

7

At first Fair enjoys being alone in Marion's shack. Well, not quite alone. There's an old cat named William, entirely black except for one splotch of white like a bow tie under his chin. So he looks elegantly dressed even when sprawled out on the best chair, which is usually. William speaks a lot, not only when he wants something, but as a greeting, or a comment. In return, he listens politely as Fair recounts her thoughts and plans.

"Now, William," she explains one evening as they both relax after dinner. "I just don't see that I'll be able to run around all over the place like this much longer. I'm getting old, William."

The cat sees fit to comment briefly, with a small breath like a caw.

Later when she wails in tears over Terra and Sparky, William seems less sympathetic. When she recovers and blows her nose, he yawns.

By the fourth day, Fair is getting antsy. Marion had calculated two weeks absence, tops. The gang was to sabotage the fracking operation and return here directly. Meanwhile, Fair was to greet and update any fellow Stewards who stopped by. Conversing with William is becoming an inadequate substitute for human contact. Fair starts gloomily dwelling on Miles, missing him and Tully, then recalling Zed, longing for his arms around her, then moaning with grief over Sparky or shuddering with panic over Terra, then going into a frenzied worst-case scenario over Orion's current mission. So it's almost with relief that in the middle of the night she wakes to loud pounding on the door.

She quickly dons Marion's old scarf and peers out. Only three of them, but it's a rough-looking bunch. They give the Steward sign, troop in, and make sure the door is closed and locked before they begin shedding their various backpacks, wigs, scarves, shawls. Emerging are two men, one in his thirties, the other fifty or so, and a woman who looks about forty with a haggard, haunted face but still beautiful. This woman intrigues Fair, draws her into some strong, disturbing memory. Have they met before?

Without any fanfare Fair gives them the basic requirements: lots of water, bread and leftover soup, some water for simple bathing, an indication of sleeping space. The three are exhausted, in a deep lasting way that won't fade with one rest. The younger man, Garth, explains they've been travelling from the Albany enclave almost without stopping since last Wednesday.

"Plus," puts in Trist, the older man, "they sprang me from prison first, so we had to nip out pretty fast. Got over the enclave border before they even missed me, I'll bet."

A full moon illuminates the table they're sitting around. Trist has a skeletal look, as if he hasn't eaten well for ages, but he seems cheerful in spite of it.

"Trist?" Fair is delighted. "Jed Trist. You're Van's dad, Letty's son, right? I saw them in Three Rivers not three months ago. Yes, they're fine, just fine."

Jed, beside himself at this news, begs for every detail.

"I'll tell you all about it in the morning," Fair says gently. "Relax for now."

The woman says, "We don't have time to rest."

When she gives her name, Lorna, Fair's disturbing memory crystallizes. How many times has she heard her friend Vita moan that name in grief? This woman is Vita's daughter, this woman is Terra's mother. The searing memory of Lorna's one visit to Tully floods Fair with sadness. The appalling rejection of the child by the mother.

Lorna reads her expression, says, "Yes, I recognize you too. Tully Island, right? My mother's friend."

Garth starts up. "What?" He puts a protective arm around Lorna, not that she seems to need it. "You know Vita, and the…child?"

Fair is swallowing hard. She nods coldly.

He asks, "Is the child ok? Did you know her?"

"We did the best we could. She's a wonderful person."

Lorna shrugs, twists in her chair. In the subsequent silence, Trist goes to bunk down in a far corner, mumbling thanks in a fading exhausted voice. Garth tries to get Lorna to join him on their blanket, but she shakes her head, doesn't move from the table. Neither does Fair. Clearly they're both intent on talking. Fair moves to sit close enough to Lorna so the men won't hear their low tones.

"You're Terra's mother," states Fair.

"So? What does that mean?" Lorna's lovely dark eyes burn with suspicion in the eerily colorless moonlight.

"I helped your mother bring her up," Fair says. She will not give this woman an easy out, won't pussyfoot around. "Vita wasn't exactly an affectionate grandmother either. It wasn't easy."

"Thank you for doing that."

"Okay. I've always understood your pain. The priest, the father, the degradation. But I never understood how you could abandon your baby."

"If you have a child, I'm sure you loved its father. You simply have no idea."

"But as a woman, I can get an idea. Give me a break. You opted out. That child didn't ever hurt you, but you hurt her forever."

"I can see that you loved Terra. I appreciate it. What's become of her?"

"She's a prisoner now, held by Boss Jones in the Hampshire settlements."

Lorna finally breaks. No tears. She simply begins to tremble. "Not the Hampshire Project!"

"Yes."

"They're doing to her what they did to me."

"I'm afraid so, pretty much. It all has different staging, a different excuse. I believe she belongs to one man, not several. But it adds up to the same thing. Rape."

Lorna reaches out a pale hand with long thin fingers, grasps Fair's arm tightly.

"Can you save her?"

"Of course we're going to try. Are you with us?"

"That's where we're headed too."

Lorna rummages in a deep pocket in her trousers, pulls out a tiny gun. It's small enough to fit into the palm of her hand.

"A Ruger revolver," says Lorna. "Antique but dependable. I know how to use it."

Fair starts back in astonishment. Nobody has guns any more. This woman is more and more amazing. She doesn't doubt that

Lorna has already used that gun, lethally. Fair studies the beautiful, hardened face, realizes she's actually only about thirty-five, feels a stirring of pity. Lorna's blond hair is ungroomed, in a blunt cut not flattering to her round face, but her large dark eyes are luminous.

"Look," Fair says gently. "You really do need to get some sleep. Rest up here for a few days, you'll be better able to help us, to help Terra."

Lorna shakes her head. "Let's leave in the morning."

"We have to stick to our plan. We all have to agree on every detail. That's the way we operate."

Lorna gives Fair a long, assessing look. Clearly feels no match for her, decides to go along. At once, her body slumps, eyes start to close. "Oh I'm so tired," she mumbles.

Fair takes her by the shoulders and guides her to the blanket beside Garth. He reaches out for her, wraps her in his arms. Fair keeps this image as she curls up in her own space, conjures up Zed, remembers their bond. But knows that it would be her own husband Miles who would comfort her so, just so, wrapping his arms around her, asking nothing but to keep her safe.

8

Finch tries to dissuade Orion one more time.

"We can still catch up with them."

"We can." Orion concedes. "But I won't. Go ahead, go on back, you know I won't blame you at all. What I'm doing is not exactly risk free."

"It's not exactly sane."

Orion stirs the little fire they've dared make to cook their squirrel. The meat turns on a stick serving as spit, browning nicely. It even smells good, gamey but rich. When he doesn't answer, Finch adds, "Your mother will have a fit when she finds out."

"Poor Mom. She will. But she's just as nuts as I am when it comes to taking chances."

"No, Orion. She has more sense."

Orion looks across at his beloved buddy crouched on the other side of the fire, his narrow bright black eyes alive with anxiety. He's still wearing the hat he uses to pose as a refugee, a big wide brimmed straw number, eaten away at the edges by some hungry mouse. All around them trees form dark shadows. The nearest safe house was out of their way, and they outpaced the refugee group they could have hidden in, so here they are on their own in woods identified on their map only as Bellows Falls. It's probably about nine o'clock; the setting summer sun has left a sliver of rose low in the sky, the stars are sprouting their glory. Their blankets are already spread out on the ground with extra clothes as pillows.

"Ohonte," Orion responds with an affectionate grin.

Finch shakes his head, but grinning too in spite of himself. "So far so good anyway. We sure did mess up those machines."

Orion chuckles maliciously. "Those idiots were running around like rabbits, trying one after the other. The damn things choked and spluttering and not going anywhere."

Finch takes a swig of tea, gestures with the cup. "Wish we could've stayed longer to watch the show."

"But we had to get out of there fast. I wonder how far our gang got yesterday after that, a good ten miles anyway?"

"Maybe, but Diego was falling behind a lot. I think they'll have to slow down for him."

"For sure. They might be back at Marion's in a few days though. You can still make it."

"If I leave right now? Oh crap, Orion, you know I'm not going anywhere without you. It's just too bad you had to fall so hard for Terra."

Orion turns the spit, says, "It's ready. Hand me your plate."

"Not that I blame you. A gorgeous girl."

Orion slides the roasted animal onto one plate, divides it up, sinks his teeth in, looks up at the pulsing stars pricking every inch of the night sky.

"What those stars have seen," he murmurs.

"What they will see," intones Finch. After a long pause, he adds, "I can't believe we're going back there."

"Yeah. We worked so hard to get away. Ironic, isn't it? But it's lucky we already know it, know the layout, the routine. That will help a lot."

Finch wipes up the last of his meal with a crust of bread, drains his tea. Looks over at Orion half whimsically, half grimly. "What's the plan?"

"Plan. Hum. Well. Let's make one right now. I figure we only have a few hours' travel in the morning to get close enough to spot it. At that point if not before, there'll be plenty of lookouts and guards."

"How about if we take a prisoner, grill him?"

"Then what will we do with him." It's not a question.

"Bad idea. Well, let's see, what've we got. Two knives and a bow and arrows. Is that it?"

"And Diego gave me his hatchet."

"Okay. Let's grab some guns first thing…"

The friends plot into the night, each trying to be hearty and optimistic for the other's sake. Orion feels strangulated with fear for Terra, whom he loves more deeply than he ever thought possible. He's sure he couldn't survive without her, it's that bad. When an image of her sexual situation creeps across his mind, he feels crazy. Chides himself he's got to be careful, not do anything stupid. He listens to every word of caution from Finch, who grabs onto his role as rational seer with gusto. They fall asleep still talking.

But before dawn both of them are countermanded by young Malloy. It seems Marion had taken it upon herself to alert a Steward group near their route, who sent Malloy to track them down.

They wake to find him standing over them backlit by early light, a tall, gangly, very young blond man with sunburned face and unconvincing moustache. He gives the Steward fist sign, states, "No, you are not going to take on All Joy by your little lonesomes."

Orion jumps up angrily. "Who the hell says so?"

Finch gestures hospitably. "Sit down, friend. Sorry we've got only tea to offer you."

Malloy glares back at Orion, snaps, "You can't take things into your own hands at this point. You could derail the whole operation." Before Orion can spit out an answer, he replies calmly to Finch, "Thanks, I'm fine. I do have a bit of breakfast."

Malloy collapses himself into a sitting position, pulls out a chunk of bread, divides it into three, and offers a share to the others. Finch takes his, stirs up the fire. Orion is still standing, arms folded. Malloy takes off his moustache, stuffs it in a shirt pocket, produces a small crock of plum jam, jabs a stick into his bread to toast it over the fire. Finch greedily slaps jam onto his toast, and eats producing purple rings around his mouth.

Orion watches them devour their breakfast, so angry he doesn't dare speak. At the same time, he's completely aware that this youngster is on the up and up. He seems brave and honest too, the kind of comrade the Stewards need. Orion is gradually mellowed by admiration, and by a creeping sense that he's in the wrong. He sits down, glumly chews his untoasted and unadorned very stale bread.

Malloy and Finch are eagerly exchanging scraps of information. Finch describes details of the inner workings of All Joy, Malloy explains the creation of a secret entrance into the old parking garage in the basement.

"Reached by an incredibly long tunnel, took months to dig," Malloy says. "We have folks on the inside. Organizing things from their end, to coordinate with us. But we have to get them out before we make our move. We know how to turn on their party dope, the Morgala mist. Knocks 'em out great. So naturally every Stewie going in has to have an oxygen mask. Taken care of. Some from old airplanes, some from military bases, some homemade from facemasks. See, that's why we have to stick to a very specific schedule. And thanks to your superb sabotage, their delivery trucks are disabled so the so-called Sealing has been moved up, giving us more leeway. So now we only need to mobilize at our entrance within a week or so. We need that time. Stewards are coming from all over and communications aren't easy. No computer parts. We're using pigeons sometimes, and hand-cranked radios."

Finch turns to Orion with a shining face. "Orion, this is just what we needed," he urges. "A real plan. Real help. A real chance."

Orion shakes his head. "You're talking about waiting weeks? Such a waste of time. Think of what could happen."

Finch tells Malloy, "You've got to realize the man's in love. His girl's been taken there. For Boss Jones, we hear."

Malloy gives a sympathetic shake of his head. Even in all his youth, or maybe especially because of it, the romance grabs him. "Oh, hey, that's hard." Orion swigs his tea as if he's murdering it, but nods reluctantly.

Malloy adds, "I see your point. We can make sure you're one of the first ones in." He reaches into his pack and pulls out an oxygen mask, hands it to Orion, who seizes it with gusto if not gratitude.

Clouded sunlight breaks though yellowing trees in a sudden harsh shaft heralding another oppressive day. They'll have to hole up somewhere at noon for awhile, just in order not to faint. Water's a problem too, now that Excells are guarding every drinking source.

From his pack Orion pulls out the map he took from the guardhouse. Malloy seizes it eagerly.

9

In the pool crowded with naked girls, Trudy swims over to Terra and cries, "No, you're not stretching properly. Let me show you."

She grabs Terra's leg, pulls it forward, whispers, "I need you. Meet me after lunch by the kiddie park."

The water aerobics instructor yells, "Okay, Trudy, let's keep going. And one and two and three…"

Terra kicks half-heartedly into the soapy water. Aside from occasional brisk walks around the second tier, this is the only exercise she gets and it feels good, but is extremely boring. Now the naked women have to jump up and down, swinging their arms. Accompanying music consists of one flute, poorly played and ill suited to these rhythmic gyrations. Every once in a while a guard or officer strolls in and watches complacently. These are "the girls" after all, hardly a level above servants, meant for viewing and whatever else. For now they belong to the Boss, so hands off, but they know that many will eventually be downgraded to serve the priests and the military.

The murky water is cold. Terra tries to think about the lentil soup she knows is waiting in the cafeteria. She wonders what Trudy wants, hopes it's not too complicated, but at the same time prays it means news favoring their escape. Her fertility week with Armand has just ended and she's been returned to the dorm. Now begins the horrendous waiting to see if she gets her period. What she will do if she ever gets pregnant here, she can't imagine. But the prospect has given her painful insight into her own mother's situation. For she herself, Terra herself, was a baby made this way, by callous force.

Before lunch, the women must attend the newly instituted religious ceremony mandated every noon by Father Karl. The Zorians now claim as their temple a large area on the tier above the entrance. The space looks as if it must once have housed a fancy shop; the words "LoveCulture" are still faintly etched several places in the wall. Terra and the rest of the harem sit on long benches in the back, while officials and their wives or favorites have special seats up front near Boss Jones' throne. Terra vaguely wonders what kind of goods would have been displayed here. Clothes or furnishings, cosmetics? Her hair's still wet. She's not allowed to cut it or even to tie it back, so it spills damply down over her shoulders. At least she doesn't have to wear that silly crown any more. Well, not until next time... The Boss enters with fanfare, looking very smug. Terra withers him with her eyes, but he doesn't even look in her direction. Her father the venerable Hall Hudson comes in with the Boss' entourage, takes a seat among the favorites at his feet. Terra can't stop staring at him; his beauty enchants her as ever, though she's begun to detect more than a trace of disillusion in her adoration.

Father Karl is a mountain of a man, not so much fat as over developed, with muscular arms, ham legs, double chin. Clean-shaven and almost bald, he sports one tuft of white hair over his top lip, more like an afterthought than a moustache. He has a voice that is oddly both sonorous and high-pitched.

"My children, welcome to our first service of many and on into eternity here in our blessed sanctuary of All Joy. You are here because God chose you above all others to survive and flourish in the destruction of the corrupt old planet Earth. Call us the second Noah's Ark."

Father Karl lifts his arms to the skies, creating a dramatic fall of his wide white sleeves. His throbbing little voice trembles with emotion. "Our great Zoria herself will soon be here to honor us with her revered presence, to live and preach among us. Her sacred son Jesus Christ awaits in her womb the amazing moment when she declares you finally free of sin so he can be born again. I believe, my children, this stunning moment may even arrive in our lifetimes. Think of it! He will be born again unto us, the chosen ones, and we will prosper in this beautiful, beatified place forever."

Wow. Heady stuff. Many in the audience look suitably impressed. But Terra has been too well educated in Tully to be much of a dupe for this kind of pitch. She's been hearing since childhood about the incredibly obese woman who claims to be pregnant with Jesus. So she works on controlling her expression: seriously devout should do it.

After Karl's speech and a lot of cheers from the crowd, Boss Jones rises royally. Terra's flesh crawls at the sight of him. She remembers his groping, his noises, the taste and smell of him, wants to vomit. But like the zombie she's meant to become, she sits demurely, hands clasped in her lap, blankly obedient.

The Boss says, "Greetings, my friends and companions in this great and divine undertaking. We are doing God's work, purifying the planet, saving ourselves for his sake, dedicated to his blessed vision for us. Every one of you has been chosen, and don't you forget it. There are still evil forces gathering around our beloved sanctuary, bent on destroying us, bent on Devil's work. Be vigilant! Even among your neighbors here, traitors can be lurking. Report any devious behavior you see or even suspect."

The Boss gets angry, threatens awful punishments both here and in the afterlife for anyone caught even thinking about defection. He turns purple and venomous. But then he wraps up his tirade with benevolent advice, and ends up smiling paternally, sighing, "I know you'll all be good, because you are good, my friends. Our time has come."

In the cafeteria Terra devours her lentil soup, which is really very tasty, listens to the other girls giggling and whispering and showing all the proper signs of girlishness. There's wine for lunch, probably laced with just enough Morgala to mellow anyone.

Trudy is waiting by the path to the children's park, casually checking a pocket mirror and fussing with her hair. She takes Terra's arm firmly and guides her forward, chirping, "We'll just go observe the little kiddies, see how you might want to help out."

Terra whispers, "What the hell's going on?"

But she doesn't get an answer. They pass knots of guards, most of whom make rude, salacious remarks, then some berry bushes, a bench, a latrine. To the left farther on, work is progressing on the small fish pond. Beyond the fence, made up of fragments like rusted cable twisted with bits of wire and only high enough to contain a seven-year-old, a few children are tossing a ball back and forth. No teachers are evident, so Trudy resumes her normal voice.

"The Sealing's been rescheduled for November 20th. We've got to get all our comrades out of here before that. Which includes you."

"Oh, fabulous… But who are the others? How many? How…"

"It's better if you shut up for now, my dear." Trudy gestures toward the kids, indicating to anyone watching that they are observers here. "The signal's going to be a blackout. We'll shut down the lights in the middle of the night on October 24th. You have to be ready, I can't come for you. You have to be out of here way before we turn on the Morgala machine to put everybody to sleep. Listen now. You'll go straight to the opening I showed you, during the tour, remember? If you turned around right now—no, don't turn around—you'd see it, that space between buildings. No, don't worry about being stopped. There'll be chaos enough. We'll make sure of that. So keep a packet of clothes and necessities ready, but select them carefully because you can't carry much. You'll have to crawl through a tunnel."

One of the little boys waves to them; they nod and smile vigorously.

"Trudy, this is more than I can handle…"

"No, it isn't. I know you. Anyway, you have no choice. Now, we're going to turn around and go back, talking excitedly about training children. When we get to the end of the path, I'm turning left. You go straight to your room."

And then she starts babbling idiotically about blessed children, hope for the future, pure souls devoted to Zoria and virtue and the Boss. She's holding Terra's arm, shakes her.

"Perk up, Terra. You're not free yet. This will take some doing."

10

On the evening of September tenth, Fair is roasting chestnuts for dinner when the front door opens unceremoniously and Marion lumbers through. She throws a bunch of dead pigeons onto the kitchen table, leans over to scratch William's ears, and grabs the wine decanter, pouring a cup and sucking it down. She's followed by the rest of her group, all in various states of exhaustion, especially Diego. They spoon him some soup and put him to bed. Jed Trist has gone back to Three Rivers, so Lorna and Garth help greet the newcomers and make them comfortable. Lorna is clearly trying to be compassionate, but makes an awkward job of it. Garth is much more hospitable and caring, a sweet-tempered man who must find his fierce beloved Lorna an enigma, Fair concludes.

Fair is upset at Orion's absence, but not surprised. It's so like him to snatch opportunity out of nothing, and swagger onward. Just like his father Seth, she mourns—that's how he got himself killed. As dusk falls, and the Stewards are fed, mellowed with wine, Fair goes out to pump water from the well. On her way she notices a purple splotch in the sky and a mean wind springing up.

"Storm coming," she comments, ladling out the water. "Hope Orion and Finch are out of it."

"Oh they can manage anything," Marion assures her.

"Their own fault," snorts Sammy, "for breaking rank and taking action before it's time."

"Finch will keep him sane," Fair notes hopefully.

Garth goes to take a look outside. "It's bad. Marion, can you board up your windows?"

"Oh, yeah," Marion replies and gets to work, summoning him and Sammy to help.

Just an hour later, as the storm is breaking, the wind screaming, hailstones pelting the little shack, the sound of pounding on the door distinguishes itself from the rest of the chaos. Standing there pouring wet are Finch and a stranger, a lanky fair-haired youngster. Marion stands aside, gestures them in without a word.

"You found them," Marion says to the stranger. "Where's Orion? You two get those clothes off. Sammy, stir up the fire."

"Yep, Marion. Malloy stopped us, just like you told him."

"Good thing too, but where's Orion?"

"Gave us the slip."

"Here, sit by the fire, drink this."

Everyone's talking at once. The newcomers strip and put on whatever stray clothes they are handed. Finally Fair yells, "Shut up! What do you mean? Don't tell me he went on over to that cursed Joy place by himself!"

Finch nods in the silence. He's wrapped in a pair of women's pants and a shawl. His coal-black hair is a soggy tumble, sticking up all over from being rubbed.

"That's right," Malloy growls. "We looked around and he was gone. Stupid idiot."

"I can't believe he left without me," Finch mourns.

"Well," taunts Malloy, "the man's in love, so you said."

"What, what?" Fair challenges them. "You mean Silk? She's not worth…"

"No," Finch sighs, "I mean Terra."

"His little sister."

"No, his lover."

Fair falls back stunned. "Oh, no. No. Wait. It must've happened on the boat…"

"On the boat, while we were gone," finishes Finch, crouching closer to the fire. The wind makes a fierce swipe at the shack, shaking the very floorboards.

Lorna goes up to him, reaches out her hand. "Finch, I am happy to meet you. I am Terra's mother."

Fair puts another log on the fire, hiding her stricken expression. What will the others think of her if she rants as she wants to against this perversion of her children. Terra and Orion are adults in anyone else's eyes and she's a jealous, interfering old woman. She pokes viciously at the logs, sending up sparks. What she primarily feels is a sense of loss, picturing them, both so beautiful, together and happy and not needing her any more. These spiteful thoughts are quickly superseded by gripping fear for both of them. Terra trapped in a fanatic's delusion, Orion on his way alone to try to rescue her. What if she never sees them again? She finds her face wet with tears, from anger or terror or both. Then Marion's thick arms are around her.

"Hey, hey, Fair my friend. Stop fretting. It's all going to be fine. Don't you doubt it."

Marion smells of lard and sweat, but her bulk is a refuge. Fair finishes out her sobs in her ample folds.

During the night, Fair wakes many times to listen to the raging storm, cracking trees, pelting hail. Sometimes it seems to cry with a human fury, beating on the shack as if to purposefully punish it. She hugs herself in her blanket, not cold but lost and afraid.

Morning dawns in perfect calm. Looking out, the Stewards see the sun shining sweetly on wrecked trees, mud ponds, and the vegetable garden pummeled to shreds. Nobody forgets for a minute that another scorching September day is just beyond the horizon. But at least the cisterns are full, and everybody has a good wash, with lots of soaping each other and laughing. Spirits are further pumped by the recovery of a pile of squashes that soon become rich soup.

After lunch Marion calls a council around the kitchen table.

"Malloy has a report to make," she announces. "He brings word from Central."

"Central Command," Malloy elaborates sedately, "in Williamstown." He adjusts his shirt sleeves sternly. "The plan is set. Countdown starts October 20th. Takeover is October 24th."

Fair looks around the table at faces expressing variations of confusion and skepticism. Clearly nobody quite believes orders can come from such an angelic looking lad. Besides, whoever heard of a Central Command for Stewards? They've been clutches of motley crews ever since they began. And they're proud of this, and comfortable with it. Leave the dictating to the bad guys.

Sammy asks him, "What are your credentials, friend?"

Marion says, "He's officially designated."

Garth says, "We met him earlier in a raid outside Albany. He's good."

Finch comments, "You're kind of young, Malloy my man."

Lorna objects, "Why do we have to wait? Let's go now."

Malloy looks startled by their skepticism, clears his throat. "I'm twenty-one, guys. Get over it. Here's what we have to do. This here's part of the southeastern node, we're meeting up with the rest at Merrimack Junction. A safe house there that used to be a factory. We leave in small groups, starting next week. Diego's staying here to man this safe house for any more Stewards. We have to get our folks out of that dome before we do the final action."

Fair decides that whatever calls itself Central Command is probably just another bunch of brave Stewards like themselves, and she's glad someone's in charge. Malloy may only be a kid, but he sure has guts. And his confidence is catching. By the time he's done, he's addressing a group of converts eager to follow his instructions, their adrenaline rising.

11

Great fanfare accompanies the arrival of the sacred Zoria and her entourage of priests and other flunkies. Among them is the gorgeous Silk, serene and shimmering as always, jabbing pins of jealousy and fury into Terra's heart. Silk is wearing some diaphanous floating garment in Zoria's colors of red and white, so suited to her persona of both goddess and whore. What is she supposed to be? Some kind of handmaiden, novice, nun? Silk is just one more outrageous and grotesque twist to this whole diabolic invention.

Zoria is of course obese, with arms and legs mere hunks, her mean little face dwarfed by the rest of her. She apparently can't walk so must be carried along by an army of men in a flamboyantly decorated rickshaw. Her meaty hands bear half a dozen shining rings as she waves them in regal condescension at the cheering crowd. She bears within her immense bulk her son Jesus Christ, so the priests are all beside themselves with fervor. Of course an elaborate ceremony is held in the temple. First, food is served to Zoria, and they must all kneel while she devours it, as if her life depended on it. It's not yet time for dinner, but Zoria will eat any time.

Once more, Terra is seated towards the back with the Boss' other girls. She's growing more and more anxious because it will soon be her turn again to serve him. Only a few days to go: she feels she'd rather die.

Zoria's voice has the breathy strain of an asthmatic. She blesses everyone and calls upon them to give thanks for God's forgiveness.

"God the Father has ordained that evil Earth shall perish for its sins. But you, my precious little ones, will live on forever in his blessed All Joy."

The roof panels are in place now. All Joy is completely protected from the elements. The sky can turn blue or purple, it may rain or sleet or not, but within the dome the temperature is always the same, a gentle warmth. People continue to come in and out, especially servants, many of whom still have families outside. But come the Sealing, only one very heavily guarded entrance will admit deliveries of food and supplies. Nobody will be allowed out, ever again, including the servants who will never see their families again. Indeed, this is the best assurance that servants and military will remain loyal and obedient: loved ones will surely suffer if those inside don't toe the line. Besides, from what Terra can see, many of the service folks buy the myth that those ruling the dome are the chosen ones, to be honored and obeyed. How comforting to believe that God has ordained all this. So much suffering has had a purpose after all.

After dinner, Trudy and Terra find a few minutes to chat, standing by the railing outside their dorm, looking down at the usual passage of people going about their business or just enjoying a stroll.

"This will all be over soon," mutters Trudy. "I can't wait. I am so sick and tired of grinning when I don't mean it, doing their dirty business."

"Hush, don't say it," warns Terra, looking about, then gesturing downwards and loudly proclaiming admiration for the peaceful scene. Glancing over to Armand's quarters, she sees that the velvet doors are wide open, and there he is standing at the railing, with Silk draped around him. She subtly calls Trudy's attention to them.

"Well, well," whispers Trudy. "The old Silk is at it again. I wonder how your father feels about that. Not that it matters to anyone. She just may save you your stint this time, or at least delay it."

Terra gasps with hope. If only.

That night she has such a vivid dream about Orion that it feels like some kind of omen. He is lying right there beside her just as he used to, *Miranda* rocking them softly. Their arms and legs are intertwined, lightly coated with sweat from love making and the lingering heat of the day. She listens to him breathe, slips her hand down to caress him. He moves and moans in his sleep, smiles before he wakes.

Sure enough, in the morning Trudy finds her right after breakfast and whispers, "Tonight. Be brave."

Then they both return their rapt attention to Grozen's pep talk on manicures.

Terra sits there demurely, heart racing. This is it. Her only chance. And it's so dangerous, so unlikely, so risky, so impossible.

206

That she should actually succeed in eluding her fate here does not ring logical or sane. It's a dream that will get them all killed, or worse. But she's only too aware that her established time to serve the Boss has already started, merely postponed as Trudy predicted by Silk's services first. Any moment, she could be summoned to begin the dreaded ritual of preparing for his attentions. This knowledge, and the still vivid dream about Orion, steel her to action.

She has dozed off, but when the lights go out, she's wide awake at once. She knows exactly what to do. She has put on her nightgown over her clothes, so she wiggles out of it, stuffs it under the covers, retrieves the red apron Trudy hid there earlier, pushes it into the bosom of her dress. Grabs her shoes and tiptoes in utter blackness past her sleeping roommates. The door's not locked, as Trudy promised. But unplanned, a half moon glows weakly through the ceiling panes on this end of the mall, illuminating figures of scurrying guards in the distance. Towards the other end where the roof is solid, complete darkness beckons and Terra hurries towards it.

Someone is shouting, people are rousing now. Usually there are lamps everywhere, dim solar tubes not sparing any secret corner. This black void is frightening, welcome as it is. She has to feel her way along the railing. She slips into the nearest latrine to pull out the apron, tie it on. Just in time, as outside she notices two guards running past give her a cursory glance.

Her goal is down one tier and some yards ahead, but as planned she runs up the stairs to the third tier. Here's where the servants live, in small crannies with dozens to a room, not a likely target for the guards. The railing she feels her way along changes texture and width, made of old materials from iron grills to plastic molding. Now and then she passes a scurrying servant, who pays no attention to her at all. Then she takes the stairs at the very end, down two flights to the main floor. Here guards are swarming now, but they have yet to figure out what they should be doing, so a degree of chaos favors her invisibility. She can dimly see the buildings that she must pass between. How will she find the entrance to the tunnel? Surely there's nothing to mark it. She dashes forward, and runs straight into the arms of a startled guard.

"Hold on there, young lady. Where so fast?"

Terra babbles, feigns tears. "Oh officer, I'm so sorry. I'm so worried about my sister."

"Turn around, you're going the wrong way. Back to the dorm where you belong."

He hustles her forcibly by the elbow, escorts her to the stairs. "Come on, now, don't give us any trouble. You're too pretty for that."

She hurries away. She crouches at the top of the stairs, waits until he's gone, then runs down again, and notices a small door under the stairway. A good place to hide for a short time. She opens the door, sees a light at the end of a corridor. Strange sounds reach her ears. A whimpering animal? No, a person in pain. Of course she should flee at once. But something keeps her there, poised. A woman's voice, a man's moan. The man sounds like her father. Of course, it can't be. But how can she leave if it's even a possibility?

Terra creeps slowly towards the light. Through a crack in another door, she sees her father lying on the floor, blood oozing from his leg.

The woman's voice says, "It hurts, doesn't it? Oh yes, that's good. I like to see you suffer. I'm going to watch you suffer."

She comes into view: a tall thin blond woman holding a small gun, which she shoots at his other leg.

Hud screams in pain. "Please don't. Please stop. You're going to kill me."

"That's right. But not yet. Not yet."

"Please, I didn't mean to hurt you," he begs. "We didn't realize what we were doing. We were young, we thought it was for God."

"The hell you did." The woman's voice is harsh with hatred. "You animals were just mad with lust for young girls."

The woman spits on him, and Terra knows. It's her mother, torturing her father. His beloved face is contorted in agony and horror. Thinking abandons her, and she rushes into the room.

He lifts a bloody hand towards her. Terra falls to her knees, cradling his head in her lap, crying, "Leave him alone!"

Lorna rushes at them, furious. Terra glares up at her. Lorna stops dead. Her hand with the gun drops to her side.

"You!" Lorna stands over them, staring. "Terra, the baby."

Terra stares back. "You've hurt him enough. You've hurt both of us enough. Go away."

"You can't stay here," Lorna says. Then she turns to the door, shouting, "Garth, Garth!"

Running footsteps. A dusky-skinned man in black rushes into the room, comes to stand between her and them, knife raised.

"I wasn't really going to kill him," Lorna says. "I only wanted him to taste it."

Garth says, "Let's go, Lorna."

"Garth. It's my daughter. That young woman."

Garth cries, "The child?"

"She has to come with us."

"Yes, yes, Terra, we've come for you," he says in a deeply tender voice. "Your mother wants to save you."

"Leave him alone," Terra repeats. "He's my father."

"I won't hurt him any more." Lorna's voice is cold but cracking.

"Let us help you." Garth steps forward and pulls Terra away from Hud, letting him drop. Hud lets out a piercing cry, aimed straight at Terra's heart. But Garth's grip is firm.

Lorna jabs her gun into her belt, puts her arms around Terra. They carry her back into the corridor, where from outside too many voices have risen to panic. So as he opens the door, Garth says, "Stay here. Let me create a diversion."

That's the last they see of him. In another moment guards have surrounded them, have found Hud, are barking orders. Lorna and Terra are half shoved, half carried in a rush of shouts and thrown into a wagon, door slammed.

12

Orion runs along with the rest of the guards through All Joy passages so dark he stumbles now and then. He's wearing the official black and gold uniform, with the beaked hat pulled over his forehead for security, but his comrades in arms no longer look at him twice. It's been two days since he ambushed and strangled the former owner of these clothes.

Orion has gleaned some idea of what's going on. He was able to make contact with a Steward who infiltrated here months ago, a cook he sought out as soon as he crept from the tunnel. He even knows where Terra's dorm is, though he hasn't been able to get anywhere near it; his unit has been busy practicing knife-wielding maneuvers at the other end of the dome. In any case, the cook has told him that tonight, with the lights-out signal, Terra will be on the move and could be anywhere. Orion desperately hopes she'll make it to the tunnel undetected, but he's frantic with worry.

He carefully follows every order to the letter, and when his unit swerves left, he obeys, head down. It was a lot easier to be confident when All Joy was running on routines. This chaos leaves everything wide open. Orion is not sure what to do. Abruptly the men are pulled up to a stop, in rigid lines, at full attention. It's then that he sees Terra and another woman being hustled into a wagon, carted off. But how can he make a move without creating suspicion, discovery? He watches the wagon disappear into the gloom, headed to the entrance end of the dome. There's an incline there, he knows, leading to the basement of the old mall. He has to get there.

Ten minutes later, he sees his chance. The captain has ordered his men to disperse and search for the breach where the rebels are somehow entering. He's able to slip away from the few guards accompanying him, and heads fast in the direction the wagon took. The incline is black as pitch, but temporary lights are springing up here and there. All too soon, the whole light system will be fixed. That will be the signal for the Stewards to turn on the Morgala steam, overcoming everyone. He and his Steward buddies all have oxygen masks with them, but they must then move fast to get out of All Joy. Orion knows he's taking a huge risk running down this dark sloping corridor. He isn't even sure if he's headed in the right direction, and he only has precious minutes.

Orion feels his way along the rough concrete wall, distractedly concocting a good story in case he's questioned. But nobody stops him, in fact pretty much nobody can see him. Then suddenly there's bright light, illuminating a space directly to his left, and there they are. He pulls back against the wall, watching, feeling for his knife.

Terra is disheveled and wearing some kind of strange outfit with an apron. Her face is twisted in anger and fear. Orion has to use all his will power to stay put. The two women are prodded into a closet-sized room, the door locked. One guard is posted, the others move on. Now comes an eerie quiet, where distant shouts sound muffled as if under water. The guard, relaxed, whistles a disjointed tune, yawns. Orion emerges, saunters towards him, salutes friend to friend, and still smiling grabs him around the neck.

A short time later Orion is running back along the corridor, wearing his oxygen mask, a heavy sack over his shoulder. All the lights have come back on, but everyone around is slumping down and falling asleep where they lie.

The safe house Orion has chosen is nestled against a cliff pitted with old mudslides, but firmly anchored among sturdy pines. It's so close to the tunnel entrance, it only takes him half an hour to get there, even with his heavy burden. Dawn is suggesting fog as he plunges through the door, heads straight for the cellar. An old woman wobbles to her feet from her chair by the stove, but nods when he gives her the fist sign, and he mutters, "Steward emergency." Nobody else is there. Of course, they are all still finishing the business at All Joy. The cellar stairs are narrow and rickety, but the space below is outfitted with bedding and provisions. Gently, gently, he puts down the sack and opens it to Terra's pale unconscious face, the Morgala still drugging her. He kisses her forehead, pulls the sack off carefully, wraps her in a blanket, and sits for a long time gazing at her: the person most precious to him in all the world. Safe, with him, at last.

"Got your message."Finch stands in the doorway mock saluting. "Came as ordered."

"Finch, old buddy. Ohonte!"

The two men share a hearty hug. Orion hustles his friend into the cottage, explaining, "Granny and I were just having lunch."

From her chair by the stove, Granny waves a spoon in greeting.

"Where's your girl?" queries Finch.

"Downstairs. Doing fine."

Finch chugs the bowl of soup Orion hands him. "Starved."

"So how's it going?"

"As planned." Finch bites off a chunk of bread. "Stewards got out and all exits are blocked and guarded. Not a peep from inside. They're all drunk of course. But not for much longer."

"Terra's already started to wake up. She did get a lot less of the dose, but it varies."

"We need to go in while they're still out cold."

"You need some sleep."

"Yep. But I'll be ready to go back in a few hours. You?"

Orion paces, stops in front of Finch, stricken. "I can't leave her."

Finch swallows a particularly big bite, slowly offers, "I can wait until morning. If I know your Terra, she'll want to come with us."

Terra's voice flutes from the stairway. "Oh I will, will I?" She emerges, uncombed but smiling, floats towards them, arms outstretched. "Finch, our man!"

She and Finch hug, all of them laughing, Granny joining in gleefully. Orion takes Terra in his arms, engulfing her, not letting go.

"Anything to eat?" she finally says.

So they feed her, share a hearty dessert of spicy pumpkin pie, Granny's specialty, she crows. As the day fades, they weed and water Granny's garden, chop vegetables for dinner, milk the two goats, make a few repairs. The autumn heat relents after dark, and the friends linger over their wine, reminiscing, plotting, dreaming of the new world they hope to usher in with the defeat of Sanmart.

Terra grows sleepy as a child, and Orion takes her downstairs to bed. He starts to help her undress, but she reaches for him in a whirlwind of passion. They tumble together almost violently, with cries almost of pain, their joy and their desire beyond thought.

13

Terra, Orion, and Finch travel fast in the early morning cool. They come upon the distant dome of All Joy suddenly, like an apparition, looming gigantically against the pale sky. Terra has begun to worry about what she will do or say when she sees her father again, and whether she and her mother will have any affection between them when this is over. And above all, is Fair ok? A lookout steps out of the bushes. It's Sammy, who greets them triumphantly.

"We did it," he crows. "There must be thousands of Stewards here, we've got the whole place surrounded. We won, we won!"

"Hold it, Sammy," Orion warns, "We still have work to do. Think about it. What are we going to do with all those prisoners?"

"Keep 'em in there till we build a stockade to put 'em in. We're working on that already."

"A lot of them are not Sanmart converts," puts in Terra. "I can tell you, many servants are on our side. It'll be a job to sort them out."

"Not too bad," Finch reminds her. "Our inside Stewards all pretty much got out in time. Forewarned, just like you."

They worm their way through the crowds of Stewards in various poses of resting, washing, or eating. From Barrytown, from Merrimack, from Albany, Hartford, and places even farther off, the motley crew ranges from teens to middle-aged, from mothers to grandfathers. Several groups are singing as they pass. All wear expressions of exhaustion and radiant relief.

Fair of course is in the middle of the medical area, rushing around creating concoctions and giving crucial instructions. At the moment they find her, she's spooning cranberry juice into the mouth of a thirsty Trudy, who's propped up on a blanket among rows of other wounded.

Terra rushes to embrace her.

"Watch it. Got a knife in my shoulder," Trudy croaks.

"Could be infected," explains Fair. "That's why she's getting cranberry."

"This is my Aunty Fair," Terra explains.

"No wonder she's an angel," smiles Trudy. "So here we are. We made it."

Terra grins happily, indicates Orion. "This here's my man I told you about."

"Mighty handsome."

With that remark from Trudy, Terra knows she's on the mend.

Meeting up with Marion and Malloy, the three friends are part of the first unit to enter vanquished All Joy. The tunnel is wide at the opening but gradually grows narrower, and darker in spite of their solar lamps, and for a distance they have to hunker down to pass under the roof that's crumbling in spots, trickling dirt down their necks. Terra is glad she's wearing a close fitting cap along with loose clothing, cobbled together with any castoffs she could lay her hands on, a pair of faded trousers, a shaggy shirt. Of course all of them are wearing oxygen masks, in case the drug is still potent. She's wide awake now, free of the bizarre dreams spiked by the Morgala, scared to death but euphoric too, being here with Orion, as victors.

The first sign that something's wrong comes as they emerge from the tunnel behind the barracks. The prostrate guards they pass look more dead than asleep. Marion prods one, and he lolls over like a corpse, pale and stiff.

She turns to Terra. "Is this what the drug looks like?"

"No," breathes Terra with dawning horror. "They're supposed to look comfortable, peaceful."

Malloy kicks the man, shakes him, feels his pulse. "Gone."

"What killed him?" queries Marion.

But they all know. Morgala.

Malloy says, "We gave strict orders about the dose. I'm sure this didn't happen on our watch."

Terra wants to shout, what about my father, but she's silent. This apocalypse is not about her own personal demons. She only begins to pray he's still alive.

Everywhere they turn, the occupants of All Joy are frozen in place. It's clear they died in their sleep, where they fell when the elixir first caught them, all over the place, in attitudes not of fleeing or fear, but of lassitude.

214

"They didn't feel any pain," whispers Terra.

Orion, hearing the tension in her voice, studies her eyes behind the mask, holds her around the waist as they progress, slowly, all overcome in spite of their triumph, by the ghastly situation. How many deaths? Hundreds. This was not supposed to happen.

"Well, we won't need a stockade now," says Finch. "Just a great big enormous grave."

"Maybe we should leave them all here, just like this," Marion suggests.

"Seal the place up," adds Malloy, "let them rot."

Terra feels the tears starting to her eyes. "We have to find him."

Orion presses her to him, but doesn't speak agreement. She feels lost in a swamp of bitter loneliness, loss.

Malloy insists they head for the Morgala tank to try to find out what happened. They pass the entrance to the children's dorm, where half a dozen in pajamas dropped as they fled. They look like little wax figures, all rosiness bleached from them. At the Morgala machine's controls where the switch had to be pulled, a woman still clings to the dial. It's Lorna, overcome as she continued to pull with all her might toward the highest possible dose.

Terra sinks to her knees, pulls off her cap, lets her hair tumble over her mother's body, gazes at the haunted frozen face, and tenderly closes her vacant eyes. She says for the first and last time in her life, "Mama."

Silk is lying at the entrance to Armand's suite, Armand sprawled a few feet away, his face a permanent blotch of pallid fury. Silk still looks incredibly beautiful, even as death continues her descent into dry pallor. She's wearing some kind of silky robe, which has fallen open to reveal her breasts and milky thighs. Orion stumbles past her, averting his eyes. Is he crying? Terra doesn't want to know. She gives herself over to grim satisfaction at the now totally impotent Boss Jones, no threat to anybody ever again.

Hud, still in bed with both his wounded legs bandaged, has an enigmatic smile on his ashen face, looking for all the world as if the events unfolding around him were his doing. Terra, prostrate over him, fervently believes that he knew this all meant her escape. She's convinced that he welcomed her freedom, sent her his love even with his last breaths. She smoothes his handsome brow, kisses it, brushes her tears from it, calls to him, "Father, Father."

Orion tries to pull her away but it's a very long time before she can let go, leaving as she does part of her heart.

About the Author

photo by Alison Woodman

Kitty Beer's stories and articles have appeared in print and online in the U.S. and Canada, including her work as an environmental journalist. Her screenplay, *Home*, placed in the 2004 International Screenwriting Awards contest. She is a member of the National Writers Union and the Society of Environmental Journalists.

Kitty Beer grew up in New England and raised her two children in Canada, Germany, and upstate New York. She holds a B.A. from Harvard University, and a M.A. from Cornell University. She now makes her home in Cambridge, Massachusetts, where she is active in political and environmental efforts.

The Hampshire Project is the third novel in a series titled *Resilience: a Trilogy of Climate Chaos*, reflecting Beer's emphasis on the courage of people to overcome disaster. The first two novels, *What Love Can't Do* (2006) and *Human Scale* (2010), are also published by Plain View Press, a 40 year-old literary publishing house focusing on issues of sociopolitical importance.

Visit Kitty Beer's website at http://kittybeer.net and her blog at http://planetprospect.blogspot.com.

CPSIA information can be obtained
at www.ICGtesting.com
Printed in the USA
BVOW08s0354270317
479266BV00001B/1/P